Praise for Jennifer Colgan's
Interview with a Gargoyle

"...surprisingly fresh, innovative and just plain fun."
~ *Long and Short Reviews*

"...a fantastically engaging story from start to finish."
~ *Literary Nymphs*

Look for these titles by *Jennifer Colgan*

Now Available:

The Rebound Guy

La Mirage

Strange New World

The Matchmakers

The Soul Jar

The Concubine's Tale

Uncross My Heart

Print Anthology

Sand, Sun and Sex

Interview with a Gargoyle

Jennifer Colgan

SAMHAIN
PUBLISHING

Samhain Publishing, Ltd.
11821 Mason Montgomery Road, 4B
Cincinnati, OH 45249
www.samhainpublishing.com

Interview with a Gargoyle
Copyright © 2012 by Jennifer Colgan
Print ISBN: 978-1-60928-786-3
Digital ISBN: 978-1-60928-533-3

Editing by Linda Ingmanson
Cover by Kanaxa

First Samhain Publishing, Ltd. electronic publication: October 2011
First Samhain Publishing, Ltd. print publication: September 2012

Chapter One

The acrid scent of demon blood tainted the crisp autumn air, drawing Blake DeWitt swiftly into the shadows behind the bakery on Chelsea Street. Once hidden there, he cut the engine of his Harley and strained to hear the scratch of curved claws on the pavement, the scrape and shuffle of a nightmare's passage through the alley.

He'd been tracking the creature, or more accurately, following the wispy stirrings of power emanating from the artifact it carried, since midnight. The odd tang in the air was the first indication he'd had that he might not be the only one on the Gogmar's trail.

DeWitt cursed the amateur demon hunters. They'd grown more troublesome and more numerous in the past year, probably in response to the sudden and disturbing proliferation of their chosen prey.

He glanced at his watch and mentally calculated the hours and minutes until sunrise. He had no desire to grapple with a human tonight, but with the cursed artifact on the move, he couldn't waste any time. If the Witch's Cabochon found refuge in the hands of a new demon queen, he faced an indefinite amount of time in the purgatory-like half-life that had become his existence.

Anxiety rising and mixing with the illicit thrill of the hunt, he tightened his gloved grip on the handlebars of his bike and watched the play of shadows against cold brick. After ten years in darkness, he craved sunlight more than most men craved food or sex. If he failed to retrieve the gem before this transfer was complete, he'd go mad waiting for another remote opportunity to free himself from the family curse.

Nothing could stop him tonight. He'd do whatever he had to in order to save his own life and the lives of his male heirs, and damn the consequences.

"Oh, damn. Not again." Melodie McConnell knew it was going to be a bad night when the antlers fell off her moose.

It happened as she was sliding an aluminum tray out of the industrial refrigerator in the back of Gleason's Gourmet Bakery, where she worked nights decorating designer cakes. One slight bump and the antlers she'd cast in melted sugar crumbled to shards, landing at the base of the chocolate-fondant-covered body of the creature she'd nicknamed Marty.

Marty had a date at the Amberville Moose Lodge's Annual Initiation Dinner tomorrow night, and without antlers, he couldn't be the guest of honor.

Right now, he looked more like a dark brown camel with an extra set of eyes where coconut sponge cake showed through the holes in his head. This latest setback left Melodie with six hours to recast his antlers in sun-yellow sugar and figure out how to keep them mounted long enough for the other Moose to ooh and ahh over him before he was eaten.

She had Marty's tray balanced on one hand and was lifting her sneaker-clad foot to kick the fridge door shut when the phone rang, nearly scaring her out of her skin. Gleason's had been a family-owned business for fifty years, and the back room still sported a black, rotary-dial single line that had been around since before Ma Bell had kittens. The old monster had a ring that could shatter glass. The sound echoed off all the newly installed stainless steel cabinets and countertops like machine-gun fire and always, *always* caught Mel by surprise.

Marty's tray tipped, and his cocoa-dusted body shifted just enough to give her a minor coronary. With a yelp, she righted him, dashed the tray onto the counter at her workstation and jumped on the phone before the second ring could rattle her skull again.

"Gleason's Gourmet Bakery. Melodie speaking. We're closed right now, but I'd be happy to take your order and get back to you with pricing in the morning." She chirped out the whole after-hours greeting without tripping over her tongue—a first. She would have patted herself on the back, but she was still busy picking pieces of antler from around Marty's artfully folded moose knees.

A vaguely familiar voice croaked in her ear. "Mel? Cuff-cuff-*cuff.*"

Mel held the phone away from her ear for a second. "Calypso? Is that you?"

The froglike voice muttered something that sounded like, "Yeah, it's me," then another bout of painful coughing exploded from the earpiece.

"Are you all right?" Obviously a dumb question, but what else do you say to someone who just reached out to hack up a lung in your ear? Calypso Smith, Gleason's premiere cake designer, was supposed to be at work in ten minutes.

"Oh, I'm ok-k-kay, Mel. Asthma's acting up. I'm on my nebulizer tonight cuff-cuff. I'm sorry to do this to you."

"Cal, Arnie left half an hour ago." Mel knew the difference between a phony cough and a real one, but their boss, Arnold Gleason, did not.

"Oh, cool." Calypso's slightly smoky voice returned to normal, and rather than continue coughing into the phone, she whispered, "Angelo's in town. Will you cover for me?"

Melodie chucked a handful of antler shards in the trash and sighed. What could she say? The moose-rack rebuild was only a minor catastrophe in the overall scheme of things, and whatever designs Cal was working on could probably wait until tomorrow night. Mel just wished Calypso wasn't going to waste her time with Angelo. Calypso's deadbeat ex-husband was a mooch, but she loved the bum to distraction, even though he'd divorced her—twice. "Sure, hon. Do what you've gotta do."

At least Melodie would get to hear about Cal's romantic adventures tomorrow night. Calypso was the queen of kiss and tell, and given Mel's own ex had only divorced her once and never bothered to come back searching for forgiveness, she got to live vicariously through her friend.

"Love ya, baby!" Cal made a smooching sound and hung up. Mel cradled the four-pound receiver and glared at Marty, who grinned foolishly with his shaved sugar-cube teeth.

"Don't give me that look," she warned him, shaking a sliver of antler. "She's a big girl. I can't tell her what to do."

The rest of Marty's cleanup went well, and in no time his little moose head was ready for re-crowning.

Melodie had just dumped a pound of sugar into a double boiler and adjusted the flame beneath it when all hell broke loose in the alley behind the store. Trash cans rattled, and something thumped around by the Dumpsters.

"Damn cats and raccoons." She swiped her hands on her apron and grabbed the broomstick Arnie used to keep the local fauna out of his trash. Making as much racket as she could, she flipped on the back light and opened the rear door. The stray cats usually scattered fast enough, but the raccoons seemed to get braver every year. The last time she'd encountered one of the black-eyed bandits filching egg shells and fondant scraps, he'd given her what sounded like a dressing down for interrupting his dessert. Fortunately she didn't speak racooneese or she'd have probably been insulted.

Just as she suspected, something had torn open a garbage bag and trailed some of the contents in a viscous mess down the side of the nearest Dumpster. Snorting sounds coming from the far side of the green metal bin suggested whatever it was had found something sumptuous in the trash and was chowing down. The thought of having to clean up the remains of a scavenger's dinner didn't leave Mel in a charitable mood, so she whacked the Dumpster with the broomstick. Two solid shots rattled the steel box and all the bones in her arms.

"Come on, move along, you little rat."

The snuffling stopped abruptly as though whatever it was might be hoping she'd go away. Must be an opossum. Raccoons usually argued before waddling off like surly little winos, but didn't opossums prefer to play dead?

She didn't want to look, but if she went back inside, she'd have a bigger mess to clean up later. A whiff of something vile wafted through the alley then, and she knew she was in for it.

It had to be a skunk. The little stinkers were normally scarce on this side of town. They preferred the fast-food joints down on Main Street where they could gorge on all-beef patties and golden fries. Then, drunk on saturated fats, they'd play chicken with the end-of-rush-hour traffic and wind up perfuming the entire west end of town. On a warm night like this, the stench could linger until dawn.

While Mel debated with herself, the snuffling began again in earnest, coupled with an oddly pig-like squeal. That didn't bode well. Curiosity and annoyance in equal parts drew her forward. She brandished the broom like a baseball bat, firm in her belief that there were no wild pigs in Amberville, Maryland.

She whacked the Dumpster again, and this time something horrible stood up and looked her in the eye.

The furry scavenger she'd expected turned out to be six feet tall, covered in lizard-green skin dotted with scaly pustules. He had a face like Clive Barker's worst nightmare. Half a dozen fangs protruded haphazardly from a gash of a mouth, and the clawed hand he thrust at her looked like it had at least eight fingers.

Nonplussed, she did what any red-blooded, half-Irish divorcee with three older brothers would do. She jabbed him in the gonads with her broomstick and screamed from her diaphragm.

Creature Boy grunted and doubled over, which was the effect she'd been after, but she hadn't counted on him losing his balance and lurching forward. She backed up fast, but the Dumpster blocked her escape, and she ended up pinned against the brick wall with him slobbering all over her green and white Gleason's apron.

He seemed to be whimpering in pain or some other less wholesome emotion. Mel used the broomstick to shove him backward. Sad, rheumy eyes met hers in the amber light filtering down the alley from the tiny parking lot out back, and he clutched his stomach just above the spot where she'd nailed him.

"Oh, crap. You're not going to hurl on me, are you?" She was about to bolt when he turned his scaly palms up as if to show her the crimson blood seeping from his middle.

His pumpkin-shaped head jerked to the side, and he glanced toward the parking lot, obviously afraid. That gave Melodie the sinking feeling something scarier than he was might be in pursuit. "Look, why don't you just sit back down behind the Dumpster, and I'll call 911?"

Ugly as he was, his blood looked very real. Could this be a frat prank gone sour? The kids from the U of M were always finding new and creative ways to humiliate one another, and this just smacked of a "costume party turned tragic" lead on the eleven o'clock news. Mel felt a minor pang of regret for having attempted to castrate him, and her guilt increased exponentially when he pressed something about the size of a cell phone into her hand.

The odd, oblong shape was smooth and cold and glowed faintly blue. It looked more like a giant sapphire than a phone, though. He muttered something unintelligible and tried to fold her fingers around the object. She slapped his crusty hands away. "Where did you get this?"

Amberville had one jewelry store, and the biggest stone they carried was a two-carat cubic zirconia. This looked...priceless. Not that Mel was any judge of jewels, being perpetually unable to afford any of her own.

"Look, why don't you just—" The words "sit down" stuck in her throat when a solid ton of slimy flesh crashed against her again. She dropped the gem into the pocket of her apron and made a frantic grab for his shoulders.

Her knees buckled under his weight, and her well-honed panic instinct took over, bidding her to kick and scream at the same time for maximum effect.

Before he managed to flatten her completely, his whole body jerked once. A questioning sound escaped his lipless mouth, and he backed away. Or, at least it seemed like he backed away.

Free of the burden of his scaly carcass, Mel hauled herself up and confronted something worse than a costumed frat boy tossing his cookies. All six feet of him hung limp as a rag doll, like a big green puppet with its strings cut. He seemed to dangle in midair, and from the now much larger bloody spot in the middle of his belly protruded the gleaming silver tip of a sword.

Melodie gaped at the thing that had killed him.

Easily six-four, surfer-blond and poured into distressed

denim and a well-worn white cotton T-shirt, Lancelot wore the smug expression of a quarterback who'd just made a game-winning touchdown.

With a clearly practiced move that showed off muscles sculpted at the gym, he shook Creature Boy's corpse from his blade and cavalierly wiped the residual blood off on the body.

"Are you all right, miss?" he had the nerve to ask with a lopsided, somewhat self-effacing grin that begged the question, *How cool am I?*

Mel stuttered something that was supposed to sound like, "I think so," then pointed her broom handle at the heap of suppurating flesh now stretched across the alley. "You killed him."

"*It*," he corrected as he slid his impressive weapon back into the long, black scabbard he wore attached to a wide leather belt which canted across his lean hips. "Gogmars are sexless. He's not a *he.*"

Mel blinked. "Gogmars? Uh...well, this Gogmar took a jab to the groin like a guy."

Lancelot shrugged and strode over to nudge the body with a steel-toed alligator boot. It might have been faux alligator, but in this light, Mel couldn't be sure. "You probably hit him in his third heart. Gogmars have three in their thoraxes."

The words "Gogmars" and "thoraxes" held little relevance for her, so Mel ignored them. More importantly, this "Gogmar" was now dead.

"But you killed him." Mel just couldn't get past that little detail. It didn't matter what the guy was dressed up as, he was still dead.

Lancelot cocked a golden brow at her. "Of course. Otherwise he'd have torn you apart looking for food. Gogmars are a lot like bears. They're very destructive when they're hungry." He held out a surprisingly well-manicured hand. "I'm

Palmer Van Houten, demon hunter."

"Melodie McConnell," she replied automatically before her sense of self-preservation returned. She let his hand hang there, unshaken, while his introduction sank in. "You hunt demons? In Amberville?"

"Well, all over, really."

Right. "You won't mind, then, if I call the police?" She backed up, broom at the ready, and glanced at the body behind him. *Fraternity prank gone bad, news at eleven* flashed in her mind again. Or maybe Crazy Palmer liked to play *Dungeons and Dragons* for real and had run one of his buddies through on the roll of the dice.

Palmer favored Melodie with a weary glance. His eyes were dark, a little bit sparkly in the dim light, and might have been mesmerizing if she hadn't just watched him impale someone. "The body won't be here when the police arrive. Gogmars usually melt after death. It takes between fifteen and twenty minutes, and it can be kind of smelly. Baking soda helps with that. You might want to shake a box or two around out here."

"Baking soda."

"Yeah. Look." He nodded to Creature Boy, who looked much more creature and much less boy at the moment.

"Eeew. Oh my God." Green sludge had begun to ooze across the alley, seeping from beneath the corpse, which seemed to flatten out a bit as she watched in horrified fascination.

"Sometimes they leave a stain."

It was times like this that Mel missed the good old days when a girl could simply swoon her way out of a difficult situation. Despite feeling a little light-headed and a lot queasy, though, she wasn't about to lose consciousness. She had no hope of waking up snug in her bed to discover this had all been a dream.

She gave Palmer a skeptical once-over and decided that he

was probably right. The body was almost completely—yech— liquefied now, and there didn't seem to be a reason to call anyone, except maybe an industrial clean-up crew. She figured tomorrow would be soon enough to contact her HMO and get the name of a good psychotherapist in her plan. Right now, a dignified retreat seemed to be her best option.

"Well, Palmer, it was nice meeting you. Thanks for saving me. I've got to get back to work. And by the way, you have a little Gogmar on your T-shirt."

He glanced at his chest, and while he was distracted, she bolted for the back door.

She'd have made it too, except she forgot she was still holding the broomstick, and it barred her hasty getaway. She turned to chuck it next to the Dumpster, and that's when hell itself roared into the alley.

Chapter Two

The blinding beam of a single headlight swept the alley. Palmer and Melodie both put their hands up to shield their eyes, which did little to increase visibility. The strong scent of diesel accompanied the belly-rumbling thunder of a six-cylinder on low idle.

Fortunately, the rider cut the light, leaving Mel blinking at the phantom color dots that swirled in front of her eyes. When her stunned retinas recovered, she focused on the movement of leather-clad arms reaching up to remove a gleaming black helmet.

Next to her, Palmer drew his sword and shoved one broad shoulder forward in a move that said, "Get behind me, wench." Annoying as it was, though, the attitude suited him.

A masculine wave of dark hair tumbled from the helmet, and Hell's angel revealed a face that could stop traffic. A day's growth of sexy stubble shadowed a granite jaw. Sculpted lips curved in a humorless grin, and deep-set hawk eyes zeroed in on the puddle of Gogmar evaporating around their feet.

"Oh, crap, it's DeWitt," Palmer muttered near Melodie's ear. She might have commented, but she was currently bewitched by a stare that made her palms slippery on the broom handle and her heart beat triple time.

Here was a man who sizzled.

She'd never been the type to be rendered speechless or weak-kneed by a show of testosterone, but Sugar Honey Iced Tea, this man was *fine*. Correction: This leather-wearing, Harley-riding, ally-skulking thug was *fine*.

He tucked his midnight black helmet under one arm and cocked a perfectly arched brow at Melodie's sword-wielding savior. *"You* killed the Gogmar, didn't you?" His words held an exotic lilt, just the hint of a Scottish brogue.

"I don't know what you're talking about. I was making out with my girlfriend. We didn't see anything. Right, sweetheart?"

Palmer wrapped an arm around Mel's shoulders, and the weight of his embrace nearly knocked an inch off her height. "Huh? Oh...right."

She assumed she was protecting them both by agreeing with him. Nevertheless she wasn't fully comfortable with Tall, Dark and Dangerous thinking Palmer was her boyfriend, or— and more importantly—that she was the kind of girl who would make out in an alley.

"You do realize you're standing in Gogmar guts," the mysterious DeWitt said.

"Umm..." The smell in the alley had grown into something no skunk could hope to emulate, and Melodie's desire to flee before *she* started to melt had become unmanageable. She decided to rat Palmer out and ducked from under his arm. *"He* did it."

The back door of Gleason's was two steps away, and she could have had it slammed, locked and dead bolted in a heartbeat if only she could have torn her gaze away from DeWitt's piercing stare.

"So what if I did?" Palmer stepped up, sword ready, while Mel inched back.

Leather God shrugged. "That's fine with me. All I want is the cabochon it carried, and I'll be on my way."

"It had no cabochon," Palmer replied.

Skepticism lit those fathomless eyes, and DeWitt smirked.

Mel conveniently forgot her desire to flee when he lifted a massive thigh and swung himself off the seat of his Harley. Leather boots, stone-washed jeans, black T-shirt, and a scuffed bomber jacket completed his bad-boy ensemble. As he stretched to his full height, her gaze dropped to his silver belt buckle, which looked big enough to hold tea service for four. She wondered guiltily if he were compensating for a small...id. Nah. A guy like this had the goods to back up that swagger. No doubt about it.

"I've been following it since sundown. I know it had the Cabochon, and I want it. Now." His demand held no room for argument, and the commanding tone of his rich, slightly accented voice made Mel want to give him whatever he asked for.

While Palmer postured, though, she slid another inch toward the door.

"You're welcome to search the remains, but trust me, there's no cabochon here."

"I can feel it. It's here." DeWitt advanced, Palmer brandished his weapon and Mel bolted again, figuring she'd just be in the way when they came to blows.

Rather than go for the armed opponent, though, DeWitt lunged for Melodie. Palmer ran interference, for which she was grateful, and she ducked inside the shop, cringing as a scuffle erupted behind her.

Once inside, she turned to shove the door shut behind her, but a booted foot wedged in the sliver of space between the door and the jamb, preventing her from closing it completely.

She screamed and thought about stomping on the intrusive instep, but her rubber-soled Keds wouldn't do much damage, so she ran. The door banged open, and the clatter and clang of armed combat followed her through the kitchen.

"She's got the Cabochon, I can sense it. Get out of my way and you won't get hurt, Van Houten." Blake concentrated on keeping the door to the bakery wedged open while behind him, the demon hunter took aim with his still somewhat bloody weapon.

The tip of the sword jabbed Blake in the ribs, and he momentarily forgot his preference not to harm humans in his quest. He whirled around, forgetting his prey, and wrapped his hand around Van Houten's sticky blade. Ignoring the bite of steel into his palm, he yanked the weapon out of the demon hunter's hands. It wasn't a move any man could get away with, but Blake didn't have to worry about scars, and physical pain had little meaning for him when his entire life was hell.

Disarmed now, Van Houten reared back. His fancy boots found no traction in the spreading puddle of rapidly disintegrating Gogmar entrails, and he went down on his denim-clad backside with an embarrassing yelp. With a disdainful glare at his nemesis, Blake flipped Van Houten's sword in the air, caught it by the hilt, and turned his attention back to the lissome brunette who, by the sound of crashing cookware, hadn't gotten very far through the bakery.

She possessed the Cabochon. Why and how were questions he could ruminate on later, when he was free. For now he had to get it from her before she had the chance to pass it on to a demon queen. He flung himself after her.

She slipped away from him, swift as the wind, and dashed through the bakery's stainless-steel kitchen on deft feet, her chestnut ponytail swinging.

Blake lunged, grabbing for the silky rope of hair, but missed. She skidded on her rubber-soled shoes and swung herself through the narrow door that separated the kitchen from the front of the shop.

He could have slung Van Houten's confiscated sword at her legs and tripped her easily enough, but she reminded him too much of a frightened doe, both skittish and curious, graceful and untried.

Even in his darkest hours since inheriting the Witch Hunter's curse, he'd remained loath to hurt anyone unnecessarily. He didn't want to consider what he might do if the day came when he had no choice.

The Cabochon had been entrusted to demon rather than human caretakers for that very reason, so the men of his cursed bloodline would never find themselves in the position to kill or harm a human being to end their exile.

Blake launched himself after his target again, but just as he rounded the counter that bisected the kitchen, Palmer crashed into his back. Incensed, he whirled around and grabbed his nemesis by the shirt. He might not have the stomach to hurt the girl, but at this moment, he had no qualms about causing Van Houten a little pain and humiliation. If the two were friends, maybe he could play on her sympathies if he threatened to hurt the demon hunter.

"Run! Get out of here while you can." Palmer's strangled command stopped Melodie halfway around the front display counter. She skidded to a halt and glanced back over her shoulder. DeWitt had Palmer by the stretchy collar of his T-shirt and was lifting his linebacker body about a foot off the floor.

Ignoring Palmer's gasping and his ineffectual kicks, DeWitt turned his predatory gaze on Mel. "I only want the jewel. Don't make me hurt him to prove how desperate I am."

And there went her escape plan. In a strange way, Palmer had saved her life, and weird as he was, she couldn't let him suffer on her account. "Jewel? You're looking for a jewel?" Why hadn't he just said so in the first place?

"The Cabochon is a cursed jewel. It will bring you nothing but tragedy. Hand it over to me, and you'll escape its curse."

"Ah, okay. I think I know what you're talking about. The Gogmar gave me something in the alley, right before he...died."

Tortured eyes searched hers, and she had the distinct impression he could see into her soul. The oddly naked feeling made her shiver.

"It *gave* you the Cabochon?"

"It gave me a sapphire. Now, put Palmer down gently, and I'll give it to you if you promise to leave us alone, okay?"

She made a "down boy" gesture with both hands.

"If you give me the Cabochon, I promise, you'll never see me again."

That seemed reasonable to Mel, but apparently not to Palmer, who still dangled in midair.

"Don't do it, Melodie. He's pure evil. He'll kill us both if we give him what he wants."

"Oh, please." DeWitt dropped Palmer then, totally ignoring the "gently" part of Mel's request. "Get over yourself, *demon hunter*. There's nothing *pure* about me."

Clutching his chest, from which DeWitt had likely ripped a handful of hair, Palmer slithered away along the floor. With a lot more bravado than she felt, Mel inched back into the kitchen and put herself between DeWitt and Marty, who still sat grinning like a fool on the very edge of the center workstation.

"Okay. Nice and easy," she said, holding up her hands like this was an old-fashioned stickup. Since it appeared the only weapon DeWitt possessed was Palmer's sword, she probably could have made a break for it, but she really was more than willing to part with whatever it was Creature Boy had given her.

"It's in my pocket." She reached slowly for the gem that the

Gogmar had pressed into her hand. DeWitt's tawny gaze followed her movements, skeptical but anxious. Judging by his expression, Mel held all the power. He wanted the cursed jewel just as badly as she wanted to get rid of it. When her cold fingers scraped the crumb-dusted bottom seam of her apron pocket, her heart shriveled a little. With a reassuring smile for DeWitt, she felt to the left, then to the right. Nothing.

She held open her pocket and glanced inside. There was nothing there but a few shards of antler and a little ball of bright green lint. "Um…"

DeWitt's accusatory glare made her spine tingle. "You lied to me, lass." The timbre of his voice brought to mind the windswept hillsides of Scotland and the icy depths of a cold hell. He was not amused.

"I *did* have it. I swear. It must have fallen out of my pocket in the alley. It's probably still out there under the…ooze."

DeWitt wasn't buying it. His ire wilted her. Under his alluring golden gaze, she *felt* guilty.

"I swear, I don't have it."

"Yes, you do." The accusation hung in the sweet-scented air of the kitchen for a second; then DeWitt lunged for her.

Melodie ducked out from under his two-handed grasp, leaving Marty to take the fall for her, and fall was exactly what he did.

Two handfuls of chocolate-fondant-coated coconut sponge cake went flying.

Mel dove, and just as she hit the floor, Palmer jumped up. He grabbed the naked stainless-steel handle of the double boiler and flung caramelized sugar and boiling water at DeWitt.

The pots clattered to the floor, colliding with what was left of Marty. Melodie yelped. DeWitt roared and clutched the hot goo now plastering his T-shirt to his chest. Before she could decide who needed her help more, Palmer grabbed her hand and dragged her out the front door of the shop.

"Oh my God! I can't believe you did that." Mel struggled to keep her arm attached to her shoulder as Palmer pulled her along the darkened street toward a bright blue Jeep Wrangler parked on the corner.

"He would have killed you. I appreciate you buying time, but it's a bad idea to lie to Blake DeWitt."

"Well, if he was evil before, he's going to be a little more evil now with third-degree sugar burns all over his front. And I wasn't lying. The Gogmar did give me a jewel, a big one, right before you skewered him."

Palmer yanked open the passenger door of the Jeep and literally shoved Mel inside. She had a split second to recall all her mother's warnings about never getting into a car with a stranger before she settled in and pulled the seat belt across her chest. Palmer threw his empty scabbard in the backseat and slid behind the wheel with a backward glance at Gleason's front door.

A second later, the engine roared, and the vehicle lurched into the empty street. "So you've still got the Cabochon?" he asked.

Mel grabbed the dashboard as the Jeep careened around a corner and took the straightaway of Garden Street at a cool sixty miles per hour. "No. Like I said, I must have dropped it in the alley. DeWitt will probably find it, and then we won't have to worry about him, right? Who the hell is he anyway, and why are you so scared of him?"

Her dubious savior gave her a sour glance. "I'm not scared of him, though anyone who knows of him probably should be. He's cursed. Seriously cursed. And rumor has it he can transfer his curse to someone else through the Cabochon. Oh shit, he's following us."

The rumble of DeWitt's Harley tickled the hairs on the back of Mel's neck, and she turned in the seat to look out the Jeep's back window. A single headlight glared back at her. "How fast can this thing go?"

Palmer grinned wickedly and stomped on the gas pedal. "Just watch—and hang on!"

Chapter Three

Each breath Blake took stretched the burned skin of his chest, sending sparks of energy along every nerve ending in his body. He wanted to crawl away and nurse these temporary wounds, but the misery of his injuries paled next to the prospect of spending the rest of his life in thrall to the Witch Hunter's curse.

Instead of giving in to it, he ignored the pain, just as he'd trained himself over the past decade to ignore all the other hardships of this unwanted existence.

This young woman had the Cabochon, his only ticket back to the land of the fully alive, and all he had to do was take it from her. The chance to finally end the curse was worth a little discomfort. Or a lot.

As he leaned into the next turn in hot pursuit of Van Houten's Wrangler, he pictured her face. Waves of chestnut hair framed unblemished porcelain skin. Eyes the color of rich chocolate had assessed him as a threat. More than his burns did, it pained him to recall the terror in her expression when he'd reached for her. Thanks to Van Houten, she probably believed he was nothing more than a soulless monster, and she'd run from him, making his task all the more difficult when it didn't need to be.

The Wrangler increased speed, and Blake cursed. He'd

burned up most of a tank of gas following the Gogmar, and now he was riding on fumes. He couldn't afford to be stranded in the open at dawn, so, reluctantly, he veered off when his prey took a sharp turn around the corner of the Sure-Shop.

He might have to suspend his search, but it wasn't over by a long shot. The woman obviously worked at the bakery. That meant he could locate her again when he had more time to convince her to cooperate.

With his nerves on fire and his tortured skin aching, he gave up the chase.

Temporarily.

The shops on Garden Street whizzed by in a blur of light and shadow. Behind Palmer's Jeep, the roar of DeWitt's Harley rose in pitch. Mel didn't think a Wrangler could outrun a motorcycle, but having just finished reading *The Secret*, she believed wholeheartedly in the power of positive thinking.

Palmer did some fancy three-pedal footwork, and while Mel's knuckles went white on the passenger-side panic handle, the vehicle pitched a ninety-degree turn into the parking lot of the Sure-Shop on the corner of Garden and Ross.

They bounced over half a dozen speed bumps and cut behind the building. Beyond the rear parking lot there was nothing but an empty field bordered by a rambling copse of very old walnut trees. The Jeep galloped through the field, and when Mel dared to look back, she saw nothing behind them but the winking lights of the convenience store's loading dock.

"We lost him," she said, careful not to bite her tongue when the front wheels dipped into a hidden gully in the tall grass. The hood shot up again on the other side of the dip, and the Jeep rumbled toward the trees. "He's gone."

"No, he's still around. We won't be safe until sunrise, but I know a place where we can hide."

"Sunrise?" That was in three hours. Sunrise was when Arnie Gleason would stroll into the bakery with his thermos of dark French roast coffee from the new Starbucks on Fourth Street and discover moose droppings all over his kitchen.

Sunrise was when Mel would lose her job.

"I'm not hiding anywhere until sunrise. I've got to go back to work. Now pull over...somewhere." She gestured at the last few yards of overgrown field before them.

"I can't do that. DeWitt will torture you for that cabochon, and once he finds it, he could transfer his curse to you."

"What curse? Let me guess, he's a vampire? Is that why we'll be safe at sunrise?" She'd heard rumors about vampires. Calypso had a friend in Ocean City, a practicing witch who knew a lot about vampires. The whole business of blood sucking made Mel a little squeamish.

Palmer twisted the wheel, and the Jeep slid between two trees. An old slab of pavement that looked like it might have been a road at one time cut through the little stretch of walnut forest. The bumpy ride smoothed out considerably once rubber met macadam.

"He's not a vampire. He's a lot worse, but he still can't move around during the day. We'll be safe in here, trust me."

There were no lights here, and the tall trees blocked out any moonlight. The only things visible in the twin beams of the Jeep's headlights were an overgrowth of crabgrass and a dizzy swarm of gnats.

Crickets chirped, and the little, invisible tree frogs sang in harmony with them. When the short run of pavement ended, the tires crunched on gravel. Palmer pulled to a halt in front of an eight-foot-high chain-link fence topped with razor wire. The reflection from the white three-foot-by-three-foot NO TRESPASSING sign bolted to the gate filled the interior of the Jeep with a chalky glow.

"I don't like this. I don't like this at all." Melodie flung her seat belt off and leaned toward the door, but Palmer put a hand on her arm. His touch was gentle and reassuring, but nevertheless the knot in her stomach tightened. She didn't know this guy from Adam.

"It's okay. This is just the rear entrance of Taylor Tools. My uncle owns it, and I work out of the back."

Taylor Tools was over on Gordon Avenue. Mel didn't spend much time in hardware stores, so she wasn't familiar with the place. She imagined they carried a lot of high-end yard implements like those fancy ride-on mowers and four-burner gas grills, but why would a hardware store need razor wire atop its fence?

"Look, Palmer, I appreciate you saving me from the Gogmar and from DeWitt, but I'm not going into a deserted tool warehouse with you. Under. Any. Circumstances. I'm getting out now, and I'm going back to the bakery to clean up the mess we left so I don't get fired."

Palmer sighed and settled back in the driver's seat. "I don't blame you for not trusting me. This must all seem pretty bizarre."

"Well, yeah. I don't get many demons in my Dumpster, you know." Just saying the words made the whole incident seem like a tabloid fabrication.

Palmer shrugged in an odd way, as though debating whether or not to comment on that. "Well, actually...you do."

"Oh?" Mel eyed the passenger-door handle. She didn't relish the idea of walking all the way back to Gleason's, but she was ready to make a break for it and take her chances.

"In the past couple of months, there's been a lot of supernatural activity around Gleason's. Demons are naturally attracted to sweet smells, but I suspect there might be a vortex or something under the bakery. This wasn't the first Gogmar

I've seen in the area, and a couple of weeks ago, I tracked a Fremling to your alley."

"A Fremling?" First Gogmars, now Fremlings. What next? This just had to be some kind of college prank, even though both Palmer and DeWitt seemed a little too old to be frat boys.

"Yeah. They're much smaller than Gogmars but pretty nasty. Your boss, Arnie, came across it, and I had to kill it."

"Arnie encountered a demon in the alley and didn't mention it?" Mel laughed. Arnie talked nonstop about everything. He didn't floss his teeth without there being a story involved that he had to share with everyone. A demon encounter would have kept him jabbering for days, but all he'd mentioned in the last few weeks was how voracious the raccoons had become.

"He doesn't remember it. I used pixie dust on him."

She gave him a vapid grin. "Pixie dust."

"Seriously." Palmer shifted in his seat and pulled a small cloth bag out of his front jeans pocket. He reached into the pouch and pinched some purple sand between his thumb and forefinger. It fell, glittering in the pale light, when he rubbed his fingers together. "Pixie dust makes you forget encounters with demons, ghosts, warlocks and vampires. It's standard demon-hunter equipment. I'd have used it on you tonight, but I can't let you wander around not knowing DeWitt is after you."

As entertaining as his demonstration was, Mel finally summoned the willpower to pop open the passenger-side door and swing her feet out. "You're completely insane. Thanks for the ride, though. I gotta go."

To his credit, he didn't try to stop her from getting out of the Jeep, but the weight of his disapproval settled on her as she exited into the buggy darkness.

"Melodie," he said in a familiar tone. She'd heard it all too often from her mother whenever she insisted on doing something Laura McConnell considered foolish or frivolous.

Sadly, she'd heard it more now in her late twenties than she had during her rebellious teenage years.

She peered at him. "Palmer, I don't believe in pixies, demons or curses."

"Fine. But do you believe in DeWitt? He's dangerous, and he's not going to give up until he finds the Cabochon."

She would have protested, but the distant growl of a motorcycle made her skin prickle and panic creep up her spine. She gave the dark swath of forest a skeptical glance.

"I'll drive you back to the bakery at dawn. Scout's honor." Palmer held up three fingers in the traditional salute.

"You were a Scout?"

"Made it all the way to Eagle, and I have all my badges." He patted the passenger seat, and with another sweeping glance at her surroundings, Melodie climbed back in. It wasn't the Scouting thing that made her trust him; it was a sudden, abject fear of DeWitt. That motorcycle seemed awfully close, as if he might have been circling the blocks systematically tightening his search radius. With a shiver, she pulled the door shut as quietly as possible and turned a hard stare at Palmer.

"Okay. I don't need to tell you that one false move and I'll see that you end up like the Gogmar, do I?"

He smiled. "On my honor, you're safe with me, milady."

She wasn't quite buying it, but her alternatives weren't any better. She watched while he pulled what looked like a garage-door opener out of the glove compartment and aimed it at the fence. The gate rolled open on small, squeaky wheels, and he eased the Jeep into the deserted lot beyond, then killed the lights.

The gray, corrugated façade of a temporary-style warehouse loomed in front of them, broken only by a narrow black door. Palmer got out and, ever the Scout, hurried around the front of the Jeep and opened Mel's door for her. She followed him across the weedy, cracked asphalt to the door, which he opened with a small silver key.

"So tell me about this curse," she said as he bumped the door with his hip to open it. He reached around the jamb and flipped on a series of lights, illuminating what could only be described as a fantasy gamer's war room.

Two computers sat side by side on a metal desk which overflowed with papers, notebooks and empty Styrofoam coffee cups. The monitors glowed green with the scrolling code from *The Matrix.* Maps of Amberville and the surrounding towns, including areas of West Virginia and Pennsylvania, covered three of the walls. Little red pushpins dotted the maps with the largest concentration falling between Amberville and Baltimore.

Palmer seemed unconcerned by the mess. He shoved a pile of papers off one of the two ergonomic desk chairs and offered Mel a seat before answering her question. "Blake DeWitt comes from a cursed bloodline. An ancestor of his was a witch hunter who, legend has it, was sentenced to turn to stone by day by the coven of the last high priestess he murdered. The jewel that holds the spell, a cabochon of some unidentified mineral, was given to a demon queen to keep it safe. Story goes, only when the Cabochon changes hands, when it's passed from one demon queen to the next, can the cursed witch hunter retrieve it. When he possesses the gem, he can transfer the curse to someone outside of his bloodline. Otherwise, on his death, it merely reverts to his closest male heir."

Mel listened with half an ear while she scanned the sketches of demons and other odd creatures that filled the spaces between the maps. She recognized a Gogmar, not a bad rendition, but most of the other creatures looked like things out of someone's drug-induced nightmares. She didn't want to ask which fanged, clawed ball of nastiness might be a Fremling.

"So DeWitt turns to stone during the day?"

"So I'm told. I've never seen him do it. He must have a pretty good hiding place of his own."

"And you've dealt with him before? He seemed to know you back in the alley."

"We've crossed paths. He hunts demon queens, naturally, searching for the one who holds the Cabochon so he can intercept a transfer."

"If he hunts demon queens and you hunt demons, one would think you'd be on the same team."

"Well, if he wasn't looking for someone to take that nasty little curse off his hands, and he wasn't a stone-cold bastard, things might be different."

Mel nodded. She really didn't want to know more about how bad DeWitt was. She already had the heebie-jeebies about him possibly stalking her for a jewel she didn't have. "How are we going to convince him that I don't have the cabochon he's looking for?"

Palmer crossed his arms over his chest. "As soon as it's light, we should go search the alley again. Are you sure you had it in your pocket?"

"I'm sure...ish. I was about to be bled on by a Gogmar. I really wasn't thinking clearly. I remember dropping it into my pocket. Then he fell on me, then you shish kebabbed him. End of story."

"So it's probably still in the alley somewhere. We'll find it, and I'll figure out a way to pass it along to a demon queen. If a Gogmar was walking around with it, there's got to be a queen somewhere waiting to receive it. Once the transfer is complete, DeWitt won't be able to do anything."

"What if he already found it?"

"If he had, he wouldn't have followed us. He'd be out looking for someone to transfer the curse to."

"Maybe he just wants to sell it. It looked expensive."

Palmer shrugged. "Believe what you want. You're in danger as long as he thinks you have it."

Melodie checked her watch. Still almost three hours until sunrise. As far as she was concerned, that was way too long.

After filling up his Harley at the Sun Station, Blake returned to the bakery. Fortunately neither the front or back doors were locked, so he had free run of the place. He started with the alley, where little remained of the Gogmar but the faint essence of unwashed carcass and a few greenish smudges on the lower bricks.

Cursing Van Houten, Blake tore through the alley. He searched every piece of rubbish that had fallen from the few plastic garbage cans and even hauled the Dumpsters around on their rusted wheels to look beneath them. He didn't expect to find the gem out here or anywhere in the vicinity, actually. He'd lost the trail. That strange silvery tingle that had been making the hair on the back of his neck stand up the past few nights had disappeared. An uneasy feeling in his gut told him the transfer wasn't complete yet, fortunately. He'd know when it was too late to save himself...he would taste defeat. That meant the girl still had the jewel—a point in his favor, and finding her again would be a lot easier than trailing a demon.

A quick recon of the bakery turned up her purse, hanging on a hook in a coat closet next to the employee restroom. Without remorse, Blake filched her wallet and rifled through it. She carried less than twenty dollars, a few pictures of people who appeared to be family, judging by their resemblance, and a MedicAlert card bearing her name. Melodie McConnell—a Scottish lass?

According to her Maryland driver's license, she was five foot five, a hundred and twenty pounds, and she lived less than a mile away in a small duplex development near the railroad station on Mortimer Avenue.

Satisfied with his snooping, Blake stuffed her things back in her bag. He toyed with the idea of swiping her keys and paying her a visit before sunrise, but if Palmer was worth his salt, he'd be doing everything in his power to hide the girl until then.

Tomorrow night, he'd resume his search for the Cabochon, and now he knew exactly where to begin.

Chapter Four

As promised, Palmer delivered Mel back to Gleason's at 6:07 a.m., one minute after sunrise. An inch-by-inch survey of the Gogmar-scented alley turned up nothing more gem-like than a few pieces of broken glass and left her eighteen minutes to clean up the mess in the kitchen and concoct a believable explanation of why Arnie would need to bake a brand-new moose for the Lodge Initiation Dinner.

Palmer gave her a sympathetic look when her shoulders drooped. "I'll help you. Give me a dustpan, and I'll work on the cake crumbs. For what it's worth, it looked delicious."

Without preamble, she handed him the dustpan. While he collected Marty's remains, Mel mopped up the water from the double boiler and chipped hardened sugar off the countertops and the floor.

Despite Palmer's wild story about DeWitt's curse, or maybe because of it, she found herself feeling a little bit sorry for the guy. He hadn't seemed all that evil, and she imagined being turned to stone, for even part of the day, had to put a major dent in one's social life. Could she really blame him for wanting to foist that burden off on someone else?

She shook her head as she dumped sugar in the trash. Right now she needed to concentrate on keeping Arnie from freaking out. She needed to stop worrying about there being a cursed witch hunter on her trail, at least until night fell again. By then, hopefully, someone would use a little pixie dust on her and make her forget all this ever happened.

Palmer finished his cleanup, left her a card with his number on it and made himself scarce barely seconds before Arnie arrived. To Mel's shock, Calypso strolled in on his heels, looking fresh as a daisy in her thigh-high boots and leather skirt. Over those she wore a man's button-down shirt cinched at the waist with a yellow-and-black-striped silk tie. The shirt's crisp white collar was turned up to hide the runes tattooed on the sides of her neck.

Cal had a sixth sense about her, and though she hung back while Arnie and Mel exchanged pleasantries and discussed his morning's coffee-buying adventure, the moment he wandered into the back to get started on his next culinary masterpiece, she pounced.

Her kohl-rimmed eyes bore into Mel's. "You've been fooling around, haven't you?"

Torn between wanting to confess to the only person who might have half a chance of believing her and wishing the whole sordid evening would go away, Mel gaped. She decided a good offense was the best defense and turned the tables rather than spout her wild story just yet. "*Me?* That's Angelo's shirt you're wearing, isn't it? I recognize the smell of his aftershave. *And,* what are you doing up at this hour anyway?"

Cal blushed beneath her Goth makeup and brushed at her straight black bangs. "Honey, I'm too jazzed to sleep. I figured I'd come in and do a little work on the Augustine wedding cake before I crashed. Now enough about me. Spill. You've had a man in here. I can smell testosterone."

"That's creepy." Mel pulled Cal aside, out of earshot of Arnie, who was whistling his way through the kitchen. In a moment, he'd open the fridge and find Marty gone. "I've got a problem."

Calypso snickered. "How many times have I told you, I can hook you up with a guy just like that. All you have to do is—"

"The moose is toast."

Cal's fake eyelashes fluttered. "There's a sentence you don't hear every day. What do you mean? What moose?"

"Marty. The moose, you know, for the Lodge Dinner, *tonight.*"

"Oh. *Oh!* Shit. What happened?"

Mel deflated a little. "It's a long, strange story. Will you help me make a new one?"

"Sure, but Arnie's going to find out."

"Will you help me keep it from Arnie? I don't want him to freak. The Mooses...*Moose* gave him so much trouble about the design, the deadline, the flavors. If he finds out we have to start from scratch because I wrecked the cake—well, I didn't wreck it, but it got wrecked—he'll have a coronary."

Calypso glanced over Mel's shoulder at Arnie. "I owe you one anyway. I'll do whatever you need me to do on one condition. You have to tell me absolutely everything you did last night and who you did it with."

"You'll never believe me, Cal."

"Good. The more outrageous, the better. Let me make a few phone calls and see if I can arrange to get Arnie out of here early; then we can get to work."

Mel sighed. Complete relief would come only when the Lodge took possession of a fully functioning moose cake, but with Calypso on the job, she at least had a chance of keeping hers. The day might not be a total disaster after all.

By the time the scent of coconut sponge cake wafted from the oven, Mel had begun to feel almost normal.

She stood at the stove, stirring a pot of melted sugar. The details of the previous evening spun around in her head like the gnats that had danced in the beams of Palmer's headlights. Demons. Witch hunters. Pixie dust.

Calypso had been staring at her for twenty minutes now, since the moment she'd gotten Arnie out of the bakery on a hunt for the perfect silver-coated nonpareils she required for the Augustine wedding cake. "Come on now. A deal's a deal." Cal wiped her hands on her apron and planted her fists on her hips. "How did the moose bite the dust?"

Might as well jump right in. "He was attacked by a witch hunter."

A strange shadow crossed Calypso's indigo eyes, and her dark red lips quirked. "Did he at least put up a good fight?"

"I'm serious, Cal. I knew you wouldn't believe me. It was a circus here last night. I heard noises in the alley, and when I went outside, there was this...guy out there with a sword." Best to leave the Gogmar out of it for the moment. "Then this other guy showed up on a motorcycle, and he chased me around the kitchen."

"On a motorcycle?"

"No. He left that outside. You're not buying any of this, are you?"

Cal turned her attention to the sheet of chocolate fondant she'd just rolled out on the coldstone at her workstation. "Hey, I've asked you to believe some wild things. Who am I to judge? What did this witch hunter look like, anyway?"

Mel returned to her stirring to hide the self-conscious flush that crept up her cheeks. How could she describe Blake DeWitt? A man who was both drop-dead gorgeous and utterly terrifying defied description. "He was handsome, in a rugged way. Dark hair, light brown eyes—you know, whiskey colored? And he had a bit of an accent. Maybe Scottish. He wore leather."

Cal raised a sculptured brow. "Leather, you say? I thought your men wore flannel or they wore nothing at all." She giggled, but there was a nervous undertone to the laugh that made Mel even more self-conscious. Did Calypso think she was lying?

"So Larry worked in construction. He might have been a jerk, but he looked damn good in a tool belt." Mel's marriage had taught her all too well that looks weren't everything. DeWitt's piercing stare and craggy voice might have caused her a tingle or two, but the fact remained he'd been ready to do to her what he'd done to Marty.

"So he hunts witches. Does that come with health bennies and a 401K these days?"

"Apparently it comes with a curse."

Cal dropped her rolling pin. The thick wooden cylinder clattered to the floor and rolled away.

"You okay?"

"Fine." Cal chased the pin across the floor, scooped it up and dumped it in the sink. She swept the kitchen with a suspicious look. "Mel, let's not talk about this here. We can have the moose ready to go in two hours. Then we'll jet, and you can tell me more about this witch hunter, okay?"

Something about her tone didn't bode well. Mel scanned the kitchen too and then spared a quick glance at Calypso. She seemed rattled, and nothing, except Angelo, rattled Calypso.

Either way, Mel was certain now that Blake DeWitt was every bit as evil as Palmer had said, and Cal obviously knew a lot more about him than she was willing to let on.

By 1:00 p.m., Marty the Second reclined in the industrial fridge, his antlers tall and proud and his sugary teeth pristine and straight. Mel was dead on her feet.

After working the night shift at Gleason's for more than a

year, she'd gotten used to sleeping from dawn to early afternoon, so by the time she and Calypso managed to slip out and dash down Garden Street to Starbucks, she felt like a zombie.

Calypso pushed a double-tall, full-caf chocolate latte into her hands and herded her to a secluded booth at the back of the coffee shop where the comingled scents of cinnamon, peppermint and rich Colombian roast swirled around them like a grandmother's hug.

Mel sighed into the first hot sip of her latte. If she closed her eyes now, she'd be out before the double shot of caffeine made its way into her bloodstream. The only thing keeping her awake was Calypso's deadly serious expression.

"Tell me everything you know about the witch hunter," she began. Her own half-caf mochaccino sat untouched between them on the freshly polished table.

"I don't know anything, really. Palmer said his name was Blake DeWitt."

"Palmer...Van Houten?"

"Yes, he was the guy in the alley. He had a sword, calls himself a demon hunter. Do you know him?"

"I know of him."

Mel rummaged in her purse and pulled out Palmer's card. Cal grabbed the little white rectangle and studied it as though it might hold the secrets of the universe. "What was a demon hunter doing in the alley behind Gleason's?"

Somehow, staring into Cal's dark blue eyes, the details of the early morning hours didn't seem as farfetched. That realization only served to make Mel even more nervous. "Hunting demons?"

"What kind of demons?"

"Um..." Mel lowered her voice. "Gogmar?"

"Oh crap." Cal finally sipped her coffee, and under the

table, her three-inch boot heels made a nervous rat-tat-tat on the tile floor. "How many were there?"

"Just the one. That I...saw." Mel whispered the word "saw". She glanced around at the other patrons of Starbucks. No one seemed particularly interested in their conversation, though Calypso drew a few sidelong glances from several of the men. Her jet black hair, ruby lips and nosebleed heels never failed to garner a few double takes wherever she went.

She leaned in closer to Melodie. "So you saw a Gogmar."

"Wish I hadn't."

"What happened to it? Where did it go?"

"Remember that essence of decay around the back door this morning?"

"It's dead?"

"I assume. Unless it can recover from being impaled and then melting into green sludge." The memory of it dulled her enthusiasm for the latte. It occurred to her that Calypso didn't seem quite as freaked out as she should have been. It wasn't every day someone confessed to a run-in with a demon.

"Van Houten killed a Gogmar in front of you, and you *remember* it?"

Mel set her cup down. "Are you humoring me because you think I'm nuts, or does this conversation not seem that strange to you? We're talking about demons here. And I'm gathering you know about the pixie dust too. Maybe you *have* met Palmer before and you just don't remember."

"I don't think you're nuts. And pixie dust won't work on me." Cal dove into her mochaccino and resurfaced, innocently licking foam from her lips.

"Why? Because you're a witch?"

Cal's nervous laugh died quickly. "Why would you... All right. Yes."

Ah, well, that explained a *lot* about Calypso. "I always

suspected, you know. I figured you didn't think I could handle it."

For the first time in Mel's memory, Calypso looked embarrassed. "I'm sorry I never told you I'm a witch. I'm sort of in the closet."

"Oh. Why?"

Cal dropped Palmer's card on the table and slid it toward Mel. "Because of witch hunters like Blake DeWitt. If he's around, and there are Gogmars roaming the streets, that means trouble."

"I don't understand. It's the twenty-first century. How can he still be hunting witches? Isn't that illegal?"

Cal nodded. "He isn't trying to kill anyone. Only a witch can break his curse. It's been in his bloodline since 1729."

"Palmer told me about the Cabochon and the transfer from one demon queen to another. If Blake gets a hold of this jewel, he can give the curse to someone outside of his immediate family, right?"

"Yes. So far that's happened only once. When a man named Wendell Blake managed to transfer the curse to his nephew, Calvin DeWitt, rather than passing it on to his own son. I think that was in the 1860s."

The caffeine had begun to transform Mel's fatigue into nervous energy, and she fidgeted. Ignoring Calypso's wide-eyed stare, she grabbed a sugar packet from the carafe on the table, tore a corner off the blue paper pouch and dumped the sweetener into her cup just to keep her fingers busy. "I don't understand. This curse was originally placed on a witch hunter in 1729 and it's been passed down through his male descendants for all these years, even if they don't kill witches anymore? Isn't that sort of excessive?"

"Key word *curse*. If you look in the dictionary, you won't find it anywhere near 'justice'." Cal sipped the last of her coffee.

"The original witch hunter was Percival Blake, an English nobleman. He murdered at least thirty-five women, and not all of them were practicing witches. Some were just herbalists or midwives, women of vision or exceptional skills who made their contemporaries jealous enough to suggest they might have come by their talents from a questionable source.

"When Birgid Cooper cursed him, she put vengeance for thirty-five deaths into her spell—thirty-six if you count Percival's last victim was rumored to have been pregnant. It takes a long time for that kind of anger to play out. Plus, at the time, it was assumed that fear of witches and witchcraft wasn't ever going to go away. And it hasn't. Murder might be illegal now, but prejudice against practitioners of magick isn't."

"But Blake DeWitt isn't really a witch hunter, is he?"

"Birgid Cooper believed Percival would train his progeny to do what he did and carry on his legacy. She wanted to make sure they *all* suffered for it, I suppose, whether they were guilty or not, just like Percival's victims died whether they were witches or not."

Mel gaped. She'd never heard such conviction in Cal's voice before or seen such pain in her eyes. "Wow. I had no idea. Palmer said Blake DeWitt was evil. Do you think he's capable of hurting a witch to force her to break the spell?"

"A desperate man will do anything. The important thing is that the Cabochon gets into the hands of the next demon queen. Then DeWitt will lose his chance to transfer the curse to anyone else. We just need to figure out where the Cabochon is."

Mel's heart fluttered a bit. "Well...DeWitt thinks I have it."

Cal arched a brow and scoffed. "Why would he think that?"

"Because the Gogmar gave it to me."

Chapter Five

Blake might not have minded his daily incarceration so much if the cold, silent darkness had been complete. Oblivion from sunrise to sunset each day might have been a blessing at times, but since it was a curse, after all, why should it have an upside?

Rather than feeling nothing during his imprisonment, he dreamed. Day after day, for ten years, he'd walked in the shoes of Percival Blake, a man who'd lived more than two hundred fifty years ago. Each time Blake closed his eyes and succumbed to the icy embrace of the stone, he lived those horrifying years of an eighteenth century nobleman's life—from the heart-wrenching moment of his true love's betrayal, to the last plunge of a well-worn blade into innocent flesh and beyond, into the decades of torment that followed the moment of the curse's inception.

Each night when the sun set, he woke shivering in the basement room where he hid himself away, and he stretched stiff muscles and flexed tired limbs that ached from being motionless so long. On waking, he suffered the shame and remorse that Percival never allowed himself to feel.

This had to end. He couldn't go on hating himself for the sins of another man, living half a life and never seeing sunlight. He'd grown to envy vampires. They, at least, could look out a window now and then and see the day-lit world.

As far as Blake DeWitt was concerned, the sun had disappeared, and it wouldn't return until he broke the curse or, in desperation, passed it to a new bloodline.

Maybe the Van Houtens would do...

Calypso's jaw dropped, and she stared at Melodie over the lipstick-coated rim of her coffee cup. "*You* have the Cabochon?"

"Noooo... I seem to have lost it."

"So you *had* it?" Her sharp whisper drew glances from every direction. She bent her dark head and pulled Mel's hand into hers.

"I thought I dropped it into my apron pocket, but when I looked, it was gone. It's not in the alley or in the kitchen, and Palmer and I looked everywhere."

Cal's skin seemed paler than usual under her makeup. "We've got to find that jewel."

"That's what Palmer said. The Gogmar certainly doesn't have it. But where else is there to look?"

"I don't know yet. I've got to make some calls." Cal tightened her grip on Mel's fingers, and their gazes locked. "Mel, this is serious. I have no idea what Blake DeWitt is capable of, and I don't want to find out. Tonight you can't be alone after dark. Come to my place...and be there by sundown. If DeWitt thinks you have the stone, you won't be safe anywhere until we find it."

Tonight he traveled down the winding footpath as he had so many times before. He knew the way by heart. He knew the shape and size of the stone on which young Percival Blake stubbed his left big toe while hurrying to meet Rebecca Thorne in the glen. He recalled exactly where it lay among the scattered dry leaves and brambles, and he knew the toe would be sore for days afterward. Nevertheless, no matter how many times the blasted curse dragged him through this scene, he could not avoid that stone. The pain arced up his leg, and he yelped and stumbled, then laughed at this own foolishness.

Haste makes waste, he would always admonish himself. Better to be a few minutes late for their rendezvous than miss it altogether because of an avoidable injury.

Percival slowed his pace and struggled to calm his racing pulse. These stolen afternoons with the beautiful Rebecca lent wings to his soul, but he dared not let anyone see him acting so giddy. If he was to eventually request her hand, he had to present himself at all times with the dignity and decorum befitting a young man who would one day take his place in the peerage of England.

After a few deep breaths, he pressed on, careful to hide the slight limp he'd acquired. He couldn't have his beloved Rebecca worrying about his careless injury.

Her voice reached him on the summer breeze, and his heart fluttered. How could the mere sound of her affect him so? This had to be love just the way the poets described it. Theirs was a meeting of souls destined by God to be joined as one.

Her words were low and reverent. Percival guessed she was praying. To have a pious woman for a wife was a gift he would cherish. Rebecca's deep, spiritual nature made her an excellent choice—even his mother had been caught in an offhand comment that she might deign to approve a match between them—though not if their secret meetings ever came to light. He had to take care to hide his true feelings in public for now, lest he compromise them both.

At the end of the path, he parted two crossed willow branches and caught sight of a vision in rose-colored satin. Rebecca knelt at the edge of the glen, just before a stand of alder, where last spring her brother, Charles, had cut several fat boles to make a set of parlor chairs. She often sat on one of the stumps in the late afternoons, doing needlework while Percival read to her from the works of Chaucer.

Today, instead, she knelt before the stump, her skirts spread on the ground, her golden head bowed. She stiffened at Percival's approach, and rather than greet him with her usual radiant smile, she turned frightened eyes on him. Her gaze rose no higher than his cravat, and slashes of high color showed through the white powder that covered the pale skin of her face.

"You are early..." It was an accusation, not a greeting.

"I daresay I'm a bit late. It's after two."

A delicate hand rose to cover her mouth, and she glanced at the shadow he cast across her makeshift altar—an altar that bore the mark of the Devil.

Rebecca rose swiftly, upsetting the cup of wine that sat amid a wreath of flowers on the alder stump. The liquid spilled, red as blood, into the black gouges that formed a five-pointed star and circle in the wood.

"Percival..." Her pale hands fluttered ineffectually like doves startled into flight. She reached for his arm, and he pulled it away, loath now to submit to her touch where moments ago he'd craved it more than breath itself. "This is not what you think."

A cold fist closed around his heart, and his lungs faltered. The rich golden light of the late-summer afternoon seemed to dim. Color drained from everything around him. "I think you are not the woman I love. Rebecca...what's happened to you? How have you come to this atrocity?"

Tears filled her dark eyes. "Percival, please. You must understand, this is not the Devil's work. I swear to you."

He stumbled back, his legs weak and his gut aching as though a blade were twisting in his entrails. "In the light of day, before the eyes of God, you consort with the Dark Prince? Rebecca, think of your family... How could you?"

She straightened her shoulders and set her jaw. "My mother taught me. I have inherited her gift. If you give me a chance to—"

"God in heaven!" A sob caught in his throat. Percival Blake had not shed a tear since he'd left childhood behind, but now grief like he'd never experienced overcame him. "Tell me you're only playing at this, that you're mocking the rites of evil. I can forgive you if you've done this in ignorance, and together we can ask for absolution from our Heavenly Father."

She hesitated, as if she might repent. In that moment, Percival would have forgiven her. He would have gratefully made himself forget what he'd seen. But rather than accept salvation, she stood tall and proud.

"I'm not playing. I'm giving thanks to the Lord and Lady for this perfect day and for your love and companionship in my life." She looked away from him. "I had meant to be finished before you arrived..."

"You meant to hide it from me." Percival clutched his chest. He could never have imagined the pain of a broken heart would dwarf every other discomfort in his life. Losing Rebecca this way would haunt him for all eternity.

She rushed at him then, a foolish move perhaps but one clearly born of desperation. "Please, sit down before you fall. Let me tell you about the way of the witches, and you will see that we mean no harm to any living soul." Her fingers clutched at the lapels of his overcoat, and her sweet breath caressed his cheek.

She smelled of elderberry wine.

Fear and anger welled up in the empty spot where his heart had been, and he grabbed her wrists and threw her away from him. She stumbled back and landed next to the stump.

"Percival, please!"

"No. Do not speak my name. Do not look at me." He whirled around, and his wild gaze fell on a stone similar in size and shape to the one he'd tripped upon earlier.

Clutched in his trembling hand, it felt solid and real—his only connection to the earth from which God had fashioned mankind. All the rest was nothing but a devil's dream, an illusion created by Satan to mislead a righteous man. Mad with grief, Percival turned to Rebecca and raised the stone in his fist.

"Keep your distance, vile thing."

She sobbed so piteously that here, every time, Blake's own heart broke for her. He'd have relented. He'd have knelt at her feet and begged her forgiveness, but of course, Percival never did. He couldn't.

With all the strength he possessed, Percival Blake brought the rock down on Rebecca's temple. The sickening crack of granite against bone echoed in the quiet glen. The memory of her startled expression would never, ever fade.

She lay still after that single, vicious blow. Bright blood, darker and thicker than the wine from her unholy offering, pooled beneath her head and turned strands of her golden hair to copper.

For a long time, Percival stared at her corpse. When the shadows grew long around him, he dropped the stone beside her head, and he ran.

The moment the sun set, Blake shook himself free of the coma-like lethargy and stretched and flexed his cold bones. As he had countless times before, he pushed Percival Blake's roiling emotions out of his mind, said a brief prayer for the soul of Rebecca Thorne and emerged from his self-made prison cell to join the world for a few short hours of darkness.

Chapter Six

Despite Calypso's assurances that DeWitt wouldn't be a threat until sunset, when Melodie returned to her apartment, she locked all her windows and checked behind the shower curtain.

She needed sleep desperately, but now, with the super-sweet latte sloshing in her otherwise empty stomach, she couldn't get comfortable in her bed or on the couch. Not even the television could distract her from memories of the Gogmar attack.

She tried a hot shower, followed by a sandwich and decaf herbal tea, and she still felt wired. Even with her dark shades drawn, the apartment seemed brighter than usual. The early autumn sun would not be denied entrance through any crack or crevice, reminding her that there was a world outside that she'd missed quite a bit of in the past year since her divorce.

She considered taking a walk, but the blinking e-mail icon on her computer sidetracked her. A little Web surfing would probably tire her right out, so she curled up in her desk chair and dove into cyberspace.

An e-mail from her mom reminded her about the family gathering in Connecticut next month. Another from her oldest brother, Sam, filled her in on the antics of her twin nephews.

Spam offered her cheap Viagra, surefire investments and

bootleg software. She dumped all that in the trash bin and opened up her browser with a singular goal in mind.

"Cab-oh-kon," she said. "Is that with a C or a K? Let's try C-A-B..."

The search turned up several sites on jewels and lapidaries but nothing relevant other than what a cabochon looked like and how one was made. Next she tried "famous cabochons", which brought up almost nothing, and finally "cursed cabochons".

One hit.

The link took her to a website on demonology. The cursed cabochon was mentioned briefly in a small article about the assimilation of objects and weapons. The author mentioned priceless artifacts, magical weapons of mass destruction and enchanted objects being fused into the bodies of humans and demons for safe keeping. It sounded gruesome to Mel, but she read on.

By the time she'd scanned to the end of the article, her imagination ran full throttle, and her hands shook so badly she could barely maneuver the mouse.

She scrambled across the room and grabbed her purse. Calypso would be asleep now like Mel should have been, but Palmer had said to call him anytime.

She had to dump out her purse to find his card, and it took three tries to dial his number correctly. He answered on the second ring.

"Melodie?"

"How did you know it was me?"

"Caller ID."

"Oh...um, I think I need some help."

His voice dropped to a deep, concerned whisper. "It's too early for DeWitt. Have you seen another demon? They're not all nocturnal, you know."

"No, no. I think…" She wanted to hang up now and forget the ludicrous notions the Web article had put in her head. It was crazy after all, to think what she thought.

"Melodie, what is it?"

"I think I know where the Cabochon is."

"That's great!"

"No, it's not."

"Why? You don't mean DeWitt has it?"

"No. I mean, I think it's inside me."

Palmer arrived at Mel's apartment at dusk. Swordless, he seemed less the demon hunter and more the jock out of uniform, until he shrugged out of his denim jacket and revealed two sheathed daggers and a small, finger-triggered crossbow strapped in a modified gun holster at his side.

Mel stared at his arsenal. "Do you always carry all that?"

"Not always. It depends on what I'm after. Plus, DeWitt has my best sword, and I'll probably never get it back." He dug a familiar pouch out of his front pocket and handed it to her. "I probably shouldn't do this, but here's some pixie dust. If you run into DeWitt when you're on your own, it might confuse him long enough for you to get away."

"I'm *not* planning on being on my own." She gaped at the shrillness of her response. She'd passed all-out panic a while ago and had settled into thinly veiled hysteria. "You and Calypso have me scared out of my mind about this guy, and now I think maybe I do have exactly what he thinks I have."

"Whoa. Back up a little." Palmer set the pouch of pixie dust on the coffee table and scanned the room, hands on his lean hips. "There's only one entrance here, right?"

She nodded.

"Okay. First of all, take the dust. You never know. It should work on DeWitt. He *is* human, after all, so it might make him forget about the Gogmar encounter and how he met you. Second, who is Calypso?"

"My friend. She works at Gleason's with me. She's sort of a witch."

"A witch witch or a bitch witch?"

"A witch witch."

"Oh. Wow. You didn't tell me you had a witch friend. That's good."

"I didn't really know for sure myself until today. Palmer, we've got to do something."

He held up his hands. "Okay. Calm down. We have a few minutes 'til sunset, so sit down, take a deep breath and tell me what happened."

Mel didn't want to sit. She wanted to run and hide and forget all this weirdness. "I was looking up cursed cabochons on the Internet."

Palmer met her gaze with a blank stare. "Okay."

"The demon queens, where do they keep the Cabochon?"

Palmer shrugged. "In their lingerie drawers? I've never met a demon queen, so I'm not really sure. Demons have lairs, caves, bogs, portals to other dimensions, vicious guardian hell beasts. I'm sure they've got security covered pretty well. Why?"

"Can they assimilate the Cabochon, like...*into* them?" Reality slowed. Mel could not believe she was asking these questions.

Palmer gaped. "Um...into? Like swallowing or something?"

"Just absorbing it."

He squinted. "I guess."

"What about humans?"

"Can a demon queen absorb a human?"

Melodie rolled her eyes. "No, a cabochon."

"Can a human absorb a cabochon?" His eyes bugged out a little. Mel gulped. What if he said yes?

"I have no idea."

"But it's not outside the realm of possibility that the reason we couldn't find the Cabochon is that I've got it. I absorbed it?"

"No!" His adamant denial made her feel only slightly better. "That would contradict the purpose of the spell. The Cabochon was meant to be kept by demons in order to protect humans. Plus, demons live a lot longer, so it doesn't make sense to—"

"Well where is it, then?"

Palmer shook his head. He crossed the room and put a hand on Mel's shoulder. "I don't know, but it's not in you. Honestly, you shouldn't believe everything you read on the Internet."

His touch was warm and reassuring, and Mel began to feel slightly foolish. Lack of sleep had caused her to buy into the hokey legend of a cursed gem. She sighed. "You're right. I'm sorry. It just seemed to make sense, you know? As if stuff like that *could* make sense."

He grinned. "No problem. I'm glad you called me. I was worried about you."

"Apparently I need some worrying about. Look, it's getting dark. I'm supposed to be at Calypso's. Could you give me a ride?"

"You bet."

While Mel stuffed her spilled belongings into her purse along with the pouch of pixie dust, Palmer shouldered back into his jacket. With his weapons hidden now, he looked so normal, Mel could almost forget he was a demon hunter.

She centered herself with a deep breath and nodded toward the door. "You first."

He smiled wider. "Don't worry. I'm ready for anything. I've been doing this since I was sixteen."

She followed him out the door and turned to lock the dead bolt with her key. "Sixteen? How'd you get started? Was it an after-school gig, like a paper route?"

His complete lack of response had her worried. She'd hoped for at least a chuckle from him. Had he taken offense at her dig about his career choice?

When she turned around, his face was expressionless, eyes a little vacant. "I'm sorry. I just meant it's an odd thing for a teenager to get involved..."

Mel's gaze fell to the faint purplish residue on the collar of his T-shirt. "Oh no."

It was like shooting ducks in a barrel. Blake waited, arms folded across his chest, while Melodie McConnell locked her front door and finished babbling to Palmer. It had been too easy to puff a pinch of pixie dust at the demon hunter the moment he opened the door, just too easy.

He'd never seen Van Houten look better, in fact. The slack jaw and glassy-eyed stare fit the all-American so well. Blake would have laughed, but it really wasn't funny to see a professional demon hunter go down so quickly.

And besides, he preferred it if pretty little Melodie saw him as intimidating rather than bemused. He made sure his usual scowl was in place when she turned, very slowly, to face him.

"Don't scream," he said.

"Palmer..."

"He'll be blissfully asleep on his feet for another fifteen seconds or so. Then he'll take himself home, watch the MLB highlights on TV and turn in early. Won't ya, Palmer?" Blake nudged his nemesis, who nodded blindly and headed down Melodie's front stoop, ambling like a blond Sasquatch.

"Palmer! Palmer, no...wait!"

"He won't remember any of this. No point in following him."

She whirled around. "You stay away from me. I don't have your cabochon, and I don't know where it is."

"I know that's a lie for two reasons. One, Palmer wouldn't be hanging around here during prime demon-hunting time, and two, I wouldn't sense it around you. I'm sure he's told you all about the curse by now."

She nodded and backed up, flattening herself against the now locked front door. Her chocolate brown eyes were huge and round, and her delicate hands wrapped white-knuckled around her purse, which she held in front of her like a shield.

"Then you know, part of the irony of the spell is that whoever carries the curse can feel the Cabochon. Just another thorn in a crown of misery, a continual itch, a dull ache so that we can never forget our salvation can be had for the right price." Uncomfortable with his confession, he shifted from one foot to the other before continuing. "We're driven to search for it, to spend the precious few hours we're given each night trying to reclaim our freedom, which is always just beyond our grasp."

"I don't have it. I'm sorry, but I don't."

"You do." Frustrated with her denial, he advanced on her, and she shrank back.

On the curb, Van Houten's Wrangler started up, and the crafty little bakery girl used the momentary distraction to duck away from him once again.

She stumbled down the cement steps and hit the sidewalk running.

Blake sighed. He didn't want to hurt her, but he could no longer stand being this close to freedom and watching it slip away. He took off after her, determined to get what he wanted before sunlight stole his life from him again.

Mel ran full out, yelling for Palmer to pull over, but he paid her no mind. He took a right on Edgemont where the sidewalks ended, and she couldn't follow his Wrangler without plunging headlong into rush-hour traffic.

The ominous sound of DeWitt's heavy footsteps followed her. At least he hadn't jumped on his Harley. She could never outrun that.

Calypso lived on the opposite end of town in the garden-apartment complex that bordered the railroad tracks. It wasn't a great neighborhood between here and there, but Mel didn't know where else she'd be safe. She sprinted through the parking lot of the corner liquor store and climbed through the hole in the fence that had been there since Ricky Cartwright had taken wire cutters to it back in 1985. Voted the boy most likely to escape from prison by her high school graduating class, Ricky knew all the shortcuts through town, and he'd taught a few of them to Mel back in the day.

She'd never guessed there'd be an advantage to moving back to her hometown after her divorce, except that rents were good, and Arnie Gleason offered medical benefits to his night-shift employees.

A passel of feral cats scattered when Mel clawed her way through the bushes that separated the back lots beyond the broken fence. There were no lights here behind Rocket Dry Cleaners and three abandoned row houses. The overgrown yards were small and full of debris that had been torn out of the old buildings as part of Amberville's slow-moving urban redevelopment plan.

Mel picked her way over a pile of plumbing fixtures and skirted through the side yard of the center house. She'd emerge on Bailey Avenue where Dunbrook's All Nite Diner would be open and well lit, a safe haven.

DeWitt's footsteps had faded. She'd lost him for now, but she refused to kid herself. He knew where she lived. She couldn't spend another night at home until she got rid of the

Cabochon.

To hell with what Palmer said. She believed every word of the Web article. The Cabochon was inside her, and she had to find a way to get it out or spend her life running from Blake DeWitt and his witch-hunter descendants.

The fetid aroma of decay overtook her before she reached the gate separating the row house's narrow, overgrown side yard from Bailey Avenue. She hadn't seen any cans or Dumpsters in the yards. Everything there seemed to be construction garbage—old wood, torn insulation, cracked toilets and bathtubs.

The stench became overpowering, and Mel covered her nose with her hand and tried to breathe through her mouth.

A hiss of air drifted over her shoulders, and every hair on the back of her neck rose to attention. Whatever it was, it stank like week-old garbage, and it stood directly behind her, slavering and wheezing.

The gate sat less than three feet away, but Mel couldn't make her legs move. If she screamed now, who would hear her? If she ran, what would chase her?

She opted for both, consequences be damned.

Fueled by terror, she catapulted herself toward the gate, three of the longest steps of her life. Her hands closed over the rusty latch just as something grabbed a handful of her jacket and tossed her against the disintegrating clapboards of the house.

The impact snapped something—whether it was a bone or merely a rotted board, Mel couldn't tell. Her only sensation after that was fear. Then her vision blurred and dimmed, and she gave herself over to darkness.

Chapter Seven

Blake supposed he owed the Ak'mir demon a debt of gratitude or at least a sincere thanks for cornering his prey for him.

Miss McConnell was clever. She knew the back alleys of Amberville well enough to disappear from his radar in a matter of minutes. Had Blake been the only one pursuing her, she might have managed to vanish completely into the shadows.

Only the distinctive odor of Ak'mir clued him in. He hadn't seen one of the feathery-skinned reptile demons in a long time, but he'd never forget their smell. They were the scavengers of the demon breeds—like Gogmars, attracted to garbage, but not in search of sweet leftovers. The energy of decay sustained them. They fed on the heat generated by rot.

Lovely way to make a living.

Since Ak'mirs spent most of their lives well-hidden in dumps and cesspools, it made no sense for one to be skulking around construction projects in Amberville. This one must have been enthralled by some higher being with a more nefarious purpose. Dedication to its mission had kept it focused on the woman long enough for Blake to flatten one side of its melon-soft head with a length of board from the construction debris. Its body sagged against the peeling clapboards, and its dark gray skin faded to a deathly shade of dry bone.

After checking that Melodie was still breathing, Blake kicked in one of the row house's rectangular cellar windows and rolled the Ak'mir's noxious corpse inside. With a wet, slapping sound, the demon plopped into the cellar, where it would probably create enough of a stink to keep workers away for a day or two.

He couldn't be sure if it was completely dead. Very likely the energy from its own decomposition might be enough to revive it. He didn't want to stick around to find out.

Blake hoisted Melodie into his arms and considered his options. He wouldn't get far with her draped over the back of his Harley, and he'd probably raise a few eyebrows if he took a stroll down Bailey Avenue with her slung over his shoulder.

He glanced up at the house—three stories, probably gutted inside and not very safe, but dark, deserted and, at the moment, convenient.

Balancing his burden in a fireman's carry, he yanked away the few old two-by-fours that temporarily barred entrance through the back of the house. A half-rotted screen door creaked when he pulled it open, and the floorboards moaned under the added weight when he stepped inside.

What had once probably been a sunny little kitchen was now devoid of cabinets and fixtures. Only the scuffed linoleum made it recognizable. Blake eased through a narrow door and moved deeper into the house, where an ornate hearth dominated the former parlor.

An old mattress lay on the floor before the hearth, reeking with the scent of cat urine, no place for a lady. A painter's tarp lay crumpled in one corner. That would have to do.

A musty smell clung to the oilcloth, but compared to the mattress and the lingering essence of Ak'mir, he couldn't complain.

Melodie moaned as he settled her on the tarp. He didn't like the pallor of her skin. The Ak'mir had been brutal with her, slamming her like a rag doll against the side of the house. Odds were, if she didn't have a cracked skull, she'd at least have broken a rib or two.

He'd make an anonymous call to 911 just as soon as he retrieved the Cabochon. Guilt ate at him over the minor delay in calling for help, but to be this close and not complete his quest was suicide. The gem might never be this close again, and he couldn't go on much longer living half a life.

He started with her purse, upending it on the floor and rifling through with the skill and efficiency of a professional thief. All the usual female tools of the trade scattered on the dusty floorboards. Blake put her wallet, lipstick, compact and tissues aside first. Her cell phone buzzed in his hand when he picked it up. The caller, Smith, C., would have to wait to make contact.

With the larger items out of the way, the pickings were slim. He found keys, a pack of gum, a few crumpled receipts, and something that looked like a thick, permanent ink marker. Blake examined the object closely in the dim light.

Though it had a black twist-off cap, it wasn't a pen. It was one of those emergency epinephrine syringes used to treat allergy attacks. Blake recalled the MedicAlert card he'd found earlier, and the memory sobered him. He didn't want her to suffer any more on his account, but when would *his* suffering end?

The Cabochon wasn't in her purse. It had to be on her, which meant he'd have to search her.

He carefully repacked her purse, making sure to put the rescue pen back where he'd found it, then let out a long, slow breath. "Forgive me, Miss McConnell. I mean no disrespect, but you have something I need."

With deft fingers, he searched her pockets and frisked her

from head to toe. Unless she had a secret compartment in the heel of her shoe—and he checked there just to be sure—the Cabochon was not on her person. It hadn't fallen into the folds of the painter's cloth, and it hadn't rolled into the dark corners of the room.

Yet he felt its presence.

It teased him, tickled his senses. It called to him like a siren luring a hapless sailor to his death. Could this be some modern nuance to the spell? Could the Cabochon deceive him, lead him down a false path?

He sat back on his haunches and stared at her for a moment. With her chestnut hair in disarray around her and her pink lips soft in this unnatural sleep, Melodie McConnell was quite enchanting. Her vulnerability tugged at him. Had she been chosen by the powers that controlled the curse as a means to taunt him?

She didn't seem like a witch. She certainly hadn't demonstrated any magical power, yet she was clearly involved with the Cabochon somehow. He had to find out how, but at what cost?

For the first time in ten years, Blake felt no better than Percival. He hated himself for hesitating to get help for Melodie McConnell almost as much as he hated his murderous ancestor for inviting such misery on ten generations of men.

He snatched her purse from the floor and retrieved her cell phone, which was still buzzing intermittently with calls from Smith, C. Blake had disconnected the last call, hit clear and dialed nine when the woman stirred.

"Palmer?" Her brown eyes fluttered open, and she groaned. Blake retreated to the shadows in the ruined room, suddenly unwilling to frighten her.

He should have merely left, but he couldn't. The pull of the phantom Cabochon was too strong.

Mel pushed herself up on her elbows and looked around. She wasn't at home. She wasn't outside.

The memory of a terrible stench curdling the air around her came rushing back, and her lungs constricted. She coughed, which caused every muscle in her body to spasm in pain.

"Oh, God that hurts." Despite the stiffness in her back and neck, she forced herself to sit up. Had she been hit by a truck? No. A house.

Something stirred in the corner of the dingy room, and tawny eyes glittered in the feeble light filtering through a grimy window. DeWitt emerged from the shadows.

"Are you in pain?" he asked.

"What did you do to me?"

He spread his hands wide. "I rescued you from a demon attack."

Except for the lingering memory of that abominable smell, she might not have believed him. "There's a lot of that going around lately. Now that you have me, what are you going to do with me, witch hunter?"

"So you know about that."

"I'm not a witch, so I won't be able to help you. I don't suppose you'll believe me, though." Mel tried to scan the room without taking her eyes off DeWitt. Her purse lay on the scuffed wooden floor at his feet. Behind him, a torn-up mattress butted up against a dust-covered fireplace. The details of the room might have registered a bit more if DeWitt hadn't seemed so much larger than life. He stood with his booted feet planted wide apart, arms crossed over his broad chest. A lock of dark hair nearly obscured one amber-colored eye.

"I believe you're not a witch, and I believe you don't have the Cabochon."

She squinted at him. "You do? What changed your mind?"

"A body search." He tossed the response out with casual neglect, and Mel shivered at the implication. All her clothes seemed to be in the right place, buttoned, zipped and fastened properly. Either he was lying, or he was very efficient. She raised a brow. "It doesn't feel like you were very thorough."

"I can do it again, if you think I might have missed something. Are you really hiding the Cabochon somewhere under your skimpy shirt and tight jeans?" His fiery gaze roamed up from her sneakers to her lips.

Again she shivered. "No. I've been telling you the truth. I don't have any idea where the Cabochon is." Could he tell she was lying now?

"Well, someone or something wants me to believe you've got it. Any idea why?"

"If I had a clue what any of this was about, I might speculate, but I don't." Mel struggled to her feet. Her back ached, and the first step she took was agony. She winced, and DeWitt thrust a hand out to steady her.

"You shouldn't try to walk yet. The Ak'mir wanted to kill you. You wouldn't happen to know why?"

She shrugged. Even that small movement hurt. "I could ask you the same thing."

"You think I had something to do with it?"

"If I did have the Cabochon, wouldn't you want me out of the way?"

"Unless you're a demon queen, your death wouldn't benefit me in any way. You're not one, are you?"

Oh God. What if she was? "Of course not. Do I look like a demon queen?"

He shrugged, a casual move but nevertheless executed with finesse. "Some of them are quite beautiful, and one or two could pass for human. You don't have pointed ears or a forked tongue, do you?"

Beautiful? Had he complimented her or demon queens in general? Now wasn't really the time to consider it. "I wouldn't show you, even if I did."

The haughty tilt of her chin amused him. "Look, Miss McConnell—"

"Wait a minute. How do you know my name?"

"The same way I know where you live, and that you're five foot five and weigh a hundred and—"

She cut him off with a swift wave. "That's enough. So you snooped in my purse."

"Of course. Illegal search aside, can I propose a truce? I don't mean to harm you, even if you do have the Cabochon. I just want it back, and something tells me you might be instrumental in my actually getting it."

She favored him with a skeptical glance and took another experimental step. Blake held his breath. If she fell, he'd catch her, but she remained upright with only a slight grimace twisting her lips. "A truce?"

"I can protect you from the demons, and perhaps you can help me locate the Cabochon."

She counted on her fingers as she spoke. "One, I don't need protection from demons. Two, I have no idea where to find the Cabochon."

He mimicked her, ticking off points on his own fingers. "One, the Gogmar last night. Two, the Ak'mir tonight. Three, demons don't bother humans as a rule unless humans have something they want. Four, you smell like the Cabochon to me. I bet if I put my mouth on you, you'd *taste* like the Cabochon. You might not know where it is, but you're obviously the key to finding it."

She seemed to quiver for a moment, and Blake wondered if she might faint. Finally, she said, "Fine. I just want to be done with this. Oh, and you have to promise me something."

He raised a brow and gave her his best devilish grin. "Not to search you again? Or not to put my mouth on you?"

Judging by the color that rose in her cheeks, he'd succeeded in flustering her. Why that pleased him, he wasn't quite sure.

"No, well...that too, but you have to promise me that if you get the Cabochon back, you won't transfer the curse to me or any of my friends."

Blake sobered. All he'd thought about for ten years was freeing himself, and that's all he wanted to think about now. "I don't think I could transfer the curse to a woman, anyway, but I'll agree not to try."

"Good." She snatched her purse from the floor and, still moving a little stiffly, strolled out of the room.

Blake reactivated her silent phone and followed her. "You forgot this. I think one of your friends has been trying to reach you."

It rang immediately, and she whirled around. The look she gave him as she grabbed the phone from his palm could have melted lead. When her fingers brushed his, the spark of power, the psychic flavor of the curse, arrowed through his body like a lightning strike. He pulled his hand quickly away from the brief contact and jammed it in his pocket. If Melodie McConnell didn't have the Cabochon, she possessed something twice as powerful, and he had to find out what it was.

Calypso's panicked voice blared out of Mel's phone the moment she flipped it open. "I'm here, Cal. I'm okay." She kept her eyes on DeWitt while she spoke. He looked shaken, as if their brief physical contact had rattled him nearly as much as it had rattled her.

"Mel! Thank God. Where are you? I'm out in front of your

apartment. I've been banging on your door so long your neighbors are ready to call the cops on me."

"I'm over on Bailey. Stay where you are. I'll meet you there and...don't freak out, but I've got Blake DeWitt with me."

Of course, Calypso freaked. In between some very creative cursing, the witch managed to ask, "What did he do to you? If he's making you make this call, you tell him I'll see to it that *all* his descendants are cursed."

"Cal, calm down. I'm okay. We've struck a bargain."

"You can't bargain with a witch hunter."

DeWitt obviously heard Calypso—the whole neighborhood could probably hear her. His comment was directed toward the cell phone, but his eyes held Mel's. "I've never hunted witches. All I'm searching for is justice."

Calypso huffed. "I'll be here, but I've got spells, so tell DeWitt he'd better be on his best behavior."

"He will be." Mel snapped the phone shut. "You're in for it now. I thought Calypso was hell on wheels *before* I knew she was a witch."

"I'll behave, on one condition. No one calls me 'witch hunter'. Percival Blake was a witch hunter two hundred and eighty years ago. I'm an accountant. Or at least I was, until I inherited this curse. It's hard to keep a day job when you're not alive during the day."

Mel gave Blake DeWitt a long, thoughtful appraisal. The dark, disheveled hair, the broody gaze and day's growth of stubble on his strong chin along with the rippled muscles stretching the white T-shirt beneath his leather jacket didn't belong to any accountant she'd ever met. He looked more like a fallen angel, sinfully beautiful and sadly out of place. Something simmered in him, beneath the surface. She'd felt it when they'd touched, and she wasn't sure she had the power to resist it if she ever felt it again.

Chapter Eight

The short ride across town with Melodie settled snugly behind him, her arms wrapped around his chest, had him practically jumping out of his skin. Every nerve ending tingled as if he'd touched a live wire, not exactly unpleasant but disconcerting. The power of the Cabochon had always been a distant itch, something not quite definable. With her next to him, it transformed into something electric and irresistible.

All the way across town, he'd been edgy, as though his skin was on fire. The essence of the Cabochon rested against his spine like a blade, and the urge to claw it away and free himself from the burden of it had become nearly overpowering.

When he pulled up in front of Melodie's apartment, the black-haired witch glared at him. The weight of indigo eyes on him the moment he set both feet on the sidewalk did little to calm his soul.

Melodie swung his helmet off her head, and her dark brown hair tumbled in lustrous waves to her shoulders. The sight distracted him only momentarily.

"It's about time." The witch's smoky voice might have been sexy if it wasn't so full of disdain.

Melodie hurried up the short flight of brick steps to meet her, and Blake followed, allowing himself a leisurely appraisal of both women.

"Blake DeWitt, this is Calypso Smith. She's a good friend, so play nice."

At Melodie's introduction, Calypso flicked her waist-length hair off one shoulder but didn't offer a hand. Blake recognized the band of runes tattooed on her left wrist as a protection spell, and he caught the pleasant aroma of lavender and mint when she turned her back on him and followed Melodie into the apartment.

Calypso Smith was black lace and dark lipstick, and Blake had the feeling she could be as elusive as smoke and as deceptive as a mirror. Already he didn't trust her, but Melodie seemed enthralled by her larger-than-life presence in the tiny, neatly kept living room.

"I don't know why you brought him here, Mel. He's not getting the Cabochon from us, even if we had it." The witch crossed her arms, her body language lending weight to the unspoken message in her voice that there would be no negotiation on that point.

Fortunately, Melodie's stance was a little softer. "Cal, I think we need to consider that Blake isn't Percival. He's not a witch hunter, and this curse isn't his fault."

"It's not my place to decide that."

"Well, someone should."

"That's a discussion for the Witches' Council." Ms. Smith wasn't about to budge. If looks could kill—and he'd heard some actually could—her stony gaze would have put Blake out of his misery in an instant.

He put up his hands in what he hoped would be interpreted as a gesture of surrender. "I'm not here to debate right and wrong about the curse. Your friend, Melodie, seems to be the target of several demon species, and I offered her my protection. It feels to me as though she possesses the Cabochon, yet I can't find it. Bear in mind, I'm not the only one who can sense it. It 'belongs' to the next demon queen, and I have a feeling whoever she is, she's sent scouts out to search for it. To keep their pact with the witches, they won't hesitate to hurt Melodie to get at the Cabochon. It stands to reason, for her own safety, she should hand it over to...someone." No lie there. This defenseless human was in danger as long as she possessed the gem, or even just the secret to its whereabouts.

"I suppose by 'someone', you mean you?" The witch glanced at Melodie, but her piercing glare bounced immediately back to Blake.

"I mean someone who can handle it."

"Cal, Blake dusted Palmer, and I was attacked by a garbage demon."

"He *killed* Palmer?" The witch's already pale complexion blanched.

"No, *pixie* dusted. Palmer doesn't remember me now. And I was followed across town by a demon. I think maybe I could use a little protection."

"An Ak'mir almost killed her," Blake put in. "I hope you have some strong protection spells at your disposal, because your friend is going to need them."

Cal seemed almost as frustrated by DeWitt as Mel was, but in a more adversarial way. She could barely look at him. Her contempt for the man who was only a distant descendant of the original witch hunter seemed terribly out of proportion.

Mel wished she could tell DeWitt and Calypso about her theory, but she sensed that now wasn't the right time. She still didn't trust DeWitt enough to believe he wouldn't do something irrational, and her faith in her own intuition wasn't very strong. It seemed absurd to think she could absorb a gemstone into her body somehow, even though at the moment it was still the most likely explanation for what had happened to it.

DeWitt glanced at his watch. "I've got work to do, and I'm sure you ladies have a lot to discuss, so I'm going to leave. Melodie, I can't protect you during the day, but I'll be back tomorrow at sunset. Hopefully by then, whoever is in the know around here will have worked out a solution. I'd hate to see you spend the rest of your life pursued by Ak'mir demons, or worse." He turned to Calypso, but his next words were meant for Melodie. "I'd also hate to spend the rest of my life paying for the sins of Percival Blake. Isn't it time the Witches' Council took another look at the curse?"

He didn't wait for a reply. It was already after eight p.m., which, if what Palmer had told her about the curse was true, left him only a little over eight hours of life. Mel wondered what he did with his time besides pursue the Cabochon. A pang of sympathy for him competed with the ache in her bones and left her feeling like all the air had gone out of her.

Wearily she settled on the couch. Without the "witch hunter" to glare at, Calypso seemed a little directionless and fidgety. A strange energy permeated the room, and it made Mel's heart race and her palms sweat.

The witch paced. "This isn't good, Mel. Not good at all. He knows where you live, where you work, and he's still convinced you have the Cabochon."

"I do." She might not have trusted her instincts, but every cell in her body was screaming it. "I *have* got it."

Calypso froze mid-step, and her jaw dropped.

Mel explained the Web article and Palmer's assurance that it couldn't be true. "I know it sounds completely insane, but what if?"

Cal sank down in the chair opposite the couch. "Yeah. Crazy insane. It's not like you're a demon queen. *Are you?*"

Mel chuckled, but her humor faded when Calypso remained staring at her. "Why does everyone keep asking me that? Don't you think I'd know if I was a demon?"

"There are hybrids, but they're rare. No offense, you're not adopted, right? You knew both your parents? There's no one in your family tree who's a little...strange-looking?"

Mel gaped. "Come on, Calypso. That's ridiculous." Didn't Great Uncle Benjamin claim to have twelve toes? Aunt Mary always said she wore turtlenecks to cover her psoriasis, but did anyone really know for sure? "No. No. My family is as normal as any second-generation mostly Irish American family can be. We've got a few characters, but no demons. And even if we did, I'm certainly not their *queen*."

"Any witches?" Cal raised her brows.

"No. My cousin Fiona used to tell people she was an elf, but a year of therapy cleared that up." An odd realization hit Mel then. "Cal, you didn't actually say it was impossible for me to have absorbed the Cabochon, did you?"

Calypso hedged. She studied her black manicure and tugged on the zipper of one of her boots. "Well, no."

"So I could have, even though I'm human?"

"Anything is possible."

Mel's stomach lurched. "So what do I do? How do I get rid of it? What if DeWitt follows me around for the rest of my life trying to get it from me?"

Cal grabbed Mel's hands to steady them. "Relax. We'll figure something out. First we need to confirm that you have the Cabochon. I've got to figure out how to do that. Then I can research how to get it out of you without..."

"What? Without what?"

"Well, the demon queen holds the Cabochon until she dies. That's the only time it takes solid form and can be transferred to another queen."

Mel shot up from the couch. "So I have to *die* to get rid of this thing?"

"No, no, no. I'm sure there's some other way to get it out of you."

"Calypso, don't lie." Mel plopped back on the couch and jammed her hands underneath her knees. "You don't know for sure, do you?"

Cal bowed her head. "No, I don't. But I'm going to find out."

Chapter Nine

Mel spent her shift at Gleason's sculpting a hundred and ten pink fondant roses for the Augustine wedding cake. Work actually kept her mind off Blake DeWitt, but with Calypso whispering into her cell phone half the night, talking to members of her far-flung coven, Mel still couldn't concentrate.

Though she kept shooting fragile smiles in Mel's direction between abrupt conversations and frantic texting, none of the calls Calypso made seemed to end on a positive note. Plagued by a sinking feeling in the pit of her stomach, Mel kept losing count of the nonpareils she was gluing to the roses with a sugar glaze. The little silver balls kept dropping and rolling away, which added to her nervousness.

When Calypso finished what had to have been her fifteenth phone call, she came over to Mel's workstation and gave the roses an appreciative look. "These are perfect. Fantastic work."

"Much easier than moose antlers," Mel said.

"I'll say. Um...I found out there is a way to test you for the presence of the Cabochon."

Mel wasn't sure if that was good news or bad news. "It isn't dangerous, is it?"

Calypso shook her head. Then her guilty gaze wandered away from Mel's. "Not if you *do* have the Cabochon."

Mel's relief died in its infancy. "Only if I *have* the

Cabochon?"

"Well, if you don't, then the good news of not having it will sort of offset a little discomfort, right?" Cal's hopeful smile was the least convincing thing Mel had ever seen.

"Spill it, Calypso. What do I have to do to find out if I've absorbed the Cabochon?"

Cal sighed. It was definitely bad news. "If you have it, then no matter how hard he tries, Blake DeWitt will not be able to spill your blood."

Blake finished his work just before dawn and rose to stretch the kinks out of his back. He kept promising himself he wouldn't spend so many hours at the computer, but he had to make a living, and online trading was the best way he'd found to keep the bills paid.

He glanced at the water bed he rarely slept in and wondered if he did lie down, would the frame be strong enough to hold the weight of his granite body. How nice it might be to wake up from his imprisonment in a comfortable position for a change.

Better not to chance it. Having replacement furniture delivered after dark would be next to impossible, just like nearly everything else in his life had been during this past decade. Fortunately, since the curse had transferred to him upon his grandfather's death, he hadn't needed to see a dentist or a doctor, hadn't needed to spend a night in the hospital or in jail—though he'd come close on more than one occasion. He'd been meticulous with his schedule, obsessive about the exact time of sunset and sunrise each day. He'd become an expert at working around his strange handicap and hiding it from anyone who might be curious enough about his life to inquire why he seemed not to exist between the hours of dawn and dusk.

With a longing glance out his bedroom window, he headed

downstairs to the basement where he'd be safe and unseen until nightfall.

He'd cut it close this morning. The change came on him only seconds after he closed the door to his sanctuary. Muscles and bones stiffened, then hardened to rock. His last breath froze in his lungs, and memories of another life lived in the darkness of the soul took over his conscious thoughts.

Grief over the death of their beloved eldest daughter crippled the Thorne family. They sought solace in the church where Percival himself had spent many days prostrating himself on God's altar, begging for mercy on his soul. His guilt, though, never drove him to confess he'd been there when Rebecca struck her head on a rock in the meadow. Even when all the other mourners had left, and only Percival remained in the transept, he couldn't actually give breath to the words.

Shame had battled with disgust earlier, when Margaret Thorne had taken his hand at the funeral and thanked him for his kindness in their family's darkest days. Rebecca's voice played in his head while her mother, bowed with grief, wept.

My mother taught me. I inherited my gift from her.

How could this woman, so well thought of in society, a patroness of the arts and mother to three gentleman sons, have had congress with Satan? How could she have corrupted her own daughter by schooling her in service of the Devil?

Only days after Rebecca was laid to rest—on consecrated ground, no less!—Percival began his new career.

A length of sturdy rope became his weapon of choice. Good faith and a kind manner were his keys to the Thorne estate where he found Margaret alone in her garden, her needlework resting untouched in her lap while she stared into the crisp autumn sky.

She fell to him without a sound to alert the less than

attentive housemaid. Hands made feeble by grief clutched at the noose he slipped around her neck, but she didn't make a sound. Her dainty feet scraped the cobblestones as he dragged her body to the corner pillar of a small grape arbor and lashed the rope in place.

"Join your daughter at your master's side," he bade Margaret, though he was unable to meet her sightless gaze. At least she would not be placed in the churchyard, another affront to the Lord. He toyed with the notion of stopping now, having purged his own life of any evil influence. Margaret's death could be the end of the internal torture, and his ravaged soul could begin to heal. That thought buoyed him, and he left the estate with a light heart, foolishly believing he would never meet another witch.

No one questioned Margaret's suicide, and if anyone wondered how a woman of such short stature had managed to tie the hanging rope so high, they never spoke of it.

The negligent servants were punished severely and dismissed from the Thorne household shortly thereafter, and Percival told all who asked him how saddened he was to be the last person to have seen the lady alive.

Since her remains could not rest on holy soil, her husband and sons buried her on the grounds of the estate, which quickly fell to disrepair. In later years, to relieve them of the burden of its expense, Percival purchased the land with his own inheritance and spent many a night sitting at Margaret Thorne's gravesite, tying nooses and praying for the souls of the witches.

Chapter Ten

Melodie should have gone straight home to bed when her shift ended, but even though she wouldn't admit it to Cal, she wasn't sure she'd feel safe at home alone. Even during the day. Calypso offered her spare key. "Mi casa and all that, sweetie. I've got places to go, but I'll be back by sundown. Don't worry. By then, I'll know how to handle this."

"Can't I go with you?" Mel hated to sound vulnerable, but spending the day alone worrying about demons stalking her didn't sound all that appealing.

"I'm sorry, Mel. I'm going to contact some members of the Witches' Council and ask about the curse. You can't come along unless they invite you. Maybe next time."

Mel wasn't sure if she should hope for a next time or not. She waved as Cal drove off and decided her next objective was putting a demon hunter back on the case. Blake DeWitt couldn't protect her from sunup to sundown, but maybe Palmer could—if he could remember why she needed protection in the first place.

His apartment wasn't far from Taylor Tools, and fortunately, at half past seven, he was still at home. At least his Wrangler was parked out in front of the building. She wondered if he had a day job and if he wore his crossbow when he went to work.

She knocked on his door, and a muffled voice responded, "Jus' a min—"

The door flung open a minute later, and Palmer stood there, wearing his trademark jeans, a damp towel draped around his neck and nothing in between. He held a Pop-Tart in one hand.

His dazzling grin made Mel's knees just a little weak. "Hey! Good morning. You're Rosa from eleven B, aren't you?"

"Uh, no. I'm Melodie from Gleason's Bakery."

Confusion creased his golden brows. "Oh. Well, I think you have the wrong apartment, then. I didn't order anything."

"I know." She sighed. The damn pixie dust really did work. "I'm here about...the Gogmar."

Palmer was the king of the blank stare. This one, though, seemed calculated. "I don't know what you're talking about, miss. I'm late for work, so if you'll excuse me..." He tried to close the door, but she took a chance and slipped one foot over the threshold. "Please, Palmer. You gave me this the other night, and you told me to call you if I needed help." She handed him his own card, and he squinted at it as if it might be a fake.

"I gave you this?"

"The other night at Gleason's, after you killed a Gogmar." She whispered the last part. "Blake DeWitt, the witch hunter, blasted you with pixie dust last night and made you forget me."

"Yeah. No. Sorry that doesn't ring any bells. I haven't seen a Gogmar in a couple of months."

"Oh, Palmer, come on. There has to be a way to reverse the effects of the dust." Mel wondered if a conk on the head would help. She was willing to try anything.

"If it could be reversed, it wouldn't be much good, would it?" Now he stepped forward, easing Mel out of the doorway.

Up close he smelled really good, like fresh shampoo and warm toaster pastry. "Palmer, what would I have to do to

80

convince you that we've met before? The night before last, you took me to your lair behind Taylor Tools. Your uncle owns the place, remember?"

That caught his attention. "Of course I remember my uncle owns the place. You know about my lair?"

She nodded and gave him a hopeful smile. "You have sketches of demons up all over the place."

Palmer glanced around and dipped his head low to whisper to Mel. "I'm sure if I had told you about my lair, I would have told you not to broadcast it all over the place and not to mention demons during daylight hours. You almost had me convinced, except for one thing—I would *never* let myself get pixie dusted. I've got to go, have a nice day, miss."

Palmer made a quick retreat behind the door, not slamming it, technically, but closing it with a definite finality that left Mel bereft.

She really liked Palmer, especially without a shirt on, which was beside the point at the moment. Without him and Calypso, she was completely alone. There was no else she could talk to about curses, cabochons and demon queens. She'd go insane before nightfall if she had to spend the day acting like everything was normal.

Unable to even think about sleeping, she went back to Gleason's. At least Arnie was always happy to see her.

At half past noon, Melodie was still wide awake. She hadn't even yawned.

Maybe it was the double-shot of espresso Arnie had bought for her, or maybe it was fear of the day-walking demons Palmer had warned her about back when he knew who she was.

She had to admit, it felt good to run on pure adrenaline for a while. She hadn't been this jazzed in a long time. In fact, she'd come to accept the fact that working nights in a bakery would be the pinnacle of excitement in her life. A sleepy, comfortable life was good, right? No surprises, no major problems. That had been why she'd come back to Amberville after two years in Boston with Larry. Now she wondered if she'd made a mistake, not about divorcing her ex-husband, but about leaving the busier lifestyle they'd had in the city.

Maybe a day job wouldn't be so bad... She was contemplating finding something to do in her off-hours when Palmer slipped through Gleason's front door.

She eyed him through the beveled glass of the display case she'd been cleaning. He looked confused but determined.

She straightened and met his curious gaze over the top of the case. "Can I help you?"

A sheepish grin flickered across his face. "I was hoping I'd find you here."

"Normally you wouldn't have. I work nights."

"I guess I should have remembered that. I'm sorry I was rude before. I realize now that you had to be telling the truth."

"Oh?" Twenty-seven years of scrupulous honesty and suddenly no one believed a word she said. "What clued you in?"

Palmer jammed a hand into his front pocket and pulled out a crumpled sheet of paper, folded in four. He spread the page on the counter in front of Melodie, and her jaw dropped.

The pencil sketch of her face was as detailed as a photograph and far more flattering. He'd given her sharper cheek bones, longer lashes and a fuller mouth, but nevertheless the resemblance was uncanny. "Did you draw this?"

"I must have. It was tacked up on the wall in my...lair."

"Wow." The idea that Palmer had taken the time to sketch her in such exquisite detail was sweet and a little spooky too. It must have been a shock for him to find the portrait and realize he had no recollection of the person he'd drawn. "You're really talented."

"With a pencil, maybe, but not much else if someone was able to wipe my memory. I was hoping when you're done working, we could go somewhere and talk. Maybe you could fill in my missing time for me."

Mel glanced into the back where Arnie and Selma, the daytime counter girl, were arguing over how many chocolate chips to put in today's batch of cannoli. Technically Mel wasn't on duty; she was only helping out because she didn't want to go home. "Give me a minute and we can go, if you're free now."

"Perfect."

Mel ducked into the back, broke up the heated chip debate and told Arnie she'd see him at ten. A moment later, she was strolling down Chelsea Street with Palmer, recounting their shared Gogmar encounter of two nights ago.

He seemed impressed with his own prowess in dispatching the scaly green demon, but his enthusiasm for the story waned when she got to the part about the pixie dusting.

"It sounds like I blundered my way into that one," he said, shuffling his Reeboks on the sidewalk.

"Don't feel too bad. DeWitt is like a ninja. He's really sneaky when he isn't roaring around on his Harley."

"I do vaguely remember DeWitt. I've run into him before."

"How much memory does the pixie dust erase?" Mel asked as they cut over to Willow Street and headed toward the park.

"It's not necessarily time. It's *things* like demons, witches, vampires, ghosts and the events surrounding an encounter with them."

"Gargoyles too?"

Palmer shrugged. "Other than DeWitt, I don't know any. Well, maybe I do and I just don't remember." The sullen edge to his voice might have invited sympathy, but something didn't sit right with his explanation.

"Palmer, what do demons, witches, vampires, ghosts and

gargoyles have in common?" she asked.

He gave her a sidelong glance. "Well...they're not all immortal. They're not all undead. They're all somewhat magical, I guess."

"And humans aren't magical."

"Witches are human...most of them. I've heard some demons can be witches, and I guess a witch could be turned into a vampire or a gargoyle or a ghost."

"But pixie dust doesn't erase someone's memories of other humans, does it? You still remember your mom and dad, your uncle. You remembered Rosa from eleven B, right?"

"Right... What are you getting at?"

Mel slowed her pace. "How come you can remember DeWitt the gargoyle, but you can't remember me?"

Palmer thought about it. "Because he wasn't a gargoyle when he dusted me, right? He was in human form."

"And so was I. Not that I have any *other* form."

Palmer stared at her. Mel didn't like what she was getting at, not at all. "I'm not a witch or a ghost or a vampire or a gargoyle, but you can't remember me."

Palmer's serious expression broke, and he laughed. "Oh come on. You're not a demon. Obviously I forgot the Gogmar, and since that's when I met you, I forgot you too. You're part of that encounter."

"But then wouldn't you remember me from last night when you were at my apartment?"

"I was at your apartment last night?" One of his eyebrows shot up, and his tanned complexion paled by a shade.

Mel gave him a playful nudge. "Don't worry. You were a perfect gentleman, *and* there were no Gogmars there. What if I have the Cabochon in me? Maybe that makes me a demon."

"No. Humans don't turn into demons."

They stopped at the entrance to the park. Mel's stomach was in knots. "Why not? They can turn into witches, gargoyles, vampires and ghosts."

"And werewolves. You forgot werewolves."

"You never mentioned werewolves before."

"I forgot about them. There aren't really that many of them around."

"Great. So maybe I'm a werewolf?"

"Well, that's more likely than a demon. Demons are usually hatched, not made."

"But anything is possible, isn't it?"

Palmer let out a slow breath as they hit the cool green lawn of the park. "You'd be surprised at what's possible."

"Honestly, I don't think I would be anymore."

Sometimes the silence of the stone was worse than reliving Percival Blake's waking life. Darkness within darkness might have been a comfort to some, but to Blake it was worse than death.

Having his existence halted between one inhalation and the next left him on the verge of madness at times. But that's how he came to understand his long family history of sudden deaths, acrimonious divorces and descent into isolation by men whose lives had previously seemed so promising.

He didn't want to end up that way, alone and angry at the rest of the world for abandoning him to a prison they didn't even know existed.

What choice did he have, though, except to hold on through the darkness and pray someone like Melodie McConnell held the key to his granite tomb?

When he awoke again, the call of the Cabochon returned stronger than ever. Still within his grasp, it would not stop taunting him until he lost his soul to darkness.

Tonight Blake had only one objective. Stay close to Melodie McConnell until she gave up her secrets to him.

"Good, you're finally here." Calypso Smith greeted Blake with familiar disdain when he arrived at Melodie's apartment. The witch, dressed tonight in formal, flowing black with dangling pentacle earrings and a matching ring on her right index finger, swirled away from him as soon as she opened the door.

Blake stepped inside, adding the scent of the takeout cheeseburgers he'd picked up on the way over to the cloying aroma of lavender and clove incense that danced through the apartment on the faint autumn breeze. Melodie stood in the living room, a virginal antithesis to Calypso in a lacy white summer dress. Barefoot and wearing no jewelry, she resembled some type of sacrifice.

"Mind if I ask what's going on?" He set the sack of burgers on the coffee table next to a billowing incense burner.

Melodie's gaze dropped immediately to the food. "That smells fantastic. What is it?"

"It's from Hanover's Hearth. I got half a dozen Big Burgers with the works. I usually wake up...really hungry." For some reason the admission embarrassed him. Right now, looking at the brunette vision before him, a different kind of hunger took over and left him wishing for a way to get the witch to disappear.

Clearly irritated, Calypso grabbed the bag and shoved it onto the cluttered desk. "Food later, I'm cleansing right now. Step back."

Melodie shrugged, and Blake obeyed, forcing himself to move out of the growing circle of incense smoke. Calypso took his place opposite Melodie with the coffee table between them.

She clasped the other woman's hands in hers and began to chant formless words under her breath.

Had it not been for the curse, Blake wouldn't have put much stock in witchcraft. He'd never been a believer in the paranormal, but he'd seen a lot in ten years—or five, if one considered he'd spent half that time unaware of the world around him. The surge of power that swirled around the two women, linked like yin and yang across the table, didn't startle him, but it did make the hairs at the back of his neck stand up.

When Calypso finished her spell, Melodie swayed a bit. Blake moved to steady her, but a fast-moving blur got to her before he did. Palmer Van Houten appeared out of nowhere, looking like a blond Clark Kent. He guided Melodie to the couch and glared up at Blake.

"Nice to see you again, DeWitt."

Blake surveyed the apartment. "Did you let yourself in, demon hunter? Because I didn't hear the bell ring."

"I was in the other room checking the locks on the windows." There was a definite challenge in his words. In this small place, there was no doubt the "other room" meant Melodie's bedroom. So the demon hunter was laying some sort of claim. Blake would have been amused, except the stakes were too high right now for him to get into a pissing contest with Palmer.

"Blake, you should apologize to Palmer for dusting him. It really wasn't necessary," Melodie said. She waved incense smoke away from her face and took a deep breath.

He couldn't help but rise to the bait. "You're right. I'm sorry Palmer isn't really necessary. If I'd known, I never would have dusted you...so easily."

Palmer glared. He might have conjured up a scathing comeback eventually but the witch cut in, literally. She handed Blake a white-handled knife, thin-bladed and razor-tipped. "Is this for the burgers?" he asked.

Calypso ignored him. "Palmer, can you spread the towel out on the table? Mel, hold your hand out, palm up. Don't be nervous, hon. It'll all be over in a minute."

Blake stepped back. "Whoa. What's going on? This isn't some kind of blood rite, is it? Or an exorcism? Because that won't work with the curse. Believe me, I've tried that."

Calypso's dark eyes assessed him. "Wish I'd been there for that. No, this isn't an exorcism. It's a test. Take Mel's hand and cut her palm, not deep. Just a scratch will do."

He met Mel's resigned glance over the table. "Is she kidding?"

Melodie shook her head. Her hair, loose from the ponytail she'd worn it in the day before, cascaded around her shoulders. "If I have the Cabochon, you can't hurt me."

A cold knot of dread settled in his stomach in the spot he'd been saving for a cheeseburger. Did the witch really believe Melodie had the gem?

"I can't...cut you, lass."

"There's no other way to be sure." Calypso folded his fingers around the cold bone handle of the knife. "It's very sharp, and it's been sterilized by flame. One quick cut, shallow and straight. It'll heal in a day."

Melodie held her hand out. Clean pink nails tipped her delicate fingers. Her skin was translucent and unblemished, inviting a gentle touch, not the harsh slice of a blade.

Blake had often thought, in his darkest moments of despair that he might kill to end his curse, but now, faced with this relatively simple task, his heart protested. "I don't want to hurt you."

"Do it. It's okay. I need to know." Her conviction galvanized him. Did he need to know? What he would do with the knowledge, he couldn't say.

He held his own palm out, and she placed her hand on top of his. Her skin was warm, and the contact made his nerves tingle all the way up to his shoulder. She had power. She had something, and for once, he prayed it wasn't the Cabochon.

She closed her eyes, and the muscles in her arm tensed.

"DeWitt, we don't have all night." The witch nudged him, and the demon hunter stared him down.

Quick, clean and straight.

He drew a steadying breath and ran the tip of the boline over her skin.

She winced but didn't open her eyes. Blake stared, dumbstruck at the bright line of blood that welled in her palm, and his heart fluttered aimlessly, unsure whether to sink or soar.

Chapter Eleven

A pregnant hush descended, followed by a swift sigh of relief from Calypso. Ignoring the sting of the wound Blake had inflicted, Mel opened one eye. Normally the sight of blood left her light-headed, and this time she swayed just a little before Palmer jammed a rolled-up towel over the thin cut.

A nervous laugh erupted from somewhere deep, and she met Blake DeWitt's incredulous stare. "See? I'm fine. I'm not a demon. This is...*great.*"

Silence. Palmer stared at the bloody towel he'd removed from her hand. Calypso gasped, and DeWitt's jaw dropped.

Uncomprehending, Mel glanced at her hand. The cut was gone. Not even a scar remained. She'd healed instantly.

"Uh...is this a bad thing or a good thing?"

Cal grabbed the knife from DeWitt and without warning jabbed the tip into the pad of Mel's thumb. She yelped and pulled her hand away, shaking drops of bright blood across the white towel Palmer had spread on the coffee table.

Cal squeezed Mel's thumb, and another dot of blood formed. Pain from the tiny wound radiated into her wrist. "Give it a minute. See if it heals."

They all stared, and a moment later, another small drop of blood formed on Mel's thumb.

"It's not healing," she said.

"Let's try a bigger cut."

"No!" Mel snatched her hand away from Calypso. "This is plenty, thanks. And it hurts. Look, there's still a red spot there."

"Cut her again." Cal jammed the bone-handled knife back into DeWitt's grasp.

Fortunately DeWitt hesitated. His bewilderment mirrored her own. "But I spilled her blood. Look at the towel."

"The cut healed. Maybe the wording was off. Maybe you can *spill* her blood, but you can't kill her."

"Could we not try to find out, please?" Mel asked.

With a fierceness Mel had never seen before, Cal snatched the knife back and gestured with it. "This is important, Mel. Everything depends on us knowing whether or not you have the Cabochon."

All eyes followed Cal's movements. The knife blade flashed as she ranted. "If you have it, your life is in danger. Now, that first cut could have just been...an anomaly."

"I don't heal anomalously, Cal." Mel stared at the spot where DeWitt had cut her. Palmer cupped her hand in his and ran gentle fingers over the soft, unbroken flesh. Under other circumstances Mel might have found the touch soothing, even sexy. She shivered but not from desire.

DeWitt pulled her hand away from Palmer. His voice went harsh, matching Cal's tone. "Give me the knife."

"I'm not a pincushion, you know. Cal, you said you would do a healing spell on me. Maybe—"

"*Would* do. Haven't yet. Cut her."

DeWitt obeyed, and Mel whimpered. Would this go on all night? After the blade sliced her skin again, she pulled her hand back. Palmer stood ready with the bloody towel, but there was no need. As they watched, the thin red line running from the base of her index finger to the heel of her hand faded to nothing.

"It still hurts, you know," she announced just in case they decided to try best three out of five.

"It's in you." Cal's conclusion silenced them. A cold sense of doom gripped Mel's innards. "It has to be."

Her shivering increased. "What does that mean? Are demons going to follow me for the rest of my life?"

"No. We'll find a way to keep you safe." Palmer didn't sound convinced. He wrapped an arm around her shoulders. The weight of it should have been comforting, but instead Mel felt smothered. She slithered out of his grasp.

"Cal? Tell me what I'm supposed to do now."

"I don't know. Of all the witches I talked to today, the general consensus was that this test would prove you *didn't* have the Cabochon. It wasn't meant for a human. No one wanted to consider the alternative."

Anger bubbled inside her, hot and icy at the same time. "Well now they'd better consider it." Her words ended with an odd growl, a snarl, and she covered her mouth with her fingers. "What the hell was *that*? Oh my God, I'm a demon. I'm a demon!"

She rounded the coffee table and scurried toward the bedroom. DeWitt's heavy footsteps followed her, and his grim reflection met hers in her bedroom mirror. "You're not a demon."

"Yes, I am. I have to be. Palmer can't remember me because I'm a demon. I absorbed the Cabochon because I'm a demon, and now I'm growling *because I'm a demon!*"

"That was your stomach. You're hungry. Have a cheeseburger and calm down."

"I'm not hungry. I haven't been hungry since this happened, and I haven't slept either." She held out her hands for his inspection. "Do my nails look longer to you? Am I going to grow a tail?"

He raised one dark brow. "You're going to end up in a straitjacket if you don't calm down." He put his hands on her shoulders, and his touch centered her. Her heart raced in her rib cage, and her whole body trembled as he pulled her back against his broad chest. "Palmer's right about one thing. We'll take care of you. We'll figure something out."

Mel nodded. It all seemed so simple. For a split second, the burden lifted, and the way seemed clear. They would help her. Between Palmer and Calypso and DeWitt, they would free her from this, and everything would be normal again. Then the crushing sense of doom returned with a vengeance. "Oh no."

"What? A tail?"

She turned in his arms and spied Cal and Palmer watching from the bedroom doorway. "This means the only way to end your curse is for me to die."

From the moment of Melodie's realization, things went swiftly downhill. She panicked and threw a bit of a tantrum, which in all honesty, Blake couldn't blame her for. He was somewhat pissed off himself. Fate had thrown a curveball he never could have anticipated. Killing a demon to retrieve the Cabochon had never posed a moral issue for him. Now, not only had he discovered he couldn't kill the demon who held the gem, he couldn't kill another human being to end his curse. Not that he'd actually considered it.

Why couldn't it have been Van Houten? *There* was a moral dilemma he might have enjoyed grappling with for a while.

As it was, he sat now with the demon hunter in Melodie's microscopic kitchen, eating cold cheeseburgers and drinking diet soda from plastic glasses.

He almost preferred his granite exile to making small talk with Joe College.

"So about how big would you say the Ak'mir was?" Palmer

asked between one burger and the next. The All-American could certainly pack away food.

The faint sounds of a feminine argument drifted from Melodie's bedroom, and both men paused to listen for a moment. "Maybe I should go in there..."

Palmer shook his head. "I have sisters. I never, ever get between them when they argue."

"But they're friends. They shouldn't be—"

Something heavy hit the wall that separated the kitchen from the bedroom. Sobbing ensued. Blake tensed. Could this sudden attack of temper be a side effect of the Cabochon?

Palmer dug into another burger. "So this Ak'mir...?"

"It was huge." Blake embellished. "Largest one I've ever seen."

"How did you kill it?" The question had a skeptical lilt to it.

"I never reveal trade secrets."

"And your trade is demon hunting now?"

Blake allowed himself a smirk. "Someone has to pick up your slack."

All-American dropped his burger and scraped his chair back. "Hey, I was doing just fine until you came along. You blew out some valuable memories when you dusted me, and like Melodie said, it wasn't necessary."

"No, but it was fun." His smirk morphed into a grin. Not much brought Blake pleasure these days, but seeing Van Houten all flustered and annoyed certainly did the trick. Blake braced for a tirade, prepared to match his nemesis insult for insult, but Melodie appeared in the kitchen then, looking reasonably calm and collected. She'd changed from her virginal white shift into an ensemble that virtually screamed Demon Queen.

Black boots laced up her calves, and skillfully faded jeans hugged curves he hadn't realized she possessed. Skull beads dangled from the fringes of her leather belt, and she wore a tooled suede vest over a ruffled shirt. Silver earrings sparkled beneath her now voluminous chestnut curls.

Palmer's eyes bulged, and his Adam's apple bobbed.

Blake would have gaped also, but with Palmer practically drooling on the linoleum, he wanted to at least hold the illusion of being a little more sophisticated. "I didn't realize getting changed could be such a battle."

"I was upset." She tilted her chin up, daring him to comment on her understatement. "I'm okay now. Calypso is going to talk to the witches again and find a way to get this thing out of me. She also promised to ask them about breaking the curse."

"She promised, did she?" Blake had his doubts about Ms. Smith. He'd yet to meet a witch both capable and amenable to putting the vengeance against Percival Blake to rest.

Behind Melodie, Calypso appeared looking rather haggard. "I keep my promises, DeWitt. It's not about you, though, so don't get any warm fuzzies about it. If the Cabochon can be absorbed by a human, then humans will be at risk. You might not be able to hurt Melodie, but someone else acting on your behalf could. That interferes with the intent of the curse."

"I often wonder what the real intent of the curse was. Percival Blake's own son, Rene, was only twenty-four when his father died and the curse transferred to him. *His* son, Paul, was only twenty-seven. There's no evidence that either of those young men hunted witches, yet they suffered for decades because of it. I've been at this half-life for ten years now, and I don't know how much more I can take." He glanced at Melodie, who might have been over her tantrum, but she looked anything but content at the moment. "At the risk of you all thinking less of me than you already do, if putting a human in danger will finally convince the esteemed Witches' Council to end this...torture, then I'm all for it."

Calypso glared, just as he'd suspected she would. Melodie only checked her watch and sighed. "I've got to go to work. Cal is going back to talk to her coven members tonight, so can one of you guys drive me?"

"I will." Palmer practically leapt over the kitchen table. Fresh from his own short tirade, Blake had little fire left in him to fight for the privilege of escorting Melodie across town. He hung back as they made their way past Calypso and out of the kitchen. "I'll follow after. I'm going to do a little demon hunting first."

Palmer ignored the jibe, but Melodie glanced back over her shoulder. "Be careful."

"Yes," the witch added with a sharp curve to her tone. "We wouldn't want anything to happen to *you.*"

"I apologize for my little freak-out back there," Mel said when she and Palmer pulled up in front of Gleason's. She had no idea how she was going to concentrate on work with every nerve in her body jangling and her brain on overdrive.

"Don't worry about it. It has to be a shock...but just because you have, or seemed to have, absorbed the Cabochon, doesn't mean you're a demon. There's obviously some sort of loophole in the curse. Maybe with no other demon available, the Gogmar had to give the gem to whoever was on hand."

"The fact remains, demon or not, the gem doesn't change hands unless whoever is holding it dies. I could have this thing in me for the next...fifty years or more." She didn't want to think about it, couldn't stand the thought of Blake DeWitt waiting for her to die so he could have another chance at ending his curse.

Palmer shut off the engine and hopped out of the Jeep. He loped around the front end and opened Mel's door for her. "I'm sure Calypso will come up with something. I don't know much about witches, but rumor has it the Council is made up of some pretty powerful individuals. Hey, look, if someone could create a curse this powerful, there has to be someone who can break it, right?"

Mel's boots hit the sidewalk, and again, a displaced sense of well-being washed over her. Sure, it would be all right. In fact, everything would be great.

She tossed Palmer a bright smile and sauntered toward the bakery. With practiced ease, she unlocked the door, punched in her security code on the alarm system and headed toward the kitchen. There would be four dozen carrot-apple cupcakes that needed autumn-leaf motif icing for the Women's Club luncheon waiting for her. She'd have plenty to do, and even with Calypso gone, she'd have someone to talk to tonight while she worked.

That, at least, was something to be thankful for.

While she mixed a batch of sweet cream-cheese icing and sorted through Arnie's collection of cookie cutters looking for the exact shape of autumn leaf she had in mind, Palmer played watchdog. After a quick recon of the alley, he stationed himself in front of the back door, arms crossed over his broad chest, blue eyes watchful and intense.

Mel would have found it amusing, and definitely sweet, except her thoughts swirled around DeWitt and the pain she'd seen in his eyes when he'd spoken of his family. Even though Percival Blake's son and grandson would have lived more than two hundred years ago, it was clear that Blake felt a connection to his forefathers. Their lives had been diminished by a curse of vengeance, and beyond blood, he obviously felt a kinship with these men.

Tears stung her eyes and the back of her throat as she rolled out the fondant for the cupcake leaves. She turned away from Palmer and used the back of her hand to dab away the first salty drop of moisture that rolled down her cheek. If the curse passed from father to son at the moment of death, what would happen to a young child if his father died too soon? Blake hadn't mentioned having children of his own, but the implications were staggering.

A full-body sob racked her as she cut the first leaf from a thin layer of orange fondant.

"Melodie? You all right?"

She squeezed her eyes shut for a second. "Fine. I'm fine." She swiped another tear and turned. Her bodyguard gave her a curious grin that seemed to morph into a hot, sexy, come-hither wink. Was he serious? Mel almost laughed at her own absurd thought. Surely Palmer wasn't coming on to her.

She shook off the tingle of curiosity that swept through her and fought to ignore the wicked hint of mischief that caused her to eye him from under her lowered lashes after cutting another leaf. Her ability to distinguish a good idea from a bad one fled after another sidelong glance at his broad shoulders.

She dropped the cookie cutter and stalked across the kitchen, drawn like a magnet to Palmer's incredibly delicious lower lip. She cupped his jaw in her floury palms and lunged in for a feral kiss, a drink of him that ended in a bite.

Stiff as a mummy under her onslaught, he tipped back against the kitchen door and uttered a muffled, "Mfflat erf yudoo...ing?"

He tasted like sin, which happened to be Mel's favorite flavor. She ignored his halfhearted protest and hitched one jean-clad thigh up on his hip. "I'm hungry. I haven't eaten since yesterday, and I want a taste of you."

"Uh..."

She had him writhing between her and the fire door. His hands seemed to be everywhere at once, which was fine with her until they ended up on her shoulders, pushing her gently but firmly away.

"I think maybe you're a little stressed," he said. His eyes were huge, and beneath her spread palms, his heart beat like a war drum.

"Come on. Don't you want me? You drew a portrait of me, for heaven's sake. You obviously put a lot of thought into my eyes, my hair, my lips..." She dove again, and he ducked, leaving her staring at the door.

"This doesn't seem like you."

"How would you know how I seem? You don't even remember me from the other day. For all you know, after you killed the Gogmar, I might have been so grateful that I threw you down on the floor and had my way with you right here in the kitchen."

He raised a brow and continued to back up until he reached the workstation island in the middle of the room. "You told me Blake came in and dropkicked me."

"Maybe I lied." She fingered the buttons on her shirt and let her hungry gaze travel down to an interesting spot just below his belt buckle. "Maybe we did things too wild to talk about."

"Somehow, I doubt that."

Mel pouted. *She* had no doubt that DeWitt would have accepted her advances and helped her slake her sudden desires. Maybe she'd go find him.

She dismissed Palmer with a wave and turned to open the back door. "Don't say I never gave you a chance, hot pants."

The night air hit her like a splash of cold water, followed immediately by the hot, putrid breath of a creature that made the Gogmar look cuddly.

Claws the length and shape of scimitars protruded from long, spindly fingers. Flesh the color of moldy bacon hung in folds from a body that had a few too many limbs and not quite enough muscle. A dozen clustered eyes, lidless and black as midnight, blinked at Mel, and a mouth that looked like a gateway to hell gaped at her.

She didn't scream.

She wanted to, but fear had closed her throat up tight and threatened to suffocate her.

Behind her, Palmer's voice reached her as if through a long, water-filled tunnel. "Maybe we should sit down and talk about thi—"

The demon struck, and everything went black.

Chapter Twelve

Just as Blake suspected, the body of the Ak'mir demon was gone from the basement of the abandoned townhouse on Bailey when he returned to continue his investigation.

The distinctive stench remained, however, which led him to believe the creature had managed to regenerate itself. It wasn't skulking around the shadows among the construction garbage, so it stood to reason this wasn't its preferred habitat. It had definitely been stalking prey the other night. Chances were, it would return to hunt again.

The ride back to Gleason's was uneventful. Though the cool evening was full of shadows and Amberville's quiet streets were empty at half past eleven, Blake saw nothing suspicious. If demons were mobilizing, they were being remarkably discreet.

Van Houten's Wrangler sat in front of Gleason's bakery, gleaming under the pink-tinted glow of the nearest street lamp. Nice car. Waxed to perfection and detailed. Spanky clean, just like its owner. Blake grumbled while he secured his helmet to the back of his bike, which he parked just close enough to the Jeep so Van Houten would have to back up in order to pull away from the curb.

This rivalry was pointless, really. The demon hunter just irked him because he represented everything Blake had never been. Growing up, he'd been a shy kid, bookish and introspective. Wrenched from his home in Glasgow at age eleven when his father's company transferred him to the States, he'd floundered socially through the rest of his teen years. Good grades hadn't been enough to make up for the fact he couldn't catch a ball to save his life, couldn't run a lap faster than the girls in gym class and couldn't hit anything with a bat but his own shadow.

Funny how ten years in darkness had changed that. He'd gone from skinny math geek who couldn't get a date, to dark, mysterious stranger who didn't dare ask a woman over for fear he'd fall asleep and crush her to death when dawn turned him into a hideous stone beast.

Palmer represented everything Blake had never been and never could be. He had every reason in the world to hate the demon hunter and no reason at all.

The bloodcurdling scream that sliced through the night gave him one more reason to despise Mr. All-Star. Clearly Palmer hadn't done his job. He hadn't protected Melodie from the demons, and now it sounded like she was being murdered.

Muttering every expletive he could think of, Blake ran for the alley.

The smell of blood reached him first, and he pulled up short, stunned by the carnage. Gogmar goo couldn't compare to this.

The bricks around Gleason's back door ran with blood. Splatters six feet high reached the small spotlight mounted over the door. Claw marks scored the green paint of the nearest Dumpster, and a bloody trail of footprints led inside the building.

Blake swallowed bile and steeled himself. It couldn't have ended this way. Not so soon. Melodie didn't deserve to die like this.

Muffled sounds made their way into the alley, and Blake

slid the blade he carried under his jacket out of its sheath. He refused to entertain the notion that if a demon had come to tear the Cabochon from Melodie McConnell's body, *he* might have a chance to retrieve it.

The thought never crossed his mind.

Much.

He hated himself for thinking it. Hated himself for hoping her end had been swift, though by the looks of things, far from painless.

He'd make Palmer pay for this, if the attacking demon hadn't already done so.

The door creaked when he nudged it open, and he froze. Nothing came after him, though, and he took another tentative step, pushing the door open far enough to slip inside.

"Good God."

"Hey...oh, shit, it's you. Do you mind getting this thing off me?"

Palmer lay on the kitchen floor in a pool of blood that now appeared more orange than red. Sprawled over him was a beast of ungainly proportions. From this angle, it resembled half a roast pig with spidery arms and legs—at least half a dozen appendages bent at odd angles. Thick claws were embedded in the terra cotta tiles of the kitchen floor, trapping the demon hunter in a cage of demon flesh.

Dead flesh, fortunately.

Relief washed over Blake and made him momentarily light-headed. "Where's Melodie?"

"She's gone. She took off after the other one...ugh. A little help here, please."

"But I just heard her scream."

Palmer looked away. "Umm, no. That was me."

Holding in a laugh, Blake navigated the pool of blood and,

with a solid kick, dislodged the Betryminar demon's nearest claw from the floor. Palmer slid through the muck and rolled out from under the enormous body, which splashed down into the remaining reservoir of its own viscera.

"Oh man." Palmer shivered and turned to the nearest sink. He hung there a moment while his complexion marched through several shades of green. "I need some air."

"Well, the alley's no better. Don't go out there. Did you say *the other one?* Melodie took off after a Betryminar demon?"

"No. The other one was a Fryyk, I think. I didn't get a good look. This one came barreling in here and started chasing us around."

Ignoring the unpleasant odor of dead demon, Blake knelt beside the body. It looked as if the Betryminar had been ripped to shreds by something even bigger and badder. A Fryyk could certainly have done the trick, but it wouldn't likely have run away and left a human alive.

"Melodie chased the Fryyk away?"

Palmer wet a hand towel and covered his eyes with the damp cloth. He nodded, swallowing hard. "Yup. She was pissed."

"Because the Fryyk killed the Betryminar?"

Palmer eyed him from under the dripping corner of the hand towel. "No. Because I...she...I wouldn't let her seduce me."

Blake ruminated on that for a split second before he laughed. Hard and long.

Palmer glared. "Would I kid at a time like this?"

"Melodie tried to seduce you?"

"Yeah. I don't know what came over her. I'm thinking maybe it's some kind of demon side effect. One minute she was sobbing over her cupcakes, and the next minute she was climbing up my leg."

"And you turned her down?"

"Well, of course."

"What came over *you*?" Blake shook his head. He had one up on Palmer now. The All-American boy was a stone-cold wuss.

Or a gentleman.

"Crap. She got mad at you and took off after a demon? I suppose you don't have any idea which way she went?"

"Sure. I think she turned left at the entrails and followed the blood splatters all the way to Oz. Come on, DeWitt. I was lying under a dying Betryminar trying not to hurl. Those things weigh a ton, and they stink like Ak'mirs."

Blake cast a jaundiced eye at the corpse. "No. They really don't stink anything like Ak'mirs. Consider yourself lucky on that count. Um...where's your weapon?"

"My weapon...oh. Melodie grabbed my crossbow before she left. I don't think she knows how to use it. We better track her down before she hurts someone."

"I have no doubt she's going to hurt someone tonight. Hopefully it will be a demon."

Palmer took two steps toward the back door, and Blake grabbed his shoulder, halting his escape. "You can't leave."

"What? Tracking demons is my job. I know what I'm doing, DeWitt."

"You can't walk away and leave this mess here. Melodie will lose her job, and there will be an awful lot of explaining to do to the authorities. Isn't the first rule of demon hunting to never leave evidence of a kill behind?"

Palmer deflated. If Blake hadn't been worried about Melodie, he might have found time to savor the Kodak moment. "You expect me to clean this up?"

"Unlike Gogmars, Betryminars don't dissolve. They come apart pretty easily, though, so you can probably hack this one up and stick it in a couple of trash bags."

Palmer's complexion turned mossy. His eyes glazed, and he shuddered. "Ugh."

"Call Calypso. Maybe when she gets back from her witch conference, she can help." Blake didn't wait to see if Palmer stepped up to the plate or ran for the porcelain altar. The tingle of the Cabochon was beginning to fade, and he had to follow Melodie's trail while it was still fresh.

The gnarled, bony hands of a monster resolved themselves into the gnarled, bony limbs of a small tree as Mel's vision returned to sharp focus. A barrel-chested guardian became one of the stone-fronted water fountains in Veteran's Park, and the caress of evil fingers became the soft touch of a gentle autumn breeze.

Melodie drew herself up from a crouch and swiped at the pine needles clinging to her jeans.

Smears of gooey orange marred the denim.

She lifted her hands in the faint bluish moonlight and stared. From the tips of her fingers to her wrists, her skin was coated with something that smelled sharp and coppery. Her white shirt bore signs of a struggle. Something had bled on her—copiously.

She staggered to the fountain and held the control lever in one slippery hand while she tried to rinse the other. The thin trickle of water served only to moisten the half-dry stains and spread them around.

Frantic rubbing and splashing and wringing of her hands only made matters worse. She might have just given up then and sunk to the ground in a miserable heap, except something caught her eye. An orange trail disappeared under the low branches of a pine tree, and for some inexplicable reason, she felt drawn to follow it.

The creature lay on the aromatic pine carpet, partially

covered with dead branches. It resembled a goat, but with a flat snout and extra horns and the potbellied body of a man.

She remembered killing it.

"Oh...my." Worse, she remembered the small army of creatures who had helped her start to bury the remains. Maybe two feet tall, they had slender bodies, hair like dirty mops and round, black, soulless eyes. They'd surrounded her as soon as the body of the larger demon hit the ground. She hadn't been afraid at all. In fact, she recalled being...pleased.

They'd been the ones to drag branches over the corpse. They were still nearby, whispering to each other in the shadows and watching her with reverence.

"Oh my God."

One foot at a time, she backed out from under the pine tree, hands out, palms down to steady her on her feet and to keep the scuttling creatures at bay. "Stay back. Don't come any closer."

They froze. Only half-hidden in the shadows now, they watched like frightened children, peering one-eyed from behind rocks and tree stumps. "Stay. Easy now."

An unrequited sob lodged in her chest. How had this happened? She'd blacked out after coming face-to-face with the monstrosity at the back door. She'd left Palmer all alone to fend for himself, and she'd gone...hunting.

Her hands bore the evidence of her success.

"Oh, no no no. This can't be happening. I refuse to—"

One of her minions—that's what they were, after all—chattered a warning to her. Something was coming. Something big and dangerous.

Mel swallowed air in an aborted attempt to breathe. What could be bigger or more dangerous than the thing lying under the branches?

A twig cracked, and something hissed out a sharp breath.

She ran, and behind her, the miniature demons closed ranks, forming a staunch line of defense.

She knew this without turning to look, because they told her they would protect her. Six of them died trying to do just that. Their screams were like the squeal of bats or the whine of rusted gears. The remaining ones fled in fear. They were only demons, after all, and couldn't be expected to march to their own slaughter when the odds had shifted out of their favor.

Now it was up to Mel to protect herself.

She stopped running and turned swiftly to face this new threat, ready to deal with anything that came at her with the same unconscious ferocity she'd shown the goat-faced demon.

He stood bathed in moonlight, his black leather jacket kissed by silver and his eyes dark and fathomless. The mini-crossbow she'd stolen from Palmer and dropped during her flight through the park rested over his forearm, cocked and ready to fire, the arrow pointed at her chest.

"I've only got one shot left," he said. "And I have a feeling it wouldn't do any damage, but that won't stop me from trying."

Relief swept over her, followed by a wave of debilitating embarrassment. She sank to her knees in the grass and covered her face with blood-sticky hands.

He was next to her a moment later, strong arms drawing her to him, protecting her from the cold. "I'm sorry. The Cabochon was infused with an incredible amount of power, and that must be taking a toll on you."

"Palmer?" She wrapped her damp hands around the collar of Blake's jacket. "Is he dead?"

"No. He's pretty hard to kill. Apparently, you ripped the heart out of the Betryminar demon that attacked you. You disarmed Palmer—not that hard, by the way—and ran after the Fryyk that had come to kill the Betryminar."

"There are freaks after me now too?" She thought about

wiping dirt and tears from her face, but the blood on her hands stopped her. DeWitt pulled a blue bandanna from his back pocket and handed it to her.

"F-R-Y-Y-K. It's a type of demon. I saw what was left of the body back there right before a small herd of Fremlings attacked me."

"Fremlings? Oh. They're mine." She sniffled and climbed to her feet, reluctant to leave the relative safety of DeWitt's embrace but acutely aware that she didn't belong there.

He stared. "Yours?"

"They seem to be following me and trying to help me. They covered the body."

DeWitt's stunned expression told her this was not a good thing. "We need to get inside, somewhere safe."

"I have to get back to work. Oh my God. There was blood all over the—"

DeWitt grabbed her arm and marched her toward the pathway that led to the entrance of the park. "Palmer's taking care of it. He was going to call in Calypso to cover for you. I think you might need to take a few days off if you don't want Gleason's to be the site of a demon attack every time you walk through the door."

"I can't do that. I need to work."

"Right now you need to stay where the demons can't find you. It appears the ones that aren't trying to kill you are forming a posse on your behalf. It's best not to encourage that kind of behavior."

"But if they were trying to help me...?"

"Fremlings are like seagulls or stray cats. If you throw them a few crumbs, they'll swarm looking for more. Tonight you had what, half a dozen?"

"At least that many."

"Tomorrow you might have hundreds."

Mel stopped short so fast that DeWitt lost his death grip on her elbow. He got three steps ahead of her and had to double back. "What?"

"It's because I'm their queen, isn't it? I'm a Fremling."

He looked her up and down. "You're obviously *not* a Fremling. They're the rats of the demon world, and you're no rat."

"What if I'm *part* Fremling? That's why they're drawn to me and why I could absorb the Cabochon."

"Impossible. No human could ever mate with a Fremling."

"How do you know?"

"I...well...it just isn't done. Now come on. Let's get out of here before they regroup and decide to protect you from me again."

Chapter Thirteen

Blake should have had a million things on his mind during the ride from Veteran's Park to his place with Melodie clinging to his back. He should have been worrying about the Fremlings, the roving Ak'mir and the amazing array of demon breeds that seemed to be roaming the streets and back alleys of sleepy little Amberville.

At the very least, he should have been wondering how Melodie would survive any length of time hosting the dark power of the Cabochon.

Instead he spent those twenty minutes wondering if he'd left any dirty underwear in the living room, or if he had a clean coffee cup on hand to offer her something warm to drink.

He never brought women home.

Not that he hadn't dated now and then. Nothing serious. It could never be serious. They usually got suspicious and dumped him when he refused to take them home to his place, figuring he was married or some type of deviate. Well, technically he *was* some type of deviate.

At least Melodie McConnell already knew that.

Fortunately at the moment, she didn't care. She climbed off the back of his Harley when he pulled into his narrow driveway and made her way on unsteady legs up the small flight of stairs leading to his front door.

"This is nice," she said, craning her neck to survey the faux-brick finish topped on the second floor by colonial gold aluminum siding.

"Thanks." He stifled the urge to explain his parents had left him the house. It was enough she knew his secret. Sharing the details of the normal part of his life with her just seemed way too intimate. He plowed through the awkward silence and unlocked the front door.

"Here." He handed her his cell phone before slipping ahead of her in the entry hall to turn on the lights. "Why don't you call the bakery and see how Palmer's doing."

She nodded and dialed hesitantly. He led her to the living room, which, to his relief, was reasonably clean. He'd never considered himself sloppy, nor was he a neat freak. He figured the place looked no worse or better than she might have expected of a thirty-five-year-old bachelor.

Palmer's voice exploded out of the tiny receiver, and Melodie held the phone away from her ear. "I'm fine...I'm...really sorry about what I—no, I *do* need to apologize. I don't know what came over me. Well, yes I do know. It's the demon thing, I'm..." Her words dissolved into a hiccupping sob, and Blake swiped the phone from her.

"Everything all right, Van Houten?"

"Yes. I've got most of the mess cleaned up. Calypso said she'd handle Melodie's work for tonight. Thanks for leaving me here with a dead demon."

"Would you have preferred being left with a live one?" Blake imagined Palmer's expression and smirked.

"Is Melodie really all right?"

"She's in one piece, and the blood on her clothes isn't her own. That's about as okay as can be expected at the moment." He watched her cross the room and sit gingerly on his sofa. Overall, she looked helpless, scared, tired, beyond vulnerable, except for her eyes. Something shone in them that spoke of the power lying momentarily dormant within her. It would tear her apart if she held on to it for too much longer. "Calypso is going to have to smooth things over with Mel's boss for a few days. I don't think she should be out and about. She'll stay here tonight."

"Here? Where's here?"

"My place."

"*Oh.*"

"Don't worry." Blake dropped his voice to a whisper. "If she tries to seduce me, I know exactly how to handle it." He didn't hang on to listen to Palmer's explosive diatribe. With a certain perverse pleasure, he shut the phone off and dropped it on the table beside the kitchen door.

"Don't worry about a thing. Palmer and Calypso have it all under control." He hoped that was close to the truth. The girl had enough on her mind without having to worry about losing her job too.

She glanced at him and shrugged. "Right now, I'm not worried. It's...scary and liberating. I go through these little manic moments where it feels like everything is going to be just fantastic. Then, wham, it all hits me again like a ton of bricks."

Blake crossed the living room and took a seat on the edge of his favorite recliner. "I don't mean to upset you, but demons are capricious. They can be ecstatic one minute and morose the next. All the breeds are different, but they're all known for being unable to control whatever emotions they possess."

"Oh. That makes me feel so much better. I'd hate to be an abnormal demon."

"You're not a demon. The Cabochon is just making you act like one."

"So then, aren't you afraid I might become morose and take out my malaise on you?"

He laughed. "No. Actually, I'm banking on a theory. If I can't hurt the one who possesses the Cabochon, I'm willing to bet she—meaning you, in this case—can't hurt *me*, either. That would undermine the purpose of the spell which is for the witch hunter to suffer, and believe me, at this point, I might be tempted to let a demon take me out."

Her eyes widened. "Don't say that. There's still hope to break the curse."

He smiled and rose from the chair. "Good. Keep believing that. Now, I have some clean clothes you can borrow, and then I'll see if I can round up something to eat."

"I'm not hungry. I haven't been all day."

"You should try to eat and try to sleep. If you're weak, the Cabochon will have a greater effect on you."

That seemed to strike a nerve, and she sat up straighter. "I can fight it, can't I? I can just sit here and let it take me over, or I can resist."

Blake nodded, though he wasn't at all sure it was possible to resist the power of the Witch's Curse. He hoped for Melodie's sake it was. "I have a feeling you're a lot stronger than you think you are, lass."

Mel wished she shared DeWitt's faith in her inner strength. Right now, the last thing she felt was strong. Sitting in his cozy, if sparse, kitchen, dressed in a pair of his sweatpants and an oversize white T-shirt, she felt lost, as though she were wandering through a dream world.

She'd felt that way for a long time after her divorce, as if she was stuck in Jell-O. Life went on around her, slightly muffled and wiggly, a little out of focus and monochromatic.

Right now, the only part of her world in Technicolor was Blake DeWitt, and she couldn't take her eyes off him.

He sat opposite her, sipping black coffee. Her own—mostly

milk and sugar—had gone cold while his still steamed. He held Palmer's crossbow on his lap and was examining it with the reverence of a lover.

"I have to give Van Houten credit. This looks handmade, and it's excellent workmanship. It fires like a dream. I took out two Fremlings with one arrow."

"Mmm?" She sipped the tepid coffee. He'd also made her a piece of buttered toast, which did nothing to entice her appetite out of hiding. The one bite she'd taken had tasted like sandpaper. "You seem to know a lot about demons and how to fight them."

He caught her questioning gaze. "After ten years trying to discover the one that held the Cabochon, ten years poring through old journals and letters left by the men in my family, I've learned a lot."

"So you were what, twenty when—?"

"Twenty-five. I inherited the curse from my grandfather. He died in 1998, five years after my father. My dad was the one DeWitt heir who never had to suffer the curse, because he died too soon."

Raw emotion gripped Mel, and the next lukewarm sip of coffee burned going down. "I'm sorry. Did your grandfather have a chance to prepare you for…"

His eyes darkened, and his lips thinned. "It's a hard thing to prepare for. Like most men in my bloodline, once the curse is transferred, the…cursee sort of fades out of society. It's hard to have a life or deal with family or children, if you can never be around during the daylight hours. I suppose it would be easier to be a vampire. I hear they can at least move around during the day, even if they can't go outside."

"You believe in vampires?"

He laughed again, and Mel clung to his brief smile. She'd come to crave any moment that brought a sparkle to DeWitt's golden eyes. "I killed six demons tonight and saw the rotting corpses of two more. You think vampires are a stretch for me? I've never met one, though I've had my suspicions about a few of my old co-workers back when I lived in Baltimore."

"So you haven't gone outside during the day in ten years?"

"I haven't *seen* daylight in ten years. I turn to stone at sunrise and back again at sunset. I used to think my grandfather was eccentric. He went a little crazy, they said, back in 1949. That was the year his father died and transferred the curse to him. Everybody said it was grief." He placed the crossbow on the table between them and sat back in his chair before continuing.

"My father was fifteen at the time, and he didn't understand. My grandfather never told him because he hoped he'd never have to, so instead he let everyone believe he just stopped wanting to be part of the family. My grandmother left and took my dad with her a few years later. My grandfather lived alone for the rest of his life. I didn't see him much, but when my parents died, he came over from Scotland to find me. He'd decided it was time to tell me what I had to look forward to, and he gave me all the information he'd accumulated about the curse over the years."

"So you knew what was going to happen to you, and you couldn't stop it." Hopelessness washed over Mel. How could she survive this? Feeling every emotion so acutely was already taking its toll. Her limbs felt like lead, and her heart ached so fiercely for this man she hardly knew that she wanted to rip it out of her chest.

"I figured in time I'd work it out. I have more resources than any of my predecessors did. And right now, I'm probably closer than any of them ever came except for Wendell Blake. He died in 1863 and his journals tell about an encounter he had with a dying demon. He had his hands on the Cabochon, but he couldn't destroy it in time. He didn't know how. All he could do was pass the curse on to his nephew, Calvin DeWitt, rather than his own son. That's how the curse changed from the Blake to the DeWitt bloodline. I, at least, have a witch who's willing to see about having the curse removed. I don't know much about Calypso, but I get the impression she usually doesn't take no for an answer."

Mel shrugged. Cal had her weaknesses, but DeWitt seemed to have pegged her. She was relentless when she wanted something. If anyone could make a case for the Witches' Council to break the curse, she could.

DeWitt rose then, collected their coffee cups and placed them in the sink. "I don't have a spare bedroom. You can sleep in my room."

Mel raised a brow. "Oh, really?" Dare she smirk at the implication? One innocent glance from Palmer had her ready to climb inside his clothes with him. How would her capricious demon psyche react to the possibility of sharing a bed with Blake DeWitt?

He didn't miss a beat. If he entertained even a fleeting naughty thought, it didn't show. "I don't sleep."

"Not at all?"

"It seems a waste of what little time I have."

And it did seem a shame to waste the night with small talk. Melodie rose and took a step toward DeWitt. He didn't try to back away, but his posture stiffened as if he guessed her intent. Once again, the world became bright and inviting. His eyes smoldered, and his full lower lip begged for her attention just as Palmer's had.

Before she could make another suggestive move, he had her wrists crossed firmly behind her back. She struggled halfheartedly, shocked by the swiftness with which he'd captured her and pleased by the sensation of his firm thighs pressed against hers.

"I was afraid this might happen. Palmer told me about your little indiscretion back at the bakery."

"I was hoping you'd be a little more of a man than he was." The words slipped out, and the still-lucid part of her brain regretted them instantly. Later maybe, when she wasn't so turned on, she'd take time to be properly ashamed.

"Oh, I'm a lot more man, but just like the demon hunter, I won't take advantage of a lady who's not in her right mind." His lips caressed the shell of her ear, sending shivers down her spine and all points south. "We both know, in the real world, you wouldn't have eyes for the dark, dangerous boys. You're Palmer's type, all squeaky clean. As much as I might like otherwise, as long as you're under my roof, you'll stay that way."

She growled and tried to wriggle free of his viselike grip. "I can think of things I'd rather be under than your roof."

"I'm sure you can. But for now, you'll just have to settle."

Step by torturous step, he marched her through the house to his bedroom.

She offered only nominal resistance tempered with halfhearted pleas delivered in a sultry voice that didn't match her girl-next-door looks.

"Are you going to lock me up? Tie me down? How are you going to keep me from being naughty, witch hunter?"

He might have bristled at the taunt. In this moment, he had half a mind to become just that. If Calypso couldn't convince the Council to finally break the curse, he'd find someone who could free an innocent woman from sharing his torment.

"I should do both of those things for your own protection, but I don't have time. It'll be daylight soon."

"I don't mind a quickie." She writhed in his grasp, reminding him just how long he'd been without a woman. A lesser man might have crumbled. A man pushed almost to the brink of madness would certainly have accepted the wordless invitation when her hips ground against his.

Perhaps Blake hadn't yet reached the point of no return, but God knew he was close. So close.

He tossed her on the bed, which undulated beneath her sinuous form. She grinned. "Oh, the fun we could have on a water bed! Come on, DeWitt, show me a good time."

"Don't tempt me." He didn't wait for her to try, merely turned around and left the room, closing the door behind him. With no way to lock the room from the outside and no way to block the door, which opened in, it wasn't much of a prison.

She could walk right out, but she didn't. He held the knob tight for a moment, feeling his pulse beat double time in his fingers as they tightened on the brass. After a silent moment, her quiet sobs filtered through the door.

He refused to go back into the bedroom. If he offered her comfort now, he might not be able to leave in time. Dawn would break soon, and whether the rays of first light touched him or not, the transformation would occur on schedule. He needed to be hidden away, safe from eyes that would look on him with pity or disgust.

Hopefully she'd stay put and fall asleep. If she didn't, he would be at her mercy.

Embarrassment left Melodie immobile in the middle of Blake DeWitt's water bed. Shame settled over her like a layer of ice, heavy and stiff.

Why couldn't she at least have the good fortune to forget her indiscretions? Twice now, she'd thrown herself at men while in the thrall of some demonic spell. If the shame of that didn't kill her, the humiliation of being rejected twice certainly would. Deep down she didn't want Palmer or DeWitt. Well, maybe under better circumstances or... No. She didn't want either of them. Whatever had taken over her mind was forcing her to act on any emotional impulse, no matter how slight.

How would she cope?

She tried to move, but the weight of her own indecision held her down. Her eyes drifted closed, and she let them. She hadn't slept in over twenty-four hours, and she'd believed DeWitt when he'd said physical weakness would make her more vulnerable.

DeWitt. She'd never be able to look him in the eye again.

Heat washed over her cheeks at the memory of his hard body pressed against her, the knowledge that he'd been aroused by her movements. The tickle of his breath against her ear and the commanding pressure of his hands on her skin had left her wanting. The complete loss of touch with her carefully constructed reality left her bereft.

Exhaustion claimed her before her hot tears dried on her cheeks.

Screams of vengeance filled the night. In their wake, Percival Blake walked the dark streets of Devon Crook. He noted with satisfaction the tightly shuttered windows of the thatched-roof houses. The God-fearing citizens of this tiny village knew well to keep themselves hidden on the Devil's night.

The nobleman's weary steps brought him to the cobbler's shop, where he'd been judiciously renting a spare room. It was not that he didn't possess enough gold to purchase a room at the inn, but he preferred anonymity when he hunted witches.

He opened the wooden door with a bloodstained hand, and a breath of cold air stirred the graying hairs at his temples. He froze on the threshold, listening.

The coven leader was dead. He'd left her hanging from a willow bough in the churchyard by a six-foot length of the strongest hemp. Even her dark master would be unable to resurrect her now. Her sisters in sin still keened over her. Their grief would prevent them from following him this evening, but tomorrow night their period of mourning would end, and they would come for him. He planned to reduce them to ash, though, before the full moon set again.

Dismissing the chill wind, he stepped inside his room. He was eager to wash the stains of his vocation from his hands and lie down on the straw-stuffed mattress the cobbler had graciously provided.

He felt her presence only after he'd closed the door, sealing them both in the darkened room.

"You've murdered a good woman tonight." The voice that accused him was thick with grief and rage. "And you've taken an innocent life."

Percival stiffened. Only his eyes moved, sweeping the dimness for the intruder. He wondered if he had the strength to fight again so soon. His forty-year-old bones had begun to protest his late-night activities. "She had congress with the Devil. There was no innocence there."

A lithe form stepped out of the deep shadow in the corner near the tightly shuttered window. She held a stone in one milk-white hand and a tallow candle in the other. Percival's eyes widened when a flame hissed to life around the wick. The Devil's concubine had merely inclined her blonde head, and fire rose to her command.

Percival swore he tasted brimstone. He shivered but refused to be cowed by her power.

"Our kind have no compact with Satan. He's part of your world, not ours. And the innocent life you took was the babe she carried. Will your God forgive you for cutting *that* life short?"

A lie. The witch he'd killed tonight was not a married woman. Any babe in her belly had to be the spawn of evil. Percival squinted at his accuser. "I do what I am called to do. If the witch's babe was innocent, the Lord would have protected it."

Apparently offended by his words, the woman narrowed her eyes and threw back her head, exposing the graceful column of her throat. In the flickering candlelight, she was undeniably lovely, but her beauty served only to harden his noble heart. His one true love had been like her—golden-haired and fine-boned with dark, intelligent eyes. He'd adored Rebecca until the day he found her kneeling in the glen, praying over a five-pointed star etched into the top of a tree stump and offering wine and rose petals to the goat-horned god of the underworld.

He'd known not a moment's peace since that day two decades ago.

"Percival Blake, you *will* stop killing witches. Beyond the lives of the women you've murdered, you've sinned unforgivably tonight."

"I will atone for my sins come Judgment Day." Percival reached for the still-bloody knife he carried beneath his overcoat. The sweet, coppery smell of death that clung to his weapon haunted his dreams, as would the terror he'd seen in the dark blue eyes of the coven leader when he'd plunged the blade into her soft flesh. He regretted having to do it again so soon, but...

The well-worn handle fit his palm perfectly, smooth and still warm from its earlier use, but before he drew the weapon free of his breeches and coat, the witch let loose the stone from her grip. Percival thought to dodge the ineffective assault, but the object didn't fly through the air to strike him. Instead it hung suspended above the ground, slowed in its flight as if the air had grown too thick to allow its passage. Equidistant between them, it spun, glowing the pure blue of a summer sky.

He stared, transfixed by the spectacle. The witch uttered words that might have been Latin, but he couldn't make them out. He turned and flung the door open, his terror winning out over pride. To run from a mere girl was cowardly, but to stand and face the Devil's own wrath was foolhardy.

"You won't see Judgment Day, my lord," she said as he stepped into the street. "In fact, you will never see daylight again. You skulk in the night like vermin, so from now on, you shall live only in darkness, forever."

He might have responded, but his throat closed, his eyesight dimmed and his feet grew too heavy to take another step.

All was blackness for him after that.

In the morning, the villagers crowded around a strange addition to their provincial surroundings. None was more surprised than the cobbler who could not explain how a statue of a fierce beast had sprung up in the street before his shop.

Women hid their faces from the evil countenance, and children clung to their parents, sure to suffer nightmares from looking at the frightful face wrought in dark granite by a mysterious sculptor. Man-shaped and of greater than average height, the beast had fangs protruding from his mouth and curving down toward his chin. His pointed ears swept back from a hairless skull, and heavy brows hooded wide, wild eyes that glared at the curious onlookers.

His hands were gnarled claws, and his legs ended in cloven hooves. A forked tail hung from his backside, its sharp tip resting in the mud. A terrible beast indeed, made all the more frightening by the fact that he wore a nobleman's greatcoat and finely tailored breeches.

All that day, the villagers of Devon Crook gave the statue a wide berth, and that night they hid in their homes again, still fearing the man who had come among them to hunt witches, though he never returned to their quiet northern town.

Sometime after moonset the following night, the statue disappeared, and it too was never seen again.

Chapter Fourteen

Mel woke with sunlight streaming across her face. The warmth of it soothed her, and the gentle motion of the bed beneath her would have lulled her back into a contented sleep except she remembered where she was.

She sat up fast and surveyed the room while climbing out of Blake DeWitt's bed. The half-open sliding doors of the closet across from the bed revealed a plethora of dark clothing. The oak dresser, bulky and masculine, held a few bottles of cologne, a hairbrush and a stoneware dish full of the usual detritus from any man's pockets—spare change, stray paper clips and balled-up receipts. The mirror above it was dusty, and the motes that clung to the glass caught the light and sparkled.

The room smelled like DeWitt, and so did she. How she could have his scent on her when they'd touched only briefly boggled her mind.

She ran a hand through her hair and bent close to the mirror to look into her own eyes. Familiar brown orbs stared back at her, a little bloodshot and puffy around the lids but definitely her own.

She felt utterly normal this morning.

Could lack of food and sleep have made her act the way she had last night? Chasing demons—and killing them!—throwing herself at Palmer and DeWitt?

Calypso would know. She had to get home and talk to her friend, but first...

The house was quiet except for the faint ticking of the clock on the wall in the kitchen. Blake's cell phone lay on the table in the hall, shut off. Nothing stirred.

Curiosity drew her through every room, wondering what DeWitt had done with her bloody clothes. Would he have washed them? Burned them? That's what she wanted to do, when she got them home. She didn't find them in the bathroom hamper or hanging in any of the closets she inspected. The second bedroom, she discovered, contained all the equipment someone would need to keep in shape—free weights, a stationary bike, a treadmill and a UV lamp. Stacks of towels and room-temperature bottles of spring water filled the small closet, but she found nothing that belonged to her. She doubted he'd stashed her outfit in the attic, so except for the trash cans outside, that left one place to look.

The door leading to the basement wasn't locked, nor was it open, but that didn't stop Mel. She flipped on the light switch, illuminating the short flight of wooden stairs, and descended into a very mundane-looking laundry room.

The washer and dryer were empty and very dusty. For some reason, she couldn't picture DeWitt measuring fabric softener and pressing creases into his black jeans.

"Who am I kidding?" she asked aloud. Her voice echoed a bit. "I don't care about my clothes."

The admission boosted her confidence just a bit, and she made a circuit of the basement. A narrow door stood slightly ajar opposite the stairs. There was no knob on the door, and she guessed if it had been closed, she might not have noticed it.

She peeked in, but the room beyond was too dark to make anything out. The door creaked when she pushed it open just far enough to let a little light spill into the shadows. Drawn by her unnaturally acute curiosity, she slipped inside. Panic stole her breath when she came face-to-face with him. The granite monster towered over her. Taller and broader than DeWitt's human physique, he stood at parade rest, clawed feet wide apart, muscular legs encased in stone jeans.

He'd taken off his shirt before the transformation, and it hung on the inside doorknob. His chest seemed expanded as though he were taking a deep breath, triangular pectorals pointing down to a ripped abdomen. Yes, this part was definitely Blake DeWitt, but there the similarity ended.

His strong chin and deep-set eyes had been replaced with the face of a nightmare. Curving fangs filled a wide, lipless mouth. The broad, flat nose and bulbous forehead harkened back to a more primitive evolution of man. Pointed ears curved up high over his hairless skull, and a forked tail spiraled down around one calf.

Mel fought the urge to shrink back from him. Immobile, he couldn't hurt her, except perhaps to break her heart.

She let her fingers trail along one icy cheekbone, down the corded muscles of his neck and to the center of his chest where a human heart would beat.

"I'm sorry," she whispered. "I really didn't believe you until now."

She wondered, if he came to life at this moment, would he be Blake DeWitt in a monster's body, or would he be a mindless beast? Her heart thundered, and she backed away, then sidled out of the half-hidden room.

"Um...I don't think you can hear me," she said through the door. "But if you can, I'm going home now. Thanks for letting me stay here. I'll be careful, I'll watch out for Fremlings, and I'll see you later."

She didn't expect him to answer, but she waited a moment, just in case, then hurried back up the stairs.

Half an hour later, Mel settled into a chair at Starbucks. Cal plopped into the seat opposite her and slid a warm pumpkin muffin and an iced latte across the table along with Mel's purse, which she'd left at Gleason's last night.

"This is getting serious," the witch said. Her black-tipped nails tapped the tabletop nervously.

Mel gulped her latte and glared at her friend. "You're telling me? I ripped a demon's heart out last night. With my bare hands. I can't even tell you how gross that is." The thought of it killed what little appetite the scent of the muffin had kindled. "And those *things* followed me here from DeWitt's house."

Cal's dark eyes darted from side to side. "What *things?*"

"Blake calls them Fremlings. They look like dirty dust mops with long...kind of bony fingers. They've been following me, sort of gazing at me with their beady little black eyes."

Cal gaped. "How many?"

"I don't know. There were at least a dozen last night, and Blake killed a bunch of them, but he said there'd be a lot more." Mel lowered her voice and whispered, "I'm their leader."

Calypso's dark brows shot up at Mel's confession. "No...honey. You're not. I've heard about Fremlings. They follow power, and you've apparently got enough to attract them. The good news is, I don't think they'll hurt you."

"You don't *think* they'll hurt me?" Mel gaped. Her muffin and her coffee looked gray and unappetizing now, and the sounds of coffeehouse patrons talking and laughing grated on her senses like nails on a chalkboard. She scowled.

"Just try to avoid them. The more you interact with them, the more will show up."

"Yeah, Blake said that too."

"Blake. Not DeWitt? You guys seem to have bonded." There was a question in Cal's statement, one that Mel wasn't in the mood to address.

"Let's skip to the important stuff, shall we? What did the Witches' Council say about the curse?"

Cal studied the table. "The Council hasn't convened yet. They're gathering."

"And how long does that take?"

Calypso sighed. "A while. The most important thing right now is to keep you safe until we have a solution. The consensus is that it may be possible to affect a transfer of the Cabochon from you to a suitable demon queen, but all the proper spells need to be worked out first."

"A suitable demon queen? Because there are *unsuitable* ones?"

"Yes. Like Fremlings, for instance, and Ak'mirs. Certain breeds aren't meant to have this kind of power."

"What about just breaking the curse? Isn't it time for that?"

Cal shrugged. "It's not my call. Vengeance spells are very dangerous. They've been forbidden for centuries, and breaking one can be almost as chancy as casting one."

"So they're just going to let it go on? How many more innocent men will pay for what Percival Blake did?"

"I understand, Mel, but the people who get to decide this are a lot more powerful than I am."

Mel pushed her cup and her muffin toward Calypso and rose. "Well, the way things are going, they might not be more powerful than me. Ask them if they're in the mood to deal with a Melodie-demon, because I'd say if you ask the two creatures I killed last night, I'm hell on wheels."

She grabbed her purse and strode out, secure in the knowledge that more than a few heads turned to watch her leave.

"The boy asks about you often. I've run out of stories to tell him."

Percival glared at his solicitor over the crystal rim of a brandy glass. A thoughtful sip of the amber liquid soothed the raw spot in his gut that flared whenever Thompson mentioned Rene. "I will visit him before the year is out. Assure him of that."

"I fail to see why you don't do so yourself. He's a fine boy, intelligent and curious. He could use a firmer hand in his upbringing, though. The house staff is too lenient with him."

Thompson steepled long fingers over his round stomach and leaned back in his chair. The firelight lit the man's hazel eyes, giving his appraising glance a sinister cast.

"I'd like nothing better than to spend time with my son, but if I'm to keep him fed and clothed, I can't live a life of leisure." Percival tossed a small pouch to Thompson, who caught it and tucked it away neatly in his desk, quick and efficient as always. Up until now, he'd never questioned where his employer's funds came from or what work brought payment oftentimes in foreign coins. He handled the accounts and had judiciously arranged for the woman who had borne Rene to disappear when she began expecting Percival to make an honest lady of her.

A man with only half a life would not make a decent bridegroom. He barely made a respectable father, but at least his boy wanted for nothing material.

"I appreciate you checking in on him. I will consult with the staff and see that they don't spoil him before I can return."

"No one sees you for months at a time, Percival. I've often feared you wouldn't return at all."

"Don't concern yourself with my welfare, as long as my accounts are paid and there's money enough to care for Rene."

"There's plenty to see him well into adulthood, but I question the means through which you've acquired it."

Percival set his brandy glass down and rose from the comfortable settee in Thompson's drawing room. Five years lived in darkness had taught him one thing above all else—he could never rest too long in one place. "My occupation is nothing criminal, I assure you. I'll be off now. When you see Rene next, tell him I'll see him soon, and he's to mind the staff." Under Thompson's curious gaze, he gathered his cloak and swept out of the cozy room.

Nothing criminal. He might have laughed, but there was nothing humorous about his line of work either. Since he'd become a creature of the night, he'd learned far more about the dark world that existed in concert with his own. His search for the witch who had cursed him took him all over Europe to places no God-fearing man should ever see and left a stench upon him that he had no desire to share with his precious son.

He'd once thought witches the pinnacle of all evil, but he'd since discovered things beyond description. He'd found that plenty of men would pay dearly for artifacts of the occult, objects not visible to those who walked in daylight. Small fortunes passed into his hands on a regular basis in exchange for these sacred and often unholy items. He trafficked in commodities no sane man could comprehend and that no pure soul could touch.

Leaving Thompson's cozy home behind, Percival hurried through the streets and ventured back into the deepest shadows where he felt most comfortable. No longer a witch hunter, he had put his skills to use tracking different creatures. Tonight, in order to maintain the flow of gold into Thompson's greedy hands, Percival Blake hunted demons.

Blake returned to the world at sunset stiff-limbed and shivering. He climbed the basement stairs and stopped at the top to listen. He hadn't expected Melodie to hang around, but he hoped she'd at least left in broad daylight. The Fremlings would stick to the shadows, even if they followed her, but in the half-light of early dawn, they might have been brave enough to swarm. He didn't want to think of them carrying her off somewhere to worship her as their queen.

On his way to his bedroom to change, he glanced at his computer desk, and guilt pinged his senses. He couldn't leave his accounts unattended for much longer. If he could track down Melodie again and bring her back here, he could get some work done and keep an eye on her at the same time.

The logical, conscientious part of his brain lost a swift and brutal argument with the part that was desperate for release. His work would wait, forever if necessary. He'd rather sell everything he owned and live in a tent if it meant breaking the curse. He'd find Melodie and Calypso, and tonight he'd demand some answers.

With every window in her apartment open and sunlight streaming in from all angles, Mel felt reasonably normal all day. She forced herself to eat a small bowl of soup, though she tasted nothing, and she forbid herself from returning Arnie's call. He'd left a concerned voice mail asking her when she thought she might be back to work and thanking her for the wonderful job she'd done on the Ladies' Club Luncheon cupcakes.

Guilt gnawed at her over that. Calypso had covered for her brilliantly, and she'd been petulant at Starbucks. Was it wrong to demand the Witches' Council move fast on this? After all, everyone agreed a mistake had been made. She'd been in the wrong place at the wrong time, and odds were, a human possessing the Cabochon could screw up the delicate balance of everything, so didn't it make sense to reverse the process ASAP?

Left with little to do but worry, Mel cleaned. She scrubbed

the bathtub, aired out rugs, polished all her windows with vinegar and newsprint and rearranged some furniture to eliminate a couple of small hiding spots that she deemed just the right size for curious Fremlings.

She sensed them. Even with the midday sun reflecting blinding rays off the spotless kitchen counter, she felt them watching her. The back of her neck tingled, and every time she opened a closet or a cabinet, the skin on her arms turned to gooseflesh.

By dusk, she'd exhausted herself. What would she do all night if she didn't go to work? When the last purple smudge of sunset faded on the horizon visible through her living room window, she snatched up the phone and dialed Blake's number. Before it rang twice, the doorbell chimed, and she flung the receiver down and ran for the door.

Palmer stood on her front steps, his hair mussed, wearing a sheepish grin. "Sorry I couldn't get here sooner. It's the Fall Blowout Sale at Taylor Tools, and I promised I'd help my uncle. Plus I had to do some research."

Mel stepped back to invite him in. Heat crept up from the knot in her stomach when he brushed past her. "Uh...Palmer, I just want to say about last night..."

He waved off her apology and settled himself on the couch. A sheaf of papers appeared from inside his jacket, and he began spreading them out on the coffee table. "We don't have to go there. More importantly—I got some of the scoop from Calypso on the Witches' Council. I know they're not in any hurry to break the curse, but the way I see it, if we don't get the Cabochon into the demon queen it was meant for, Amberville is going to become a hub of demon activity." He shuffled the papers around and glanced at her.

Mel crossed the living room and knelt beside the coffee table. Upside down, the papers he'd assembled look like chicken scratch. Spidery handwriting interspersed with unusual symbols and fine-lined sketches of plants, feathers and stones covered what appeared to be photocopies from very old books. "What is all this?"

"The Demon Hunters' Network has a few resources at their disposal. I called in a favor, and I got my hands on some pages from a seventeenth-century grimoire."

"That's a spell book, right?"

Palmer nodded and rearranged pages again. They seemed to be in a specific order, though none of the sheets were numbered. Palmer motioned for Mel to join him on the couch, and he scooted over on the cushion to make room for her.

He smelled slightly spicy, and his Docker-clad thigh was warm against hers. She ignored the sudden flare of awareness. No way would she allow the demon in her blood to take over again. The embarrassment would destroy her.

Instead she stared at the pages in front of her. Now arrayed like the pieces of a puzzle, the half-dozen sheets looked like one large diagram.

"It's a spell and incantation book written by an English witch back in the early 1700s. My sources tell me spells were very elaborate back then and very powerful. The old magick was stuff not to be messed with. Modern witches aren't even allowed to perform these spells."

Mel gave Palmer a sidelong glance. "And this will help us how? You don't think Calypso would use one of those old spells if it's forbidden?"

"If she won't, we can do it ourselves."

Mel might have laughed, but Palmer's blue eyes had gone steely. That tingle crept up her spine again, and she shivered. "Are you serious?"

"Yes. Nowadays, a lot of a witch's power is internal. The spells they use have been simplified, and many of the purposes of those spells are benign...protection, warding, health, happiness and recharging psychic energy. The darker spells and curses are forbidden except under dire circumstances. These old spells relied more on ambient power that anyone could summon. Because witchcraft was demonized, though, the average person wouldn't dare try casting a spell when they could be hung for something as simple as making a home remedy for heartburn."

"So what is *this* spell? It looks complicated."

"It is, but nothing we can't handle. The ingredients are relatively common, and the incantations are in Latin, here..." He pointed to some of the chicken scratch. Mel couldn't make out any of the words, but Palmer seemed confident. "It'll take a little time, but we could have everything ready in a couple of days."

"Ready for what? What does this do?"

"This is a transfer-of-power spell. It should transfer the Cabochon from you to someone else, preferably a demon. My friends in the network are willing to help me track one down."

Mel gaped. All the normalcy just drained out of her day. "You're going to capture a demon? A live demon."

"Well, a dead one won't work." Palmer smirked. He nudged her shoulder with his own. "C'mon, don't look so bleak. It's doable. We capture a demon and hold it in a magical cage, perform the spell, then get out of the way and dissolve the cage."

"Do you have a spell for making a magical cage?"

"They're easy. I have the stuff in my lair—a few crystals, some salt and a power charm."

"This is crazy." Mel covered her face with her hands. "Why can't you just pixie dust me and let me forget all about this whole mess?"

"Then you'd be chased by demons and not know why.

When all this is over, if you want to be dusted, I'll do it, but I don't know how much of your memory could be erased. Considering the circumstances, you might forget all of us."

Mel thought about that. She didn't have many good friends. Larry had managed to keep all the couples they'd hung out with in Boston, and with the exception of her college roommate, who lived in Albuquerque now, there weren't many people she could confide in. Could she afford to forget Calypso and Palmer...and DeWitt? How could she ever forget him?

"Well, let's worry about that later, then. What does this spell entail?"

Palmer picked up the first page and read a laundry list of kitchen herbs.

"This is either a transfer spell or the recipe for Italian wedding soup," she said. "I've got most of this stuff in my cupboard."

"It all has to be fresh, no preservatives—don't worry. I know a couple of magick supply shops that should have almost everything we need. We might have a little problem getting desiccated leeches this time of year, but—"

The doorbell rang before Mel could question the necessity of desiccated leeches. She rose, and Palmer shuffled all the grimoire pages together and stuffed them back into his jacket. "We should keep this under wraps for now."

"You're right. I don't think Calypso would approve." Mel hurried to the door. Blake and Calypso stood on the top step, shoulder to shoulder. His Harley was parked at the curb in front of Palmer's Jeep, but there was no sign of Cal's beat-up Toyota.

"Uh, hi?" Mel stepped back, and Cal shouldered her way in.

"I brought some warding stones to put around your apartment. That should keep the Fremlings away. Ooh, Palmer. You look like the cat that ate the canary. What have you two been up to?"

Mel's curious gaze followed Cal's sinuous sway across the room. She flipped her long hair over her shoulder and thrust one hip out, plopped her heavy purse on the coffee table where Palmer's secret spell pages had just rested, and smirked at Mel. "You look like you're feeling a lot better than this morning."

Blake sidled past Mel with an apologetic grin. "I'm sorry you had to wake up alone this morning. I hope you slept well."

Palmer glared, and Mel blushed. The strange rivalry between the two men didn't make much sense. They couldn't be fighting over her. Calypso just raised a brow.

"I've got your crossbow, Van Houten. For such a *small* weapon, I have to admit it's well designed."

Palmer rose, and Mel's heart did a small flip. Had his shoulders just gotten broader and his blue eyes darker? "I've been told accuracy and skill are more important than size. The bigger weapons can be clumsy, and they have a tendency to misfire."

DeWitt rose to the bait, and Calypso crossed her arms over her chest, settling in for a front-row seat in the testosterone battle.

"I imagine if you're used to handling something slim and compact, you'd find a larger weapon difficult to control. I've always preferred something more powerful. When I fire on something, I like it to know it's been fired on."

Palmer surged forward, and Mel planted herself between him and DeWitt. "Boys, you can compare weapons later. Right now, let's let Calypso do her warding spell."

"Aw, Mel. Things were just getting interesting." Cal pouted as she rummaged through her purse for a collection of black stones. Palmer and Blake circled each other like caged beasts, and for a moment, Mel entertained a vision of them naked to the waist, covered in sweat, ready to battle to the death for the right to possess her.

Cal caught her faraway stare and squinted at her. "You okay?"

Mel shook herself back to reality. "Fine. Let's get this show on the road."

Calypso performed the warding spell, which gave the whole apartment a faint, unpleasant scent of ozone. It took less than an hour and left the four of them squared off again in the living room.

Palmer spoke first. "Melodie, I have some more research to do. If you want to come with me, maybe you can help."

Cal eyed him. "Research for what?"

He flattened a palm against his chest. "Demon hunter. I research *demons* for a living."

Mel shrugged. Why not? But DeWitt made his move. "I was thinking maybe you should be someplace bright and full of people. You want to put some distance between you and the Fremlings, and they'd be less apt to come near you if you were somewhere well-populated...like a restaurant."

Cal gaped. "What did I do a warding spell for if she's not going to stay in her apartment?"

"Well, maybe they can't get in, but they're certainly going to congregate outside," Blake shot back. "Take it from someone who knows about being cooped up, this is no place to spend the evening. Come with me. I'll take you to dinner."

"Like a date?" Cal asked. Her eyes went flinty and narrow.

"No, just dinner."

"Research, Melodie. We—*I* have a lot of things to go over." Palmer tapped his jacket. Mel looked at Cal.

"I have to go to Gleason's and fill in for you," the witch said. "In fact, I'm due there in an hour."

"Uh, well, since I'm sort of hungry, I think I'll go with Blake.

I could use some normal time, and I really don't want to sit here listening to the Fremlings mobilize outside my bedroom window."

"Can you ward the yard too?" Palmer asked as Cal grabbed her purse. He cast a skeptical glance at DeWitt, then dismissed him with a shrug.

"I'd have to get more stones. I could do it tomorrow night."

"You wouldn't happen to have any desiccated leeches lying around would you?"

"What for?"

"Aren't they good for demon warding?"

Mel held her breath. Was Palmer trying to make Cal suspicious?

"Hmm. Sometimes. I'll have to check into that."

"Need a ride?"

Mel's jaw dropped. She'd just been ignored by Palmer, and DeWitt wore a satisfied grin that spoke of the superior size of his weapon. Mel rolled her eyes.

"I guess it's settled, then," she said. "If anyone should come across a cure for cabochon affliction while I'm gone, please text me, okay?"

Chapter Fifteen

"It gets worse at night," Mel said. She slathered sweet butter on a plump roll as she spoke. Blake sat across from her in a cozy booth near the bustling salad bar of a place called Rossie's in the Highway Mall just outside Amberville.

The clack of flatware on hot plates, the sizzle of entrées whizzing by as waitresses hurried to fill orders and the buzz of subdued conversation combined to make the place lively and fun. Mel felt good, normal and just a little flirty, not in a demony, tear-your-mate-apart-and-eat-him-raw kind of way, but in the way she hadn't felt since she and Larry had dated a million years ago.

The combined crimson glow of the small votive on the table between them and the low-hanging copper-shaded lamp suspended above lent an exotic tinge to Blake's golden eyes.

He stared at her over his own salad and the dark beer he'd ordered, and his expression filled with sympathy. "I haven't been a fan of the night for a long time. Too much unseen happens at night. I never knew, until the curse, about all the things that are out there. Most people never know what really happens after dark."

Mel bit into her roll. She waited for the flavor that should have accompanied the succulent aroma of the fresh-baked bread, but it never came. She set the roll down and shifted salad around on her plate with her fork. "I wish I could forget everything I've seen in the last few days, but maybe it's better to remember. What you don't know *can* hurt you."

"Let's forget it for a few hours. The mall's crowded, everything's lit up. You're safe here. It feels good to pretend none of that other stuff exists." Blake raised his glass, and Mel followed suit, clinking her mineral water against his beer. "Here's to a few hours of normal."

"So what will you do?" she asked, letting the glow of the small flame draw her gaze. "On your first day, once the curse is broken?"

"Are we assuming it will be?"

"We'll find a way, right? We have to."

"Okay, assuming we break the curse, I'm going to...sunbathe?" He shrugged. His shoulders remained a little hunched, and Mel wondered if this wasn't the best vein for the conversation to take. "I used to think about it all the time. I had a list a mile long. I wanted to travel, maybe go skydiving, windsurfing, snorkeling. I think I've gone beyond missing those things now. I just want to watch the sun come up. I want a whole day—all twenty-four hours of it."

"What about your family? Haven't they wondered why they never see you during the day?"

"My parents have been gone for fifteen years, my grandfather for ten. I don't have brothers or sisters... There's really no one."

Mel swallowed hard. She didn't want to eat, but the physical act of shoveling food into her mouth gave her something to do besides radiate pity at the man across the table. He was completely alone and cut off from most of the world. Sitting here in the bustling restaurant, he seemed much less sinister than he had when she'd first encountered him at Gleason's, less brooding than when he'd rescued her from the

Ak'mir. She might have believed he was like anyone else—only perhaps better-looking than most—except she recalled what she'd seen in the basement room this morning. She'd seen what he hid from the world, and it made her heart ache for him. "Well, there's no one asking hard questions, then, I suppose. You don't have to lie to anyone."

He raised a brow as if he'd never seen the upside of the situation before, dismal as it was. "That's true. All my research into my bloodline shows families being torn apart by the curse. All the men seemed to have kept the secret from their wives and children. They receded from society, gained reputations for being crazy old hermits or eccentrics. I guess it's a good thing I don't have anyone to disappoint."

Mel set her fork down. "I'm sorry. I'm not very good at this."

He leaned forward a bit, and his eyes caught the candlelight and sparkled. "Good at what?"

"Ignoring white elephants. What kind of normal conversation can we have with the curse hanging over our heads?"

He laughed, and Mel liked that. The deep rumble made her skin tingle and humor lit his amber eyes. "Let me give it a shot. How did you get into the bakery business?"

"Are you sure you can handle the excitement of that story? It's a doozy."

"Try me." He sipped his beer and nudged his own food around his plate.

"Well, I wanted to be a chef, but I've got a number of food allergies to things that are pretty common in most kitchens. It's very limiting for a cook if you can't taste your own food. I went into pastry decorating because I don't have to taste-test as much. It's more art than cooking."

"Ah, that's why you carry the allergy pen."

She nodded. She'd forgotten he'd gone through her purse,

more than once. "I haven't had a reaction in about five years, so I'm doing pretty well."

"Why do you work nights?"

"I don't sleep much. Last night was unusual for me. I guess I was completely exhausted. During the day, there are too many...people around."

"You don't like people?" Blake glanced around the bustling restaurant.

"I like people. I just prefer to work when it's quiet."

"That's no reason to hide away in the dark."

"I don't hide away. I've always been shy, and it's just easier for me to function when I don't have to interact with too many people." She allowed herself a grin, hoping he'd accept her admission.

His eyes narrowed. He wasn't buying it.

Fortunately the arrival of their dinners cut off his response, and Mel dove into conversation about the food to distract him from any more personal questions. That worked well until dessert; then he pounced.

"Do you work at night to avoid dating?"

She blinked. "Wow. I thought you left Palmer's crossbow at my place. That was a targeted shot."

He looked flustered, and she liked that. She'd punched a small hole in his armor to match the one he'd just torn in hers.

"I'm sorry. I just can't believe that you're a social misfit."

"All right, so I'm hiding out a little. There's less pressure at night to be something spectacular. I can just exist, and that's all I can handle right now."

"Bad breakup?"

"Necessary divorce and too many prying eyes." Mel tapped her chest. "I have a big family. Brothers and their wives, cousins, aunts, uncles dropping in to see if I'm okay, lining up with crowbars to pull me out of my shell and throw me back into the boiling pot of dating. I'm not ready."

"Still love him?"

"No." That was the first easy question he'd asked. "Still hurting, maybe. Still hibernating."

"Don't hibernate too long. The world might not be there when you want to come back to it."

Mel found his advice easier to digest than the food. She'd always assumed the day would come when she'd convert back to a more "normal" life—sleeping at night like the rest of the world, awake during the day to care for a husband and children. She realized now, if she let too much time go by, that conversion would never happen. Now, maybe she'd already lost the chance to reinvent her life. This curse had stripped her of those opportunities the same way it had stripped them from Blake.

It was nearly ten, and the gibbous moon lit the night, competing with the streetlights to dispel the shadows. The ride back to Melodie's apartment from the mall had been uneventful, and at the moment, Blake sensed nothing more sinister in the dark than the constant tingle that accompanied the Cabochon. Melodie's keys jingled as she attempted to fit them in the lock of her front door.

"You should come back to my place tonight," he said.

He wondered if, without the cursed gem inside her, he'd be so drawn to Melodie McConnell. If she wasn't the key to his freedom, would she seem so beautiful? In this light, her skin was translucent. Golden highlights shimmered in her dark hair, and her eyes danced with mischief.

She smiled, and tucked a strand of chestnut hair behind one ear. "Calypso went to all that trouble to ward my apartment."

A lame excuse. He could shoot that right down. "But on the other side of the wards, you're still alone. At my place, you could practice your social skills, prepare for the end of hibernation."

She smirked and turned the doorknob. "Are you trying to drag me out of my shell too?"

"I've got a crowbar in my garage. We could give it a try."

She laughed and bumped her hip against the heavy storm door. It popped open, and the faint scent of ozone drifted out. She wrinkled her nose. "I should have picked up some air freshener at the mall. Why don't you come in for a minute and we can talk about—"

Her scream pierced the quiet evening like a blade. A crackle of blue energy threw her back from the threshold, then raced around the half-open door frame like an electrical charge.

Her body hit him, and together they tumbled backward down the steps, landing in a heap on the cement walkway.

Blake recovered first and sat up, cradling Melodie in his arms. A burn, black and smoldering, marred the length of her forearm. The acrid scent of scorched flesh had replaced the sharp odor of the ward spell.

Pain clouded her eyes. "No...no. This can't be."

"Was that the ward?" He climbed to his feet, still shaken. His heart pounded from the shock, transferred through her body into his. Mindful of her wound, he helped her up, and she huddled against him.

"I can't get into my own apartment because I'm a demon." Despair tinged her words.

"No, it has to be something else." Blake drew in a sharp breath at the sight of her injury. Wisps of smoke rose from the blackened, puckered flesh. "We need to get you to a hospital. Come on—you can sit in front of me on my bike so you don't have to bend your arm around me."

"No. I'm all right. It doesn't hurt anymore."

Blake stared. Was she in shock? Half of the skin on her arm was singed to a crisp, and she'd been thrown down a flight of stairs to boot. While he watched, she brushed at the ashes that clung to her flesh. Like an old scab, the burn flaked away, leaving only fresh pink skin. Within moments, the wound was completely gone.

She raised a brow. "They can keep me out, but they can't hurt me."

Her voice didn't sound quite right.

"I guess you're coming to my place." Somehow, he wasn't as confident about that alternative now as he'd been a few minutes ago.

She smiled, but there was none of the sweet flirtiness he'd seen earlier in the evening. Her expression was more of a dark affirmation. "Let's go, then."

"Do you want me to get anything for you, from inside?"

She looked down at herself, then walked her fingers up his chest from his abdomen to the hollow of his throat. "I've got all I need right here."

An unfamiliar scent drifted on the evening breeze, and Melodie's head snapped to one side, following it like a predator. The shadows along the edges of the empty street seemed to lengthen and darken.

"We'd better get moving. I think your minions might be closing in."

She responded with a shrug and swept a feral glance around the silent neighborhood. "They won't hurt me."

Blake grabbed his helmet and handed her his spare. "Right now, *you're* not the one I'm worried about."

The shock of stumbling into the witch's barrier had rattled Melodie's nerves, jangled her bones a bit and woken a part of

146

her that had slept for too long.

Pain had morphed quickly to exhilaration when she watched her body heal. Exhilaration became lust when Blake DeWitt put his hands on her.

Clinging to his motorcycle, they fled the shadows around her apartment. He was right. The Fremlings were watching, mobilizing, preparing to do her bidding. Wouldn't it be nice to have someone do her bidding for a change? She'd spent too many years doing what was expected of her, playing by the rules, staying invisible to avoid confrontations.

Now the captive part of her psyche screamed for release from the self-constructed cage. The energy of the ward had done more than repelled her. She'd absorbed some of it. Power soaked through her skin, tickled her nerve endings and heightened her senses. Right now, the thrum of the V-twin engine between her legs drowned out every other sensation except the feel of taut leather under her hands.

Blake drove hell-bent for election toward his place. Was it fear of the demons that kept his gloved hand on the accelerator or desire to get her alone in his domain again? Last night he'd refused her advances, but something told her tonight would be different—she'd just have to convince him she was in complete control of her actions.

She'd have to play coy.

When they reached his house, he guided the bike straight into the garage and led her inside through the inner door. No wards here, nothing to keep the Fremlings out except her will.

She sensed them swarming just out of sight, a miniature army at her disposal. What would she have them do for her?

She strolled through DeWitt's house on his heels, making note of her surroundings—the doors and windows, the nooks and crannies where the deepest shadows hid. If she couldn't get into her own home, this one might do. Surely once the sun rose, the witch hunter would have no say in who or what came and went.

He led her directly to the bedroom but stopped her at the threshold. She put herself in his personal space, drank in his scent now mixed with the smoky aroma of the autumn evening and the faint scent of ionized air. "What's wrong?"

"I just want to make sure I know who you are. That shock from the ward spell jazzed you up a bit."

She feigned innocence, not easy considering her current mood was anything but. "It was seeing that burn heal. It's an incredible feeling. I wonder if it's any type of wound or only magical ones." She sidled closer and gazed up into his eyes.

"I'll look into it. The Cabochon protects itself, apparently better than I'd ever imagined."

"So I might be invincible." It wasn't a question, and somewhere deep down, she knew the truth. Nothing could hurt her.

"You might be, but let's not try to find out just yet."

"Okay." She grinned. "What do you propose we do, then?"

"Well, I've got work to do. I figured you might want to get some sleep." His gaze challenged hers. This was a test, and she wanted desperately to pass.

"That's a good idea." She aimed her lips at his and went up on her toes to deliver a quick, chaste brush against the corner of his mouth.

It might have worked to convince him she was sincere, but rather than let the moment pass, he snaked an arm around her and drew her in. His lips found hers again and came down hard, unyielding. His tongue darted inside, first tentative, then demanding, searching.

She held back from clawing his clothes off, let him explore while she surged against him, backing him into the bedroom door frame.

He was all muscle and male power, and she became a taste of feminine surrender even though she wanted so much more. Something inside her drew up tight, flexed, ready to uncoil into a lash of undeniable lust.

This was good. Very, very good.

Until he dropped her.

With just slightly less force than the ward spell had repelled her, Blake DeWitt pushed Melodie away, breaking their kiss and severing their physical connection.

His eyes bore into hers, his expression a mixture of accusation and regret. "Who are you?"

She swiped the back of her hand across her moistened lips, felt him there, tasted him. "Whoever I am, I'm apparently not good enough for you, am I?"

"You're not Melodie McConnell right now. I can tell by the way you taste."

"Oh? Do you know how Melodie tastes? You've never kissed her."

"That's right, I haven't, but I'm sure she doesn't taste like a demon."

Mel laughed. How absurd. "Oh, and how do you know what a demon tastes like?"

"Because I've kissed one before."

Chapter Sixteen

He hated to admit it. Years of chasing demons, searching for the Cabochon as his ancestors had, brought him to many places he'd rather forget and led him to do many things he'd forever wish he hadn't.

Trying to seduce a demon was top on his list of regrets.

Melodie, or rather the creature that stared out through her once-innocent eyes, tilted her chin and smirked. "Do tell. I'd have pegged you for a man with higher standards."

He frowned. Lust and attraction hadn't been part of that equation, only foolish desperation. "Helena was beautiful. She was half-human, half-something-else. There's a breed called Domaré which mate with humans successfully. The hybrids live among humans, and they can hide pretty well."

"Domaré. I've heard that word before, but I can't remember where."

Blake squinted at the woman before him. Was the demon in her fading back into the shadows or just lying in wait? He eased out of the doorway before responding. "Some have used the word as a surname. Helena's family didn't. I met her while researching demon breeds, around the time I first ran into Van Houten. She haunts some of the old libraries, collecting references to her kin. When I discovered what she was, I tried to...use her as a gateway to the demon world."

"And how far did you get?"

He wondered why he was telling her all this. Would the demon in her use it against him? "Not very far. She figured me out. My seduction was clumsy, and since it wasn't based on true feelings, I suppose I was a bit transparent."

Melodie shrugged. "You felt something when you kissed me. I know you did."

Blake took another sideways step, and his opponent inched toward the bedroom door. Tonight he was ready for her, and once he got her where he wanted her... "I won't lie. I felt something for the woman I thought I was kissing."

"There's no one else in this body," she said, and her voice rose in pitch. "It's just me, ramped up on cabochon power. This is who I really am, or who I want to be. I'm tired of being an invisible little mouse. I can be more."

Another inch and their positions had reversed. He stood in the hallway now, and she stood in the bedroom doorway.

"I know you can be but not with the power of the gem. It's not meant for humans. It will destroy the real Melodie and replace her with something dark and cold. I can see that creature in your eyes, and I know you don't want to become that."

"How do you know what I want?"

"I can guess, because we're a lot more alike than you think." *One, two...* On five he'd strike.

"We both intend to get what we want," she said. "That's what we have in common."

"I want to end the curse and destroy the Cabochon for good. Is that what you want?"

Again she fixed him with that deep, dark stare that grabbed hold of his insides. If *Melodie* had looked at him that way, he wouldn't have been able to resist her. "Right now, I want *you*."

"Well, then, I guess you should have what you want." He

lunged and had her on the bed in three steps. He'd expected a fight but got something much more sinister.

She writhed under him. With the water bed undulating and sloshing, Blake felt mildly seasick, like he had years ago in a rented canoe on a choppy lake in New York State. The Melodie-demon moved like a snake, clawing and nipping at him. A sound rumbled in the back of her throat. It might have been a sensual purr, but it sounded more like a growl.

"Go ahead," she urged him. "Do it. I want to feel something, anything."

"How's this?" He hated himself for it, but it had to be done. He and Calypso had discussed it on the way to Melodie's apartment. The power of the Cabochon had to be contained and kept somewhere safe. He only hoped the handcuffs he'd attached to the bedframe would be enough to hold her for the night.

He snapped a restraint on her left wrist and maneuvered quickly to catch the other one. She scratched him with nails too blunt for a demon, and the lack of damage she inflicted made her angry. Her growl morphed into a scream of rage.

"You can't do this! You can't keep me here."

"I can't keep a human imprisoned against her will, but right now, you're not quite human, are you? You're a little more and a little less." He bounded off the bed, stood back and watched her struggle.

She kicked and seethed, yanking so hard on the chains binding the cuffs to the bed Blake worried she'd hurt herself. He caught her flailing legs and wrestled her pumps off so she couldn't tear the vinyl cover of the mattress through the bedsheets. The last thing he needed was a flooded bedroom and a soaking-wet demon on his hands.

"Blake, please, don't do this. I'll behave, I promise!" The voice sounded like Melodie's, but there was a steely undercurrent. She wasn't herself yet.

"I'm sorry. Calypso thinks this is best for now, and I agree with her."

"You can't leave me here all day while you're...you know..."

"Don't worry. She'll be here before sunrise to keep an eye on you. She may even have a spell that will help you by then, so relax and try to get some rest. Tomorrow this could all be over."

She struggled so violently against the cuffs, the bed frame rattled. "What if I don't want it to be? What if I like the new me?"

"You can be whatever you want to be when the Cabochon is removed. Trust me, Melodie. Just trust me."

He doubted after this betrayal that she ever would, but he'd worry about that when they were both free of the curse. For now, he had work to do. He backed out of the room and closed the door, which helped to muffle her screams of rage. He had three hours until sunrise. Hopefully by then, she'd wear herself out and fall asleep.

He'd never been this close to ending the curse before. Likely none of the nine other men in his bloodline had either, yet he'd never felt less human in his life. He kissed his fingertips and touched them to the closed door before he left the darkened hallway. "I'm sorry, Melodie. I hope you'll be able to forgive me one day."

Calypso arrived half an hour before dawn with a bag of black stones and a sack of sweet-smelling herbs. She either had another spell in mind, or she was going to plant a garden. She looked paler than usual.

"What's wrong?" he asked as he secured the front door behind her.

"I saw a handful of Fremlings out there skulking around. Have you checked all the doors and windows?"

"Yes, everything's locked." Blake moved aside the curtains on the window beside the front door. He saw nothing in the shadows, but years of experience told him not seeing a demon was no guarantee it wasn't there.

Calypso bustled past him into the kitchen and set her supplies on the table. "We're lucky, she hasn't quite figured out how to summon them yet. They're just drifting around out there, like they're waiting for orders."

"She'll learn soon enough. She's already figured out that not much can hurt her. The burn she got from your ward spell on her apartment healed within minutes."

Calypso brushed her hair aside and nodded. "That's what I was afraid of. The Cabochon is transforming her."

Blake peered into the paper bag and sniffed. "What's all this?"

"I'm going to ward the rest of your house, all round the bedroom. It's probably best if she stays in there. Things could get messy, and you don't want your neighbors to get suspicious."

Blake stared at the dark-haired witch. "Messy?"

"The power of the Cabochon is increasing now that it has a new host. She's going to get more...demony, louder, stronger and a lot angrier. Your place is more secluded. She'll be safer here until we can get the proper spells from the Council to remove the Cabochon." While she spoke, she set out the collection of black stones and unpacked the bag. "I'm going to try a calming spell that might muffle the power emanating from the gem and allow the real Melodie to take over."

"I hate to keep her imprisoned, but I don't want her to hurt herself."

The witch caught him in her dark indigo gaze. "I'm her friend; neither do I. This is the best way to prevent her from doing any permanent damage to herself or anyone else."

"How long is the Council going to take on this? She might get to the point where we can't control her."

"It won't get that far. The Council won't let that happen."

"Will they let the curse continue?"

She looked away and busied herself with emptying supplies from the bags. "I don't know. I think if they can break it, they will, but there are no guarantees. Old magick is best left alone."

"So I get to suffer for the rest of my life because the witches are afraid of their own magick?" The constant buzz of the Cabochon had reached critical mass, and his anger at the discomfort of it threatened to boil over. How could he manage to have the cursed gem so close to him all the time—and how could he stand to part with it and risk losing his only chance to reclaim his life?

"It's not the magick they're afraid of, it's the consequences. Releasing that much power could be deadly."

A million replies came to mind but none he could trust himself to utter. Blake stepped back. He had only a few minutes left before sunrise, and he needed to hide himself away. Swallowing his comments, he turned and headed toward the basement door, leaving Calypso to her spells and incantations.

Chapter Seventeen

Melodie watched through bleary eyes as Calypso unfastened the cuffs which held her to Blake DeWitt's bed. The events of the night before teased her conscience, and once again shame weighed heavily on her.

"I did it again, Cal. I threw myself at Blake."

"And you ended up handcuffed to his bed. Not bad for a night's work, in my book." Calypso grinned sympathetically as she rubbed Mel's sore wrists and helped her to sit up.

"Don't joke about it. He seems to think I'm possessed. Do you think that? Is there some demon inside me along with the gem?"

"No. I think over the years the Cabochon has absorbed a lot of demon essence. That remark you made about being a Melodie-demon isn't far from the truth. You're unique, honey. You're taking on demon characteristics from the stone, and they're making you a little bit crazy. That's all."

Mel ran shaking fingers through her hair. "I don't want to be a little bit crazy or any crazy. I want to go back to work. I want to taste something. I want to sleep without dreaming of Fremlings."

"You will, soon. There are a couple of things we need to talk about first, though."

"Like what?" Mel vaulted off the bed. As usual, after a long sleep, she felt revitalized and not at all demony. How long would this period of normalcy last though? She remembered the burn she'd suffered as a result of Calypso's ward and rubbed at the spot on her arm where the injury had been. "Whatever it is, can we discuss it at my place? I want to take a shower and get changed and—"

She'd almost reached the door when Calypso grabbed her arm. "Don't. Stay right here."

"Why?"

"I warded the rest of DeWitt's house. You can't leave this room."

Mel yanked her hand out of Cal's grip. "What? Now *you're* in on it? You're going to keep me locked up here for how long?"

"Just a few days, until the Council makes a decision. They'll come up with something, Mel. You have to trust them."

"Trust them? I don't even know them. Let me talk to them, Cal. Why can't I go and talk to them?"

"It's not that simple. I'm sorry, Mel. I know this sucks, but you're in a lot of danger. The demon breeds will know about the Cabochon, and they're all going to come looking for you."

Mel narrowed her eyes. "But they can't hurt me."

"Some of them can. Just because you heal fast doesn't mean you can't be killed, and if another demon gets hold of the Cabochon, DeWitt may never be able to break the curse." Cal put her hands on Mel's shoulders. The contact served only to irritate her, but she endured it. "Mel, you're his only chance. If anything happens to you..."

"Why do I have to stay here? Can't you unward my place?"

"It's just better if you're here, away from people who might start asking questions."

Mel paced. Something didn't feel right. Not that being held prisoner should ever feel right, but for the first time since they'd met, she didn't quite trust Calypso. Clearly her friend was hiding something.

"What aren't you telling me?"

"Nothing. I'm telling you everything I know."

Mel didn't buy it. "Are you sure?"

Cal crossed her fingers. "Scout's honor."

"That's not scout's honor. It's three fingers, not two."

Calypso uncrossed her fingers. "Mel, please, trust me."

"That's what Blake said too. I'm not sure who to trust. I just want to go home. I promise I'll behave."

"You can't promise that, Mel. You're not in control. Come on, sit down and relax. I'll bring you some breakfast, and we'll talk. I've cooked up a little potion that should help you keep the demon tendencies at bay. I also brought you some clothes from your place and…uh-oh."

"What uh-oh?"

"I need to adjust the wards a little bit if you want to go to the bathroom. Sorry about that. Sit tight, I'll be right back."

Mel gaped as Calypso slipped out the bedroom door. She would have run after her, but even though her skin showed no evidence of the ward burn, the memory of the pain it caused lingered. Instead she placed herself just inside the threshold and yelled down the hall. "You owe me big-time for this, Calypso Smith! Big time!"

Every bone in Percival's body ached. His tortured muscles screamed, but still he refused to acknowledge his own agony.

He'd rather die than profess his weakness to a demon, even one as stunningly beautifully as the Domaré queen. He'd rather have died than do many things, and maybe tonight, before sunrise stole his breath again, he'd get his fondest wish.

When the dark-haired woman approached him, he strained against the leather straps that bound him to the wall of her boudoir.

"Tut, tut, my lord. Don't struggle so. I'll set you free very soon." Her voice rode over his frayed nerves like a balm, as smoky as the incense-heavy air in her abode. Violet eyes appraised him almost lovingly as she ran a manicured hand over his naked chest.

Despite himself, Percival flinched at her touch. "If you're going to kill me, do so quickly. I have no patience for your games."

She laughed, a bright sound more suited to the genteel parlor of a noblewoman than the lair of a demon. Percival struggled to remind himself that in daylight hours this creature walked the streets of Paris with her head high as a beloved member of society. At night, though, she crawled in the dirt beneath this abandoned abbey, presiding over a nest of her kind, and she reveled in their desecration of what had once been holy ground.

"My dear Percival, I have no intention of killing you. Truly. Your death would bring me no pleasure. In fact, just the opposite is true. I'd love for you to live well beyond your mortal years. Each day you survive is another opportunity for you to repent your sins."

Percival spat, and the demon queen stepped back to spare her delicate silken slippers from his own desecration.

"You were a gentleman once, my lord. You would do well to remember your upbringing."

"And what were you once? Human? Were you born to live life in the sunlight and corrupted somehow? Or were you truly spawned in darkness?" He'd chased demons so long, learned so much about their various breeds, he thought himself jaded on the subject, but these lovely ones, the Domaré, they brought a new dimension to his obsession.

If a beautiful woman such as Lady Arabel, with her raven

hair and beguiling eyes, her ethereal features and melodic voice, could be, underneath her silks and satins, a creature of such vile origin, then anyone could be.

For all Percival knew, he was the only truly human being left in all of Europe. That thought chilled his blood.

Arabel smiled at him. "I'm of noble birth, my lord. Higher than yourself, in fact, and born and raised as any other woman of my station. I suckled at my mother's breast. I played with porcelain dolls and dressed my hair in satin ribbons. I ate cakes and learned the waltz, and I've pricked my finger many a time while attempting to embroider. My blood is red like yours, and my tears taste like salt."

"And yet you are not human."

Arabel paced. Her skirts scraped the cold stone floor of the chamber in which she'd held him hostage for half the night. "No. Not human at all. Unlike my society sisters, I will live for more than a century, and I will bear two dozen or more offspring. Most of them will be male. Females of my kind are scarce, and we are exalted. It's sad that human women are considered a step beneath their men, pretty but disposable."

Percival tore his gaze away from Arabel. He'd already spent too long lost in the spell of her eyes. "If you don't plan to kill me, what then?"

"I plan to strike a bargain." Arabel stopped her pacing. She stood straight and tall before him, a statuesque vision in lavender silk. Demurely, she twirled a fat curl through her fingers, but the set of her carefully painted lips belied the darkness in her soul.

"I doubt you and I could reach agreeable terms on anything, *my lady.*"

"Oh, but I'm sure we can. You want the power that will one day be my inheritance. I know you chase the gem that controls your curse, and I know you would kill for it."

"That is true. What, then, can you possibly offer me besides your life and by extension, my own?" Percival yanked hard on the leather straps. The pain helped him focus. A month tracking the gem through France had brought him to Arabel's lair. Another fortnight would see the object safely transferred to her care, unless he stopped it.

Arabel sighed. "I have only this to offer—the life of your precious son."

Rene! Percival bridled. How dare she threaten his child. "You would harm a boy—"

"No! No. Of course not harm him, my lord. Do I look like a monster?" She laughed at the irony of her remark. "I would not harm him. I would enchant him and conspire to see him mated to a daughter of my kind. Wouldn't you like that, dear Percival? Your son as husband to a demon, father to a Domaré child?"

Bile rose, burning Percival's throat. "My son would never!" Before he completed his thought, Arabel brought her sinful lips to his and kissed his breath away.

A longing like he'd never felt stirred his loins. His heart filled with an emotion he hadn't experienced since the last time he'd raced to meet Rebecca in the glen so many years ago. Hot tears sprang to his eyes.

When she pulled back, the loss of her magical touch left a pain in his heart that rivaled any ache or injury he'd ever suffered.

For a moment, she'd made him *love* her.

"Do you see, my lord? Your son will do whatever he has to for the love of the Domaré woman I choose for him. She can enslave him with a kiss, or not, depending on whether you accept my bargain. And be aware, my death will not stop this plan if I decide to put it in motion this evening."

Percival slumped, and the leather bit into his bruised wrists. "He's just a child."

"Now, yes. But he'll be a man soon enough, and we can wait."

"What do you want?"

"Nothing." Arabel caressed his sweaty brow and his heaving chest. "I want nothing from you. Not a word. Not a sign. Not a glimpse of you anywhere near my home, my family or any of my clan. I know you earn your living hunting the lesser demon breeds, and that is not my concern. Do as you will to the others, but make me this promise that you will never touch a Domaré, and I shall make you the promise that neither will your son."

Percival hung his head.

"I didn't hear your answer, my lord. Please speak up."

"I said yes. Yes. I will leave your kind alone."

"Excellent." Arabel reached up to unfasten the evil straps.

Percival's arms dropped, bloodless, to his sides, and he sank to his knees. The scent of jasmine reached him, and his heart clenched with the remnants of her insidious love spell.

"Now, go home to your boy, my lord. Give him the one precious thing you still possess."

Percival wiped stinging sweat from his eyes and glared up at his nemesis. "And what is that, my lady?"

She bent at her cinched waist and cupped his chin in her soft hand. "Your time, dear Percival. Your time."

Calypso left Blake's house at noon, promising she'd be back before her shift at Gleason's.

Mel paced the confines of Blake's bedroom, occasionally venturing into the small section of hallway Calypso had "unwarded" between the bedroom and the bathroom. Calypso's calming potion had done little but taste bad and make her sleepy for an hour or two. Now the magick panacea seemed to have worn off, leaving her more jittery than before. With nothing to do but watch television until sunset, she'd go completely insane.

The frustration of captivity had her wrestling with the power of the Cabochon. It seemed to reside in the pit of her stomach, a hard dark nodule that, when she concentrated on it, made her feel both desperate and invincible at the same time. It scared her to think what might happen if she unleashed it all at once and what might happen if she completely relinquished control. As long as the sun shone brightly outside the bedroom window, she had a tenuous hold on reality, but something in her longed for the darkness. Just like Blake, she'd begun to live only at night.

She was poking one of Calypso's ward stones with the tip of a ski pole she'd found in Blake's closet when she heard the front door open downstairs.

"Hello? Cal, is that you?"

She raced into the hall and craned her neck to try to see down the staircase. A shadow fell across the entranceway below, and Palmer appeared, carrying a box from DeLio's Pizza and a six-pack of soda. She nearly wept with relief.

"Hey, Melodie. It's my shift. Sorry I'm a little late."

"Your shift?" She snatched the pizza box from him and retreated into the bedroom. "There are demon-sitting shifts?"

"Yeah. I hope you like pepperoni. I can hang out a little while, until sunset; then it's DeWitt's turn."

Mel set the pizza on the bed and waved away Palmer's offer of a cola. "Palmer, please get me out of here. I don't want to sit around waiting to go all *Exorcist*."

"You're not going to go *Exorcist*. This is for your own safety. Really."

Mel had always considered herself above using feminine wiles to get what she wanted, but desperate times and all. She thought about the dismal hours spent by herself in DeWitt's bedroom without even access to a phone, and her eyes misted. "Palmer, I can't go on like this. What about your spell? Is it ready?"

"Almost. I've finished the research, and I've translated the incantations."

"So what's the holdup? Why can't we do it now?"

"It has to be done at night."

"Well, how am I going to get away from DeWitt after sunset? If we're going to perform the spell, I've got to get away from here now. Please, Palmer. Don't make me wait around until the Council decides what to do. I can't spend another night handcuffed to Blake's bed."

Palmer glanced at the bed. "He handcuffed you to the bed?"

She nodded, hoping he could see the tears welling in her eyes. She hated to manipulate him, but she hated being a prisoner more. "All we need to do is move a couple of the ward stones. I tried poking them with this." She held up the ski pole. "But I get a shock. You could just pick them up in your hands and move them, and I could leave."

"Where would you go?" Palmer glanced at the bed again.

Mel thought of mentioning the kiss she'd shared with DeWitt just to capitalize on what appeared to be Palmer's latent jealousy, but the memory of that encounter made her skin tingle and the back of her knees sweat a little. Better not to think of Blake at all. "Home? Anywhere. It doesn't matter. I promise I'll come back later—if your spell doesn't work."

Finally he met her gaze. "I don't know, Melodie. I've got everything lined up, but I don't have a demon yet. Without something to transfer the Cabochon to..."

Mel eyed the window. "I can get a demon. The Fremlings. I can get a Fremling to follow me anywhere."

Palmer shook his head. "No. Bad idea. They swarm. And besides, they're not smart enough to handle the Cabochon. It would be like giving a rat a grenade."

Mel sighed and sank to the bed. "You're right. We don't know what the Cabochon would do to a Fremling. I'm better off here, chained to Blake's bed." She ran her fingers over the nearest metal cuff, somewhat lovingly, she thought.

Palmer paced. Clearly the thought of her and Blake together in any intimate setting made the demon hunter uncomfortable.

"Please?"

After a few turns around the room, he lost his inner battle. "Okay, I'll let you out. You can't go to your place, though. That's the first place they'll look, and I don't really want Calypso mad at me."

"How about your lair? No one knows where it is."

"That'll do. You'll have to stay out of sight until dark. I'll see if I can get the DHN to line up another demon for us by dark."

"DHN?"

"Demon Hunters' Network. Stay here a second." Palmer left the bedroom, kicking Calypso's black ward stones away from the threshold as he went. Mel followed him into the hall, where he slid several more of the polished river stones around on the hardwood floor until Mel had a clear shot for the stairs. She followed him downstairs and waited at the landing while he moved a few more stones, clearing her path to the front door.

Mel approached freedom with cautious steps. She would never forget the pain of the ward burn. She tapped the air within the door frame and nothing happened. No snap, crackle or pop.

Palmer grinned. "That was easy."

Mel hugged him, a quick, chaste gesture of thanks. "You're the best. Come on, let's get out of here before Calypso comes back."

"Wait." Palmer grabbed her arm, and for a second, Mel

feared he might have changed his mind. She couldn't blame him, after all, for fearing a witch's wrath, but with freedom so close she could taste it, there wasn't time for second thoughts.

"Whatever it is, don't worry about it, Palmer. Let's just go."

"We'd better take the pizza. I have a feeling we'll need to keep our strength up."

Chapter Eighteen

The moment Blake awoke, he knew Melodie had gone. The power of the Cabochon still teased his sixth sense but much fainter now, obviously farther away.

He bounded up the basement stairs and found Calypso in the kitchen. She stabbed one ebony-tipped finger in the air to silence his question and continued yelling into her cell phone. "I know it was you, you weasel. You're not doing Melodie a favor by letting her free, and I promise you, Van Houten, if anything happens to her, you won't be hunting demons anymore. You'll be hunting for what's left of your head."

She growled, much like Melodie had the other night, and snapped the phone shut. "Van Houten took Melodie."

Blake wanted to growl as well. Stupid demon hunter.

"Don't look so surprised. I told you we shouldn't let him have a demon-sitting shift." Calypso tossed the phone into her purse. "I've already been to his apartment and to the library. Where else do demon hunters hang out?"

Blake shook his head. "Doesn't matter. I can find Melodie, if she still has the Cabochon."

The witch's deep blue eyes widened, and she bit her lower lip. "You don't think he's dumb enough to try to remove the Cabochon from her by himself, do you?"

"He's no witch, but from what I understand about the old

magick, he doesn't have to be."

Calypso slung her purse over her shoulder. "Let's go find them. I'm going to show Palmer some old magick he'll never forget."

Blake grabbed his jacket and two helmets and followed Calypso out of the front door. Something dark and dirty scuttled in the bushes beside the house as they passed.

"Fremling," Calypso whispered. "A spy?"

Blake eyed the bushes. He imagined a pair of black, soulless eyes staring back. "More like a straggler. They're not the smartest of the breeds. Ignore it. I have a feeling we don't have much time."

"How long is this going to take?" Mel paced impatiently in the rectangular swatch of warehouse Palmer had cleared for the spell.

"I'm almost done," he replied. On the freshly swept concrete floor, he'd drawn a circle of sea salt. The rough crystals glittered in the beam of a two-hundred-watt work lamp he'd attached to a nearby shelf.

At five points on the circle, he'd placed quartz crystals and doused them with a mixture of vinegar and seven herbs and spices. On top of the familiar warehouse aromas, the place now smelled like a Greek deli.

"When do we bring in the Fremling?" Though she tried to ignore the uneasy feeling in the pit of her stomach, Mel had no doubt her tiny minions had rallied behind the warehouse. The chain-link fence would keep them confined to the walnut grove, but she and Palmer would have to open the gate and find a way to coax just one of the creatures inside to complete the magick.

Palmer looked up from his spell work. "Soon. Once we get it into the circle, the stones will activate and keep it there, like a ward spell, only reversed, to draw something in rather than repel. Then we do your end of the spell, and the Cabochon should transfer to the Fremling."

A small pot boiled low on a hot plate Palmer had pilfered from the hardware store's break room. The brew smelled a little like stew and probably would have been edible except for the pinch of dirt he'd thrown in and the fact that he was stirring it with a gnarled oak twig.

Mel paced around the circle once. Her hands felt clammy, and she rubbed them on her jeans to dry them. "Okay, let's do this."

Palmer glanced at her, the oak twig poised above the pot. "Last chance to back out."

"Don't give me options. I don't want options. I want to believe this is the only choice I have so I know I'm doing the right thing."

"You can save yourself and Blake once the Fremling absorbs the Cabochon...they're easy to kill."

Guilt roiled in Mel's stomach. They were talking about capturing a living creature—a vile, disgusting, creepy thing borne of evil but alive nevertheless—and killing it. The plan left a sour taste in her mouth. She tried to picture Blake as she'd seen him the other morning, imprisoned in a body of stone, frozen in time, shut off from all the things that made living in this world bearable. The life of one small demon was a cheap price to pay to give him back the sunlight.

She gave Palmer a determined nod and spun away from the circle. He followed her to the door of the warehouse and out into the cool autumn air.

The evening was utterly silent at first. No crickets chirped. No night birds twittered in the walnut grove. Mel listened for the Fremlings, and her senses tuned with little effort. The demon in her stirred, and the dark creatures gathered in the shadows of the old trees began to swarm.

First they crept on hands and knees, like ragged children, their mop-like hair swinging and obscuring their small, pinched faces. Clawed fingers, thin like dry twigs, hooked around the mesh of the fence, and in unison, a dozen of them began to rattle the chain links.

Mel shivered, and behind her Palmer tensed. The sour scent of fear surrounded them, and in the amber glow of the security lights, a short blade flashed. "You're armed?" she whispered.

"Hell, yes. Do you think you can get just one of them to come through the gate?"

Confidence flooded her like a hot wave, and she grinned. "Hell, yes."

She sauntered across the macadam, secure in her own safety and aware, even though she didn't turn to look, that Palmer hung back near the corrugated wall of the warehouse, gaping at her boldness.

Mel approached the fence and singled out one of the creatures hanging near the still-closed gate. She crooked a finger at it. Its head lifted, and two beady, black eyes followed where she pointed. "You will come with me. Everyone else will stay here."

The authority with which she gave the command would have stunned her under other circumstances, but something powerful had taken over her psyche. The Cabochon ruled her now, and she liked it.

The Fremling obeyed her without comment. Could it even speak? They seemed to communicate on a level just below telepathy. Their actions spoke to her, and she understood.

The others gathered but wisely remained outside the fence when Palmer opened the gate using the controls by the warehouse door. Just the one demon slipped inside and marched past its mistress. Mel caught a glimpse of cloven feet clacking on the hard ground, and the small shard of her human consciousness that remained gave an involuntary shudder. Odd that this devilish thing should obey her unconditionally. The others held back, anxious for her to command them as well. They eyed Palmer, who gave the passing Fremling a wide berth, then followed it into the warehouse.

Satisfied with herself, Mel waited for the clink of metal on metal as the gate rolled shut and locked. The Fremlings left outside expressed their disappointment with a collective susurration—the equivalent of a petulant sigh.

"Be patient. Your time will come," she said before hurrying back inside. Their time for what? The words certainly hadn't been her own.

The chosen Fremling waited inside for her, with Palmer hovering nearby. Clenched around the handle of his small knife, his knuckles were bone white. "I've never seen one of these things up close before."

Mel ignored him. She glanced at the circle. Would the little demon huddling in the shadow beneath an oversized gas grill continue to obey her even if she ordered it to its death? She stifled the thought and gave rein to her own demon side. "Go there." She pointed to the circle. "Stand there and wait for me."

Black eyes appraised her, and despite its obvious lack of a soul, mistrust colored the expression on its wrinkled, rotten-grapefruit face. Thick ropes of its matted hair dangled when it shook its misshapen head.

"You're defying me?" Rage bubbled in Mel like she'd never felt before. How dare this impudent little monster disobey her? Shaking off her pique, she held out her hand like a mother to a stubborn toddler. "Come on. It's okay. I'll walk you there."

"Melodie..." Palmer's voice held a warning, which she dismissed with a flick of her wrist. The Fremling balked.

Damn. It had read her thoughts. It knew the fate they intended for it.

"This might be a little harder than we thought." She moved one step closer to her minion, and the creature backed deeper into the shadows. It hugged the fat, white propane tank secured beneath the grill and shook its head until the matted hair obscured its eyes.

Irritated by this childish behavior, Mel cursed it.

Palmer muttered something that sounded like "Uh-oh", and she cursed him too, then flung herself at the Fremling. "Come here, you little brat!"

Swift but clumsy, the Fremling darted away from the grill and scuttled deeper into the warehouse. Mel lunged after it, hoping to drive it toward the circle.

"This is a problem," Palmer said. He took off in the opposite direction. "We'll never find him in here in the dark."

"*I'll* find it." Mel hurried after the demon, tracking it by its jerky movements and her own growing demonic instincts. She felt cat-like, sleek, a formidable hunter. She'd catch this little rodent and play with it until exhaustion killed it. A cold laugh replaced her rage. It might even be fun.

The Fremling ran from shadow to shadow, nook to cranny, ducking behind sacks of fertilizer and cement. It wove between stacks of paint cans and slithered among pallets of lumber. Like a monkey, it swung from the metal shelving and clattered through a storage box of garden tools. All the while, Melodie stalked its movements, loving the chase, feeling invincible.

"We got him!" Palmer yelled when they finally converged on the creature who had ducked into a display-model toilet. The lid of the commode crashed down, trapping the beastly little thing in a porcelain prison.

"Sit! Sit!" Palmer gestured at the toilet, and without thinking, Mel obeyed.

She perched on the closed lid, and beneath her the Fremling beat ineffectively on the underside of the seat. "Now what? We can't carry this over to the circle."

The Fremling squealed, and Mel sensed the others mobilizing outside, galvanized by the sudden distress of their comrade.

"I'll be right back." Palmer disappeared, leaving Mel clutching the toilet seat while the demon inside the bowl battered itself against the porcelain walls.

"You'd better hurry!"

An eon passed before Palmer reappeared holding a burlap sack. "Get up slowly. When he jumps out, I'll catch him in this."

"Are you serious?"

"Got a better idea?"

Mel huffed. "No."

"On three. Ready? One...two..."

"Slow down." She put her feet on the floor and released her death grip on the seat. The Fremling had gone quiet beneath her. Either it was biding its time, or it had knocked itself unconscious. She prayed for the latter.

Palmer loomed with the burlap, ready to pounce.

Mel held up her hand. "*I'll* count. On three. One...two...*three!*" She flew off the toilet, and just as she suspected, the surprisingly clever Fremling popped out of the commode like a nightmarish jack-in-the-box.

Palmer dove and snatched the demon up into the sack. It hissed and struggled, but the strong fabric confined it. Palmer gave the neck of the bag a vicious twist and slung it over his shoulder. "I still got it," he said with a satisfied smirk.

Mel had no comment. Silent and sullen now that the game was over, she followed him back to the circle of salt. "Are you sure this will hold it?"

The demon hunter responded with a dark look. "Trust me." Careful not to break the circle, he placed the sack inside it. As though dropping a poisonous snake, he released the bag and jumped to safety beyond the magical barrier.

For a moment, nothing happened; then the Fremling began to stir. It seemed to roll over, testing the confines of its new prison. Then, tentatively, a clawed hand emerged from the sack. Mel stared, and Palmer retrieved his discarded knife from the floor.

Little by little, the Fremling appeared. It looked around, setting its suspicious gaze first on Palmer, then on Mel. As if eager for guidance, it moved toward her in a drunken shuffle that took it toward the edge of the circle. From there, it lunged at her, claws outstretched, jagged yellow teeth bared.

Mel stumbled back, and Palmer rushed forward to protect her from the attack. A blue flash lit the warehouse, and sparks danced in broken arcs up from the salt circle. The familiar odor of ozone and singed flesh made Mel cringe. The spot on her arm where Calypso's ward spell had burned her began to ache.

With a pitiable cry, the Fremling plopped to the cement floor and lay in a smoking heap, panting, effectively corralled by Palmer's spell.

"Damn, it works."

Mel shot him a startled look. "You had doubts?"

"What? No. I knew it would work. I just wasn't sure it would...work."

Mel stifled a complaint. Now that they had a demon where they wanted it, the next step was freeing her from the Cabochon. No time to waste.

Before she could form a question, though, the warehouse door swung open on its creaking hinges, and two figures burst inside. Calypso marched up to the circle, her eyes blazing, and gave Palmer a look that by rights should have stripped the flesh from his bones.

"Are you completely out of your mind, Van Houten?"

Behind Cal, Blake DeWitt stood tall and feral, dressed entirely in black. When he turned a similar gaze on Melodie, her heart stuttered. His words, like Cal's, were anything but endearing, though.

"You're lucky we found you before the two of you got yourselves killed."

Chapter Nineteen

The relief that washed through Blake the moment he saw Melodie ebbed when she turned an unapologetic gaze on him. The power of the Cabochon pulsed in her and sizzled like the faint sparks of magickal power still ricocheting around the circle that lay between them on the warehouse floor.

Within the circle huddled a Fremling. The pitiful creature climbed to its feet as Blake watched and began to pace like a caged cat. It looked fierce, with its craggy features and snaggle teeth, but Blake knew what Van Houten should have guessed. The power of the Cabochon would tear the little demon apart. And after that, with no one but humans to serve as hosts, both he and Mel would have been in danger.

He swiveled and put himself between Mel and her slavering minion. Hands on hips, he drew up in front of her. "Calypso and I were trying to keep you safe. You have no idea what you're playing with here."

Seemingly buoyed by his wrath, she stepped up to him, toe to toe, her lithe body arched in defiance. "Palmer wanted to help me. He doesn't have anything to gain in this, so why shouldn't I trust him?"

Blake grumbled. He didn't like the way Van Houten's name rolled off her ruby lips. "Because he's a rank amateur, and he'll get you killed." He swept her out of his way with one arm.

"Stand back while I get rid of this thing." He turned his full attention and his anger toward the Fremling, which greeted him with a petulant growl.

On the far side of the circle, Calypso and Van Houten were engaged in a tug-of-war over a handful of papers and the contents of a small cooking pot. During Blake's brief moment of distraction, Melodie shifted position and put herself between him and the demon. When their gazes met again, hers held regret. "Don't kill it, please."

"It's a demon, lass. It has no place here."

She put her hands on his chest, and once again the power of the Cabochon leaped from her and raced through every atom in his body.

Random nerve endings fired, causing an inexplicable tingle to skitter up his spine. The hairs on his arms and at the back of his neck rose, and a shock of arousal hit him like a two-by-four. He'd have kissed her then, but he didn't dare.

Instead he gripped her wrists and held her away from him.

"Blake, please. *I* lured it in here. It trusted me, and I betrayed it." Her voice sounded tinny and distant as if it had traveled a great distance to reach him. This was the real Melodie, trapped behind those demon-bright eyes and the siren's mouth. She suffered for her compassion—an emotion he'd forsaken long ago.

"If we set it free, it will attack." He didn't know why he felt the need to justify his actions. Mel threw herself against him and sobbed into his chest.

Instinctively, he wrapped his arms around her, hating that her pain made him vulnerable, hating that he coveted the surge of power that came from the cursed gem inside her.

Beyond the circle, Calypso cursed. She'd won her argument with Palmer and spilled his potion out on the cement floor amid oil stains and a smattering of sawdust. Now she turned her attention to the Fremling.

The creature trembled under her scrutiny in a way that Blake had never seen a demon of any size or shape do before.

The witch put her hands out, just over the salt barrier, and uttered an incantation that set the air within the warded space ablaze.

"No!" Mel sobbed and sagged in Blake's arms. The conflagration lasted only seconds, but it left little more of the Fremling than a pile of fine gray ash.

Blake gaped, and Melodie cried for the death of a demon.

Calypso kicked the anchor stones away from the five points around the circle and swept her indigo gaze between Blake and Palmer. "I told you gentlemen I had spells. *Now*, are we going to straighten up and take care of this problem my way, or do I have to—"

Mel's scream silenced her, and she and Palmer stared. Blake struggled to hold Mel up, but some tidal force doubled her over. A violent convulsion shook her free of his grasp, and clutching her stomach, she hobbled away from him.

"Melodie—" Blake grabbed for her, but she swiped at him.

"Don't touch me. None of you touch me." With her features pinched in agony, she stumbled away, and when she was just out of reach, she righted herself. A ring of yellow rimmed her eyes, and her now-crimson lips parted in a harsh laugh. "Did you think this would work? Did you really think I'd give up all this power so easily?"

Palmer groaned. "We're too late."

Mel whirled away and bolted for the open door of the warehouse. In half a dozen superhuman strides, she was gone.

Calypso turned on Palmer again. "Great work. Now we've lost her."

"Hey, I didn't kill her demon. You're the one who made her mad."

"Stop bickering, boys and girls. We've got to find her before one of the demon breeds really does elect her queen and takes her to their realm." Blake headed for the door, but he never made it through.

A shadow, low and fluid, slithered into the warehouse and transformed into a wave of undulating gray bodies. Blake froze mid-step and stared as the tide of Fremlings washed in from outside.

A moment later, the three of them stood knee-deep in a sea of angry demons.

From the safety of the walnut grove, Mel watched the Fremlings swarm the warehouse. They scuttled by her in droves. Her betrayal of their unfortunate companion seemingly forgotten, they existed now only to protect her from the threat within.

Trembling and dizzy with power, she clutched her stomach where the heat of the Cabochon burned. With those who sought to harm her out of the way, she could go anywhere, do anything. The freedom to reach her greatest potential taunted her, though, and left her confused and directionless as she ran toward the edge of town with a small legion of loyal Fremlings in her wake.

She could do whatever she wanted now, except the one thing she should, and that was to free Blake DeWitt from the curse. With the Cabochon at full power within her, she knew she could live forever, and the witch hunter would never have another chance to see the light of day.

Consumed with guilt and grief and greed for more power, she ran.

Gnarled fingers tipped with ragged claws tore at Blake's clothes and his hair. Using each other as ladders like army ants, the Fremlings made living chains that stretched up the two-story-high storage shelves. From those upper perches, they dove on their human adversaries, biting, scratching and shrieking like wild animals.

Chivalry drove Blake to rescue Calypso from their clutches first. He literally swam through the tide of dirty little bodies until he found her grappling with one demon while another worked at ripping a dangling earring from her lobe.

She threw one Fremling off her and struggled to reach for Blake's hand. "I thought you had spells," he muttered while tossing writhing, mop-headed beasts left and right.

"If I could breathe long enough to cast one. Get me with a wall at my back, and I'll figure out the rest."

"Where's Van Houten?" Blake kept Calypso's back while they edged toward the wall, fighting the undulating wave of demonic vermin as they went.

"He went down over there somewhere." She pointed to a disturbingly violent knot of Fremlings not far off. A low moan came from beneath the crush, and Blake sighed. "Let me go help him," he said once he'd led Calypso to the last row of shelves. He waded off, kicking demons aside as he moved.

Fortunately the Fremlings' only strength was in their number. The individuals fell quickly enough to well-placed blows, but it seemed as if ten or twelve replaced every one Blake knocked out of his path.

He'd never seen anything like it. The chaos in the warehouse came close to making him long for the relative tranquility of a day encased in stone.

He reached the throbbing pile of demons and began casting small bodies off from the top. After a dozen, though, he realized the only things underneath the demons were more demons.

Van Houten was gone. Had they killed him? Eaten him? Blake paled at the thought. Maybe they'd just carried him away as a trophy.

If he'd had more time to think about it, he might have mustered some sympathy for the meddling demon hunter, even if he'd brought this carnage on himself. Falling prey to the lowest of the underworld denizens was certainly no way to die.

With no clear objective now, Blake turned his attention back to Calypso. She'd reached a set of shelves and was dumping boxes of hardware on the floor. Metal pipe fittings, screws and nails clattered down and spilled like liquid across the concrete. Fremlings swarmed over the debris, but the witch's plan wasn't to use the displaced inventory as an obstacle. She merely wanted to clear a space so she could climb the shelves and get to a safe haven above the layer of demons.

Clinging to the galvanized crossbars at the end of the shelving unit, the high heels of her black, lace-up boots hooked around the metal, she surveyed the roiling sea of evil and opened her mouth.

An earsplitting tone emerged that startled all the Fremlings and left Blake himself in stunned silence. Even Calypso looked astonished for a moment; then Blake realized the deafening sound hadn't come from the witch.

Someone had set off the burglar alarm, and the shriek of the ceiling-mounted sirens had the demon horde scurrying away like the rats they were, as if abandoning a sinking ship.

In seconds, the warehouse was empty.

Calypso hung from the shelving, looking a little dazed. Blood from her injured ear stained the collar of her shirt, and a few vicious scratches marred the pale skin of her arms. Blake stood in the center of what remained of the salt circle. Crushed herbs and ground-up salt crystals crunched beneath his boots.

Looking like something even the cat wouldn't bother dragging in, Palmer leaned against the wall near the door, next to the alarm control panel. Blake had never been happier to see

Golden Boy. "I thought you were dead," he offered and stopped short of adding, "Glad you're not."

"I'm hard to kill, remember?" Palmer sagged a bit. Not dead, maybe, but not in the best of health either.

Calypso leaped down from the shelves, and like a jaguar, she stalked toward Palmer. For a moment, Blake thought she might make good on her earlier threat to do the demon hunter some bodily harm, but rather than add to his collection of bruises and contusions, she draped one of his arms over her shoulders and helped him stand up straight. Surveying the carnage left behind by the Fremlings, she smirked. "The only reason I'm not killing you myself is because I'd hate for you to miss catching hell for this disaster. Your uncle owns this place, right?"

Palmer's pale complexion greened beneath his injuries. "Yeah."

"Well, Ace, I'd say you're out of the will, and probably out of a job too. Let's go get you cleaned up so you can face the music."

Blake eyed the mess and decided Palmer probably would have been better off facing Calypso's wrath. Unidentifiable stains covered the floor between puddles of nails and piles of pipes. Stacks of lumber had been knocked over, and paint cans lay dented, some oozing their contents into multicolored pools. Fremling footprints coated the walls in some places, and the whole place stank of unwashed evil. Later, he'd take the time to laugh about it, but right now he could only manage a hint of jaundiced gratitude that they'd all survived.

Or had they? Melodie and the Cabochon still beckoned him. He headed for the door. "I'll meet up with you two later. I've got to find Mel."

Calypso touched his arm as he passed her. "There's not a lot of time before sunrise."

"I know. I'll find her before then. I have to."

Chapter Twenty

Between the stench of Fremling and the inarguable lure of the Cabochon, stronger now than ever before, Blake had no trouble tracking Melodie. Her demonic entourage seemed to have beaten a path through every back alley in town with their ultimate objective being the little-used railroad yard on the west side.

Nothing more than an overgrown stretch of tracks that disappeared into a slab of concrete at one end and a hopper-car graveyard at the other, it offered a perfect venue for all manner of night prowlers.

Blake proceeded with caution into the deathly quiet yard. No crickets or tree frogs chirped here. No night birds fluttered. Even the eerie twin glow of feral cats' eyes was missing. Nothing worldly lived here, and that meant the place was full of demons.

One in particular would be easy to find. The Melodie-demon lurked among the abandoned rail cars. Blake knew this because every time he turned in that direction, his body tingled. The gem attracted him like a moth to a deadly flame. He'd hover around that energy until he died. Doomed to follow his only salvation anywhere, he ignored the knowledge that, as he moved deeper into the overgrown lot, a phalanx of demons closed ranks behind him.

He'd learned all his demon-hunting skills from Percival—a

man driven, as he was, to find the Cabochon at all costs. Over and over he'd followed his ancestor into the deepest, darkest holes in Europe to ferret out demons of every imaginable description, searching for the one that might have held the key to his freedom.

Those memories, shared with a dead man, guided him now to move silently and keep to the least shadowed pathways that wound between the rusted and disintegrating boxcars.

What would he do when he found her? He couldn't hurt her. Both the curse and his conscience made that impossible. For the first time since this sordid adventure began, Blake regretted not insisting Palmer come along. Two demon hunters would have better odds than one, at least in this case.

"Melodie? Lass, where are you?" Like he had to ask. The cold surge of the Cabochon's power emanated from a spot no more than a hundred feet straight ahead. A broken boxcar, its sliding door hanging from a corroded hinge, nestled in knee-deep grass. Shuffling sounds came from within and joined the array of disconcerting demon noises closing in on Blake from all directions. His instincts told him hundreds of Fremlings hovered in the shadows, but he couldn't have pointed out a single one.

"Melodie? Is this what you want? Do you want to give up the daylight completely and spend your nights huddled in a nest of stinking demons?" The only response was more shuffling from inside the boxcar, coupled with a low moan that cut off abruptly.

Was she in pain? What would the Cabochon, tainted by two-hundred-plus years of demon blood and depravity, do to a delicate human body like hers? Could it be any worse than turning to stone?

Anger at life's inequity flared in Blake, fueling his determination to beat the unjust curse and take back his existence. He could be sympathetic only so long. Now he had to act, and damn the consequences. He braced for a sprint toward the open boxcar. "I'm coming in there, lass. I'm coming to get you and take you home."

The creature's hairless skull sported a trio of black-tipped horns, around which sprouted rings of tiny but deadly looking spikes. Its teeth protruded in a wicked overbite beyond blood-red lips that glistened with spittle.

Misshapen wings beat against its hunched back, and its cloven feet stamped impatiently on the rotting boards of the boxcar's floor.

Buoyed by the sharp flavor of her own growing power, Melodie held the demon's rheumy gaze. Some queen. The thing looked like a reject from the last *Star Wars* movie. She could have taken it easily, would have torn those pathetic wings right off its knobby carapace if she could have moved a muscle. The weight of a dozen Fremlings, three on each limb, held her prostrate amid the remains of broken crates that had, judging from the stale smell and abundance of feathers, likely once held chickens or some other type of fowl.

Mel cursed the beastly little demons for their betrayal. Here she'd imagined they'd been swarming to protect her and had lured her off to this dark place to worship her and the power she carried. Turned out all they really wanted was to bring her to their true leader.

Never trust a demon. She'd learned that lesson well.

"You can't hurt me," she'd told her captor. "I've got—" A Fremling reached up and slapped a filthy hand over her mouth. The violent movement left the taste of blood on her lips, and she'd moaned while gingerly testing her teeth with her tongue.

Then Blake's voice floated in from outside the boxcar, offering assistance and freedom from this terrible nightmare.

She'd have answered him except the nearest Fremling gave her a warning glare. Silently, she promised revenge, though she remained still, waiting to see if DeWitt would make good on his promise to come after her.

The demon queen advanced, dragging her hooves—*its* hooves...was it really female? Nothing about the twisted, inhuman visage or the bony appendages appeared the least bit feminine.

Mel made a disparaging face and tensed for an attack. Her own demonic confidence faded. Maybe DeWitt couldn't harm her, but this thing with its razor claws and abundance of teeth wasn't actually bound by the Witch Hunter's curse. For all Mel knew, she was staring into the jaundiced eyes of the Cabochon's rightful owner.

She cringed away from the demon's touch, and the Fremlings rallied, gripping her tighter in their filthy claws. The demon queen snarled, then lurched backward, an unmistakable look of surprise widening "her" bulbous yellow eyes.

Mel gaped, confused, until she realized Blake had leaped into the car and grabbed the demon by her stunted wings. The creature screamed and flailed her skeletal arms. Torn between holding their prisoner and helping their leader, the Fremlings did little but tremble. Mel took advantage of their confusion and threw all her strength into dislodging them one by one from her legs and arms. She snarled as she slammed their slender, formless bodies against rotting wood.

Nearby, Blake grappled with the queen. Leathery wings flapped, and curved claws glinted in the bare moonlight filtering through holes in the boxcar's roof. Blake landed a punch to what should have been the demon's solar plexus, and it grunted, a sound of surprise rather than pain. Enraged, it fought back, pummeling him with its meatless fists until he staggered.

Mel, free now from her diminutive guards, scrambled after a retreating Fremling. She picked the creature up and threw it at the queen's spindly knees, bowling her over.

Dabbing at a bloody lip with the back of his hand, Blake lurched toward his opponent and delivered a vicious kick to the jaw. The demon's head snapped back, and this time, she wailed in pain.

He kicked again, and the demon went down in a heap that resembled rags draped on old bones. She struggled to rise once, then groaned and lay still.

Blake's dark gaze met Mel's, and the scattered Fremlings froze. With no leader to guide them, they lost coherence and bolted for the door. Mel feigned a move after them, adding her best demonic growl for effect. Squealing, they fled into the night, leaving her alone with her bloody savior.

"I could have taken her." Mel's arrogant words came from the part of her she'd been battling all evening to suppress, and she hated herself for the cavalier remark.

Blake merely grinned and swiped the sleeve of his jacket over the oozing cut at the corner of his mouth. "I bet you could have." He held out his hand to her. "Now, lass. Are you going to fight me too, or come home like a good girl?"

Mel bristled, and the demon in her clawed at her gut. She winced at the pain and guarded her stomach where the ache of the Cabochon had grown from an occasional pulse to a constant throbbing. She'd go mad if she didn't get the cursed object out of her. Momentarily defeated, she sagged and slid her fingers into his palm. "Let's go home quick, before I change what's left of my mind."

Something like sympathy flared in his eyes, and he tugged her toward the door of the boxcar. "Aye, lass, I'll drive as fast as I can."

Melodie balked at entering Blake's house. She feared being imprisoned by Calypso's ward stones again and wouldn't go inside until he collected the polished river rocks and tossed them into the front garden. Once he'd disposed of the stones, though, she followed him dutifully into the house. Exhausted, he ambled toward the couch and collapsed, wishing for a few minutes of natural sleep before the dawn stole his life again. Very soon the night would end, and he'd return to his granite prison.

Mel stared at him for a moment, then disappeared into the kitchen. Too tired to follow her, he lay there listening to the faint sound of his freezer opening and the rattle of the ice-cube tray.

She returned a moment later with a makeshift ice pack, a kitchen towel wrapped around a handful of cubes. She sat beside him on the couch and pressed the cold towel to his swollen lip. "Thanks for coming to my rescue."

He smiled, then winced at the pain it caused. He didn't have the heart to tell her the ice wasn't necessary. His injuries would be gone when he awoke from his exile at sunset—the only advantage he'd found so far to the curse. "It wasn't exactly a rescue, lass. It was a hunt."

She gave a harsh laugh, but disappointment flickered in her eyes. "How can you stand it? How have you managed all this time, living this way?"

"I don't know what else to do." He tried to keep the desperation out of his voice. How could he tell her how close he was to just giving up?

"I'll do whatever I have to," she said after a long silence. "Whatever spell is necessary. I want to set you free."

Blake's heart ping-ponged against his lungs, making it hard to breathe. He lifted a weary hand and cupped her face. "Worry about yourself, Melodie, not me. I'll find some way to break the curse, but not at your expense."

Before he could think of anything to add, she lunged in and kissed him fast and hard. Pain lanced through his split lip, but he ignored it in favor of the other sensations colliding in his gut. The buzz of the Cabochon nearly overpowered him. Being this close to it left him weak. He lifted a hand to her waist and felt the tingle of power race up his arm. His heart hammered as the flavor of Melodie, the woman, not the demon, flooded his mouth.

Sweet and warm, her tongue danced against his. Her lips soothed his hurt, and the pressure of her supple body caused other parts of his anatomy to throb.

For one delicious moment, he let everything fade away and permitted himself to enjoy the feel of her in his arms, the slide of her silky hair through his fingers, and the tantalizing press of her mouth on his.

Then he pushed her away. "You have to go. Now."

She stared at him uncomprehending. "Why? I thought I had to stay here."

"It's almost sunrise." Blake vaulted off the couch and out of her embrace. He had to get downstairs and hide himself away.

"I don't care." She stood and followed him across the room. She plucked at his sleeve and forced him to turn and face her. "I've seen you, Blake. I know what you become, and I don't care." She reached up to touch his face, but he pulled back.

"I do. I care." Shame burned in his chest. She must have found his hideaway. He couldn't meet her gaze. "Go. Please, Mel. Come back again at sunset." He whirled away and headed for the basement stairs. He'd barely make it to safety. Already he felt the change coming on. Each step became agony as his body hardened. "Mel," he croaked her name as his vision blurred. "Please go."

Blake froze mid-step, one hand reaching toward the cellar door, the other thrown back behind him to warn her away.

In horror, Mel watched his skin darken to deep gray and the lines of his muscles stiffen into sculptured angles. His hands became claws, and his beautiful face morphed into the stark, frightening visage she'd seen the other morning, hidden away from the world.

In little more than a minute, he'd transformed completely. Even his clothes turned to stone, every line and nuance perfectly preserved as if wrought by an artist with the skill of Michelangelo and the imagination of Clive Barker. He'd become a monster in jeans and a leather jacket, a modern caricature of the classic guardian beast.

Mel touched his arm, then his face, and tears of futility welled in her tired eyes. He'd want her to go, to leave him to his solitary shame, but she couldn't.

Seized by a sudden, uncontrollable bout of emotion, she kissed his cold cheek and met his granite gaze. "I won't leave you, Blake. I'll be here with you until you wake up. You don't ever have to hide from me again."

Chapter Twenty-One

Darkness had become his friend over the years, his only constant companion. He welcomed it at times, and at others, he merely tolerated its presence in a way that was almost companionable.

Tonight, he rejoiced in the utter blackness of a moonless night and the sharp taste of winter on the autumn wind. Cold darkness mirrored his inner desolation and made it easier to track his prey.

He'd followed a demon into the deep forest north of Kielder Castle in Northumberland on the orders of a new employer who'd promised him twice as much gold as that already lining his pockets. Percival would have done the job for half what the man offered—hell, a third—but he'd kept his own counsel and showed humble gratitude when his benefactor counted out a king's ransom of coins, likely on behalf of the nervous duke who wanted to keep his hunting lands secure and free of all unholy creatures. Percival took care his payment didn't jingle as he slipped between the closely spaced spruce boles.

The creature he stalked had been credited with luring young women away from the nearby village. Two ravaged bodies had already been found, their vicious wounds blamed on wolves by the authorities.

His benefactor knew better, though, and had showed

Percival a sketch of a hell beast with scimitar-shaped claws and an appetite for virgin blood.

His eyes had grown accustomed to seeing in the dark, and even on a night as black as this, he could locate his prey with ease guided only by the light of the stars. It wasn't his eyes he relied on this evening, though. Tonight he smelled the creature before he saw it.

The demon's incoherent grunting was mixed with a whimpering female voice. Damn. The beastie had already chosen its victim for tonight.

Percival picked up his pace and brandished the broadsword he carried. Decapitation, his employer had explained, was the only way to ensure the creature would not resurrect. One sure slice at the thick neck would be enough to dispatch it.

The horrid sounds grew louder, and a lilting voice rose above the lascivious grunts. "You will not harm me."

Under other circumstances Percival might have laughed at the girl's bravado. She sounded no more than a score in age, probably less, yet her conviction seemed large enough to fill the woods. He gave her credit for that bravery but held out no hope she'd survive to greet the dawn.

Silently he advanced to the next clearing, and there he saw the vile thing. It stood on hind legs, weaving drunkenly and swinging claws at its prey.

She huddled by a fat tree, draped in a pale shift that revealed a wealth of delicate skin in the silvery starlight. Auburn hair hung in a thick braid over her shoulder, and this, it seemed, attracted the unholy attention of the beast. It hooked a claw into the silky plait and tugged. The girl should have screamed—any other woman would have—but instead she slapped the gnarled hand away. Amazingly, the demon drew back a step.

"I said, *you will not harm me.*"

She held up her hands, palms forward, and pushed at the air. Foolish chit. Provoking the creature would only get her torn to ribbons more quickly, and Percival had no desire to take responsibility for a bleeding carcass...other than the demon's, of course.

He surged forward, ready to defend what would ultimately be left of her, but the sight in the clearing stopped him. From the girl's hands emanated a faint glow, which, as he stood dumbfounded, coalesced into a ball of light. With all the force contained in her thin, barely clothed frame, she hurled the brilliant missile at the beast.

It exploded in a cloud of sparks against its hairy chest, and the demon roared.

Dear God. Percival had found himself a witch!

He should have turned and walked away then, leaving one servant of evil to the other, but his feet refused to move in either direction. Could he stand here in the depths of shadow and watch the hell spawn destroy her?

The man he'd been before the curse would have relished such a spectacle, but now...

Beyond angry and no longer vaguely enchanted by her coppery locks, the demon lurched toward her. It slapped her, and with a truncated scream, she fell at its feet.

Some force he would never understand propelled Percival into the clearing. Shaking his sword and yelling—two things he would normally never have done while hunting demons—he drew the beast's attention away from the girl. He didn't stop to contemplate the best angle from which to deliver his killing blow; he merely struck with all his strength. The girl put her hands up to shield her face but could not prevent dark demon blood from splashing across her shift and her delicate throat.

The headless demon teetered and fell in a heap, and she gaped at it, then at Percival. Any other woman would have wept with gratitude, or merely swooned, but this hellion had the audacity to glare at him.

Wiping at the blood on her dress and succeeding only in smearing it, she demanded, "Why did you do that?"

"I was paid to do that, my lady."

"Ugh."

"I daresay I did you a favor."

"I'd have dispatched him eventually." She swiped the back of a hand across her cheek, leaving a smudge of demon there.

Percival bowed and wiped blood from his sword on the rag he carried for such a purpose. "Forgive me. Next time I'll not interfere when a hell beast attacks you." He sheathed his blade and concentrated on not allowing his curious gaze to drop below her chin.

She waved a dismissive hand. "Oh, well. Thank you, I suppose."

"Are you grateful in truth, little witch, or merely bored of my company and wishing me on my way?"

She stilled at his words, and he pressed on. "Yes, I saw your display of power. Tell me you've not been summoning the beast to play devil's games out here in the dark." Memories of Rebecca surfaced, and Percival's dark heart beat faster. The last time he'd threatened a witch, he'd lived to regret it. If one could call this living. Tread carefully, his inner voice admonished.

Her defiance withered. "I know not what you're talking about, good sir."

"I saw the spell you cast, the power in your tiny hands. You cannot lie your way out of this."

Now fear darkened her blue eyes, and again Percival thought of Rebecca. "You would not tell, my lord, would you?"

"I would not. If, perhaps, we can strike a deal."

She blanched in the gossamer light trickling through the

trees. "My lord, I'm...too young to...please—"

"Och!" Percival stepped back. How dare she think he'd make such a rude proposal to a mere girl? "Not that, child. I'm likely three times your age and quite unwilling to beget a brat on some peasant girl. No, it's not your body I want. It's your power. Can you break a witch's curse?"

She stared at him for so long he thought *she* might have turned to stone.

"Did you hear me, child?"

"Yes—I... No, I cannot break another witch's spell for good or bad."

Percival nodded slowly. "Fine, then. I'll be telling this tale in the village at dawn and leaving out no details." He turned to leave, and she followed him a few hasty steps, then clamped her hands on his sleeve.

"My lord, I *can't*. But I may know who can. I can take you to him."

"Him? A *man* practices this sorcery?"

"He both practices and teaches it, sir."

"Teaches? An abomination." Percival sighed to himself. Evil, perhaps, but necessary in this case. "Lead the way, child."

"Are you sure? He's very powerful, and he will exact a price for any help he gives you."

Percival laughed, and the sound echoed in the darkness. "I'm prepared to pay any price, girl. Any price a man can name."

Melodie's stomach churned as she paced back and forth in Blake's living room. "Are you sure this is going to work?" she asked for the third time.

Her impertinent question drew a long-suffering sigh from Calypso, who had just finished scattering a handful of crushed cypress needles on the floor around Blake's granite feet.

"I thought you said it was a bad idea to mess with the ancient magick."

"This curse is old, not ancient," Cal explained with forced patience. "And I'm not 'messing' with it. I'm just laying something over it. This new spell won't break the curse, but for now it should transform DeWitt back to his human form. Best-case scenario, it's permanent. He'll still be technically cursed, but he'll be human twenty-four/seven. Worst case, he'll be human for the rest of the day, then the spell will wear off."

Mel shivered. Ever since she'd called Cal at sunrise, moments after Blake's transformation, she'd been in a state of semi-panic. Daylight made her feel almost like herself again, just normal enough to remember how good and how bad all that unbridled Cabochon power had made her feel last night. She didn't want to hide behind Calypso's ward spell again, but she had no idea if she could survive another night with the gem controlling her actions and her thoughts.

"Won't it be cruel to give him just one day?" Mel stared over Cal's shoulder at Blake's transformed face. She'd do anything to see him restored to human form permanently, but how could she look him in the eye and tell him he might have only one day of freedom?

"Mel, it's more than he's expecting. And if it proves to be temporary, I can always cast it again tomorrow."

"And the next day? And the next? What if you have to do it every day forever?"

"I won't have to. The Witches' Council will come up with something. I promise."

Mel hadn't asked about her own end of the problem. She was afraid Cal might tell her the Witches' Council didn't have any options for getting the Cabochon out of her, and she didn't want to hear that right now. All she cared about at the moment was helping Blake. "All right. Let's go, then. Are you ready?"

"Yes." Calypso held up a small bottle of orange liquid, the transformation potion she'd just cooked up in Blake's kitchen. "Stand back, out of the splash zone."

Mel eyed her. "Splash zone?"

"And close your eyes. There may be flying glass."

Mel backed up, and Cal took a position a few feet away from Blake's left side. She couldn't stand directly in front of him because he was so close to the cellar door, and his stone body weighed far too much for the two of them to budge him even an inch.

After a deep breath, Cal recited the Latin incantation on a long exhale, and when she finished, she threw the small vial at Blake. It hit his outstretched arm and bounced off unscathed, landing amid the smattering of fragrant needles at his feet.

Mel gaped. "Was that supposed to happen?"

Cal huffed. "Sorry. I didn't throw it hard enough." She retrieved the potion bottle and backed up. This time she wound up for the pitch. Mel clenched her eyes shut and held her breath. The bottle shattered with a musical tinkle, and something began to sizzle.

Mel opened her eyes and rushed over to Blake. The potion bubbled on his stone sleeve, hissing and smoking like acid. "Oh, God, Cal. Is *that* supposed to happen?"

Calypso waved a hand. "Shh. Hold on, give it a minute."

"What if it burns him?"

"It won't. Look." In one small spot on Blake's arm, shiny black leather shone through the stone. The spot spread up and down his sleeve to his hand, his shoulder, his chest. As they watched, granite became flesh—rough, gray flesh.

Mel's momentary elation turned to horror when Blake began to move. He turned his head slowly, stiff and obviously disoriented. Sunlight streaming through his living room windows cast her shadow on the rug in front of her, and his gaze fell to the dark shape stretching toward him.

"Melodie?"

"Blake...it's..."

A smile spread across his frightening visage, and his pointed ears twitched. "Oh my God. Daylight."

"Blake—"

He rushed across the room in two gargantuan strides and caught Mel up in a bear hug that left only enough room in her lungs to squeal for help. He twirled her around once and plopped her back onto her feet, grinning through his upcurved fangs. "I owe you my life, lass. Everything!" He cupped her face and loomed in for a kiss. Mel stiffened, and that's when he realized something wasn't quite right.

Slowly he pulled his clawed hand away from her face. He flexed his thick fingers, then patted his head, his ears, his chest.

"You owe *her?* I'm the one with the spells, mister." Cal's complaint drew his attention, and his whole, muscle-bound upper body turned in her direction.

"*You* did this?"

Mel grabbed his arm. "Blake, we tried. Cal tried to turn you human."

His hooded eyes swept over Melodie; then he turned back to glare at the witch.

"I'm sorry. I didn't know this would happen. Maybe the spell wasn't strong enough to transform you all the way back."

Blake stood still so long Mel began to wonder if he'd turned back to stone. Only the barely perceptible rise and fall of his chest told her he was still breathing.

Finally, he sighed. "Will I stay this way even after sunset?"

The knot in Mel's stomach tightened, and the sudden pain made her wince.

Cal offered a delicate shrug. "I don't know."

"By then I'm sure Cal will come up with another spell. Right? Calypso? *Right*?" Mel brushed her hand over Blake's jaw.

He jerked away from her touch. "Don't."

"Blake, I'm sorry."

"It's all right. It's all right." He walked away from Mel and moved toward the window. Parting the sheer curtains with one claw, he peered out into the midmorning sunlight.

Mel stepped back toward Calypso. Her heart ached so badly for Blake that the crushing weight of it in her chest left her barely able to breathe. She grabbed Cal's elbow and propelled the witch into the kitchen.

"This is terrible. Can you reverse it?" Her demon half, evident in her harsh whisper, threatened to emerge.

"I could try, but I might just make it worse." Cal nodded toward Blake, and Mel turned to watch him. With one oversize hand splayed against the warm glass, he surveyed the outside world. His new prison might have been larger and brighter, but it was still a prison.

"Oh, Cal, please help him."

"I will. I'll come up with something."

"Please." Mel touched her forehead to Calypso's, and the witch gave her a quick hug.

"Will you stay with him while I go do some more research?"

Mel nodded. "I told him I wouldn't leave him."

"Okay. I'll be back as soon as I can." Cal hurried out the door, and Mel returned to the living room. She joined Blake at the window, and together they watched Calypso drive off.

"Thank you," he said after another stretch of awkward silence. His voice was thick, gravelly.

"For what? I didn't do anything except call Calypso for help, and now you're...like this."

"It's all right. Really. It's better than before. I was alone then. Just me and Percival. I live his life in my dreams, and no man was more alone than he was."

"But you still can't go outside."

He lifted one hand and rested it on her shoulder. Though the weight of it tested her strength, this time she didn't flinch away from his touch. He squeezed her shoulder, and she patted his hand. Despite her own exhaustion, she remained there with him at the window for the rest of the morning, watching the world go by.

Chapter Twenty-Two

Even though Blake could move around now in his gargoyle form, he still weighed nearly as much as when his body was made of stone. When he finally stepped away from the living room window and sat , the couch creaked.

Melodie raised a brow at him, and he shrugged. "I've got to sit somewhere."

"Are you hungry? Why don't I made you something—"

"I'm not. And I don't think a kitchen chair would hold me anyway."

"I can bring you something here."

"No. I'm fine." He wasn't, but what could he say? He'd longed to see the sun again, and now he had. Maybe he should be content with that. He sighed. "If you're—"

"No. I'm not either." She seemed to flutter around the room, obviously unsure of what to do with a living gargoyle.

He wondered how he must look to her. He'd run his fingers over his fangs, pointy ears and hairless head several times and still couldn't quite believe it. His lower jaw felt huge, and his bulbous forehead shaded his eyes. Somewhere, snaking down one leg of his jeans, there seemed to be a tail, but he didn't have the stomach to excuse himself to another room to check.

"I can bring you your laptop, if you'd like to work." She sounded hopeful, as if she could take his mind off his new predicament.

"No. I think I'll just rest for now."

"Sleep? You want to sleep?"

Yes. He wanted desperately to wrap his arms around a pillow or some other soft object and drift away, but how could he close his eyes on the first rays of sunlight he'd seen in ten years? How could he close his eyes on Melodie?

He followed her movements around the room and gazed up at her when she returned to him with a knitted afghan from a nearby chair. She handed him the blanket, her expression uncertain. "While you're sleeping, I'll see if I can track down Calypso and find out what's going on."

Blake dropped the blanket across his lap and reached for her hand. "Don't leave, please."

"I won't. I'll call her. I told you I'd stay with you, and I will."

"How can you even look at me?" He let his fingers trail out of hers and flicked the woolen ridges of the blanket with one vicious black claw. "I understand now why it's better to be turned to stone. At least then, I didn't have to see my own reflection in people's eyes."

Melodie drew in a breath and swiped a hand over the tears that had gathered on her lower lashes. "You're not ugly. Not at all. And you're not frightening." She knelt down in front of him and put her hands over his. "When I look at you now, I don't see a monster. I see a man who's done everything he can in the last few days to try to help me. You might pretend you're only in this for yourself, but I see the real you. You're not a witch hunter, and you're not evil."

He almost believed her. Staring into her warm brown eyes, feeling the slide of her smooth skin over his rough hands, he could almost imagine himself as the man she claimed to see.

Their gazes held, and he leaned over to kiss her, not thinking, only feeling.

"Ow!" She jumped back, dabbing at a scratch on her chin from one of his fangs.

"I'm sorry—damn, I'm sorry." Instinctively he reached for her, then pulled back, afraid to hurt her again.

She caught his hand and held it to her face. "It's okay. I'm fine." She rose and ran her hand over the top of his head. The contact made him shiver. "I'm going to call Calypso. Get some sleep."

"Wake me before sunset," he said as she headed out of the room. "I don't want to miss any more daylight than I have to, but I can't keep my eyes open any longer."

She nodded and disappeared, and with a heart as heavy as stone, Blake lay down on the creaking couch and closed his eyes.

Apprehension dogged Percival's every step as the copper-haired girl led him deeper into the woods. He expected a cave, or perhaps a deep, dark tunnel leading to the underworld, but instead she brought him to a cabin made of smooth, round river stones with a neatly thatched roof. The stuff of fairy tales—and probably nightmares as well.

The man who answered the rough plank door at her insistent knock looked like a woodsman. His dark eyes sparkled in a heavily bearded face, and concern creased his plump lips. "What happened, Lise? The blood—"

"Is not mine," the girl hastened to explain. "This man killed the Mendican."

Percival eyed her expectantly. In the warm light spilling from within the woodsman's cabin, her hair lit with streaks of gold and her face shone like an angel's. He cleared his throat, prompting her to continue.

"And he saved my life, I suppose."

The woodsman raised a bushy brow. He looked nothing like

a sorcerer, and Percival wondered if perhaps the girl had deceived him to draw him farther from the village.

"As recompense, he asks a favor. Can you break a witch's curse?"

The man eyed Percival now, and his lips quirked into an expression resembling a smile but without the humor. Finally he motioned them inside. "Sit by the fire, and I'll make you something warm to drink. Tell me about this curse you bear."

"I never said *I* bore the curse."

"You didn't have to. I can see it in your aura. It's powerful. You must have done something terrible to earn it." The man's eyes, set deep in his wrinkled face, seemed to pierce Percival's soul. Reluctantly he crossed the threshold into the old man's home and followed him to sit on a cushioned bench near the crackling hearth.

His apprehension eased just a bit when the woodsman placed a cup of steaming broth into his hands. He sipped the brew, grateful for its warmth, and before long, he found himself confessing his sins. All of them.

When he'd finished, shame heated his face as surely as the merry flames heated his old bones. Lise glared at him, her youth obviously heightening her emotions. The woodsman merely nodded as if none of the horror Percival had described fazed him in the least.

"Can you help me?"

"I can." The man raised a hand swiftly to still Lise's protest. "Hush, child. This is beyond you at the moment, and it is not your place to judge. Nor is it mine."

For the first time in more years than he could count, Percival's heart lifted. He'd have grabbed Lise and kissed her if he wasn't certain she'd have spit in his face. "Thank you. Thank you."

"Don't waste your gratitude. You may find my brand of help

lacking since I cannot break the curse myself. Only she who cast it should make that choice, but I can tell you where to look for her."

Percival sagged. More searching, more disappointment. "And if she won't cooperate?"

The woodsman placed a hand on Percival's arm. "It's not her cooperation you seek."

"What then?"

"It's her forgiveness."

Melodie awoke with her heart pounding, unsure of where she was or why she'd been asleep. She pulled herself upright and groaned at the stiffness in her legs and the ache in her lower back. She'd been dozing in the chair in Blake's living room, and unfolding herself from the pretzel shape she'd curled into took every ounce of effort she could muster.

An unfamiliar sound drew her attention to the couch where Blake's gargantuan form bowed the cushions. He thrashed once, his arms thrown out as if reaching for something just beyond his grasp. He moaned.

Mel scuttled across the dim room. Dusk had settled. She'd slept too long and allowed him to miss what might prove to be his one and only "day" in ten years. Racked by sudden guilt, she shook him awake, her eyes on the shadows lengthening around the room. He had only moments before the day he'd dreamed of for so long slipped away, and it was her fault. "Blake!"

He growled at her intrusion, and for a brief second, she feared he might attack. She froze when he gripped her arms and snarled at her. Then his eyes snapped open, revealing the man trapped in a monster's body.

"What time is it?"

She bowed her head. "I don't know. Maybe six. I'm sorry. I

fell asleep too. The hazards of being up all night, I guess."

The couch creaked piteously as he rolled to his feet. He crossed to the window and swept the filmy curtains aside to look out on the last few seconds of daylight. "More like the hazards of being a demon. Most of them hibernate during the day when they're above ground. I doubt either of us could have stayed awake if we'd tried."

"I'm sorry. Maybe tomorrow we can—"

"No. It's okay." Dismissing the purple light of dusk, he turned back toward her. "Where's Calypso? And what happened to Van Houten?"

"She's not back yet, and I haven't heard from Palmer all day. I hope he didn't lose his job." Mel watched Blake pace across the room. The floorboards groaned under his weight. "What's wrong?"

"The witches have to find a way to break the curse. They have to."

"They will. I know they'll think of something. We just need to—"

"Percival sought forgiveness." His words came out as a strangled whisper that Mel wasn't quite sure she heard correctly.

"What?"

"He knew he had to ask forgiveness of those he'd hurt in order to end the curse. Once he realized that, he set out to find Birgid Cooper, the witch who'd cast the spell."

The conviction in Blake's eyes and his voice made Mel nervous. How could he know what Percival's motivations had been in seeking out Birgid Cooper, if indeed that's what he'd done? "Obviously he never found her. Or maybe he did, and she refused to break the curse."

"Even so, whether he found her or not, he wanted to be forgiven. I know that. I see his life when I'm...transformed. I live in his head."

"But just now, you weren't transformed. You were only dreaming."

That silenced him. He swallowed and turned away from her. "But it felt the same. I'm still part of Percival, and he's part of me. Maybe that's why the curse can't be broken. Maybe I'm Percival's soul reincarnated, and I still have to do his penance."

Mel crossed the room and put her hand on his broad shoulder. His gray flesh was cool to the touch, so much like stone. "I don't believe that, but even if it's true somehow, you shouldn't pay for his crimes. What he did has nothing to do with you."

"No, lass. It has everything to do with me. I've been with Percival from the beginning, and I know everything he did. I feel like I'm a killer just like him, and maybe that's why the curse can't be broken."

Chapter Twenty-Three

Blake didn't expect Melodie to understand. He'd relived so many moments in Percival's life over and over again, they felt more like his own personal history than something lost in time. Though this last trip to the past had been a dream, and not quite like the too-realistic visions he experienced while encased in stone, it felt just as authentic. What he'd seen might have been a manifestation of his own desires, but his gut told him this was how the events had actually played out.

Percival had come to repent his sins, and he'd been determined to find Birgid Cooper and beg for her forgiveness.

Blake watched the streetlight on the corner begin to glow, and he sensed the stirring of Fremlings in the shadows outside. He glanced at Melodie, who watched him from the couch, and all the doubts he'd lived with over the years fled. From this moment on, he'd no longer wonder if perhaps Percival's crimes were so vile that ten men deserved to bear punishment for them.

Melodie rose. "I'll call Calypso ag—" Mid-word, her jaw dropped.

Blake felt the change immediately. Sunset cast the room in shades of indigo, but even in the strange light, he saw the difference in his skin. A cold ripple of sensation raced across his back and up and down his spine. He tensed, fearing this was the end of him for the night, but rather than turn to stone, his skin paled. His body morphed as he stared down at his own familiar self.

In seconds, he'd become human again.

When the transformation was complete, Melodie let out a cry of relief and flew into his arms.

She felt like heaven, warm and bright—an armful of sunshine. He'd have reveled in the physical contact, but the power of the Cabochon hit him like a wall. A hot arc followed the cold tingle through his nervous system, leaving him breathless.

Her own transformation would follow on the heels of his. The darkness would steal her soul tonight, the same way daylight had stolen his for more than a decade.

Gripping her arms, he held her away from him. "We've got to hurry, lass. You can't take another night of this."

"Kiss me." Her demand caught him off guard. "Now, Blake. Please?"

How could he argue? All consideration for their mutual plight drained out of him, leaving nothing but raw need. He threaded his fingers through her hair, pulled her face to his and captured her lips.

Warm and sweet, tasting of forbidden desire, she opened to him instantly, and between them as their bodies collided, something sparked.

"Take me upstairs…" she whispered against his throat.

He could do nothing but oblige. She gasped when he swept her up into his arms. The bedroom was so far—he'd have taken her on the couch, but that didn't seem right. He'd compromised for too long not to have everything perfect now.

She clung to him, her fingers tangled in his hair, her warm breath on his neck. He wasted no time, took the steps two at a time and placed her in the center of his bed.

He paused long enough to pull off his shirt and kick off his boots. Then he joined her.

Melodie reached for him and dragged his half-naked body across hers. When he'd settled atop her, she wrapped her thighs around his waist.

This intimate contact stirred the demon in her. Blake sensed the spike in power and felt it in the sharp grip of her nails along the flesh of his back. He should have stopped, should have torn himself away, but to have her beneath him, demanding his kiss, commanding his movements, felt too good.

"Blake—Blake..." She panted his name between breathless kisses and tore at his belt buckle. "I need you."

"Easy, angel. We'll get there." He helped her unfasten his jeans but refused to let her slide her eager hands into his briefs. As much as he wanted her, he had to know who, or what, was in control. Catching both her wrists in one hand, he pushed her arms above her head. He used his free hand to tease her and himself by gliding his fingers along the smooth skin of her belly, up under her shirt and over the satiny cups of her bra. He'd taken this journey before, when he'd searched her in the abandoned house. He'd struggled then to remain a gentleman. Now his inhibitions were gone. He could do as he pleased—as *she* pleased, and she let him know with a satisfied purr that his explorations did please her.

Little by little, the desperate tension left her body. She relaxed her wrists and allowed her arms to come around his shoulders gently while he kissed her.

"It's you," he told her before sliding her shirt up over her head. He pushed the delicate straps of her bra off her shoulders and ran appreciative fingers over her tender flesh his ministrations revealed. "It's got to be only Melodie tonight."

She nodded, then arched into him and moaned when he released the clasp against her back. He tossed the garment aside and bent his head to take a hardened nipple into his mouth. There was definitely a little demon in the sound she made when he flicked his tongue over the tight bud.

His own growl answered hers. Together they'd be wicked, evil and magnificent.

"I want you now." She bucked her hips up, sending a sinuous wave rippling through the bed beneath them.

"Soon. Soon." He soothed her with gentle strokes up her arms, across her breasts. So beautiful. Her skin smelled like lilac, and her lips tasted like sin.

Blake couldn't hold out much longer, but there was one thing he had to do before giving in to all of her demands. The condoms in the nightstand drawer had been there awhile, but they'd have to do. Blindly, he searched with one hand through the junk in the drawer, kissing Melodie breathless, until his fingers finally closed around a familiar foil packet.

For a moment, he thought she might protest. She seemed surprised when he ceased his sensual onslaught to tear the packet open. "I can't let anyone else inherit the curse," he said, stripping off his jeans. "I'm the last of my bloodline. Even if Calypso and the Witches' Council can't break the curse, it ends with me."

Mel's eyes glistened. She sat up and sidled into his arms, kissing his jaw, his throat, his chest. Silently, she helped him strip her bare and slide the latex over his erection.

"Right now, there is no curse," she whispered as he pushed her supple body back onto the pillow. "There's only us."

He took her mouth as he entered her, swallowing her gasp at his first full thrust. "Ah, Melodie, I've wanted this—" He couldn't express how much in words. He could only show her by giving her everything he had.

Mel struggled to maintain control of her thoughts and her

movements. The power of the Cabochon seemed to pulse each time Blake's hard body connected with hers. The inner surge left her breathless, drunk with a demonic longing for more of everything he offered her, while the feel of him moving inside her left her weak, humbled by his perfection.

She hadn't been loved this way in so long, hadn't allowed herself to let go and experience a complete release of all her inner fears and inhibitions. Blake made it easy. Every touch, every ragged breath of his told her she was everything he needed. All she had to do was surrender completely to every delicious sensation, but one lingering fear remained. If she did let go, the demon would take over.

There, under the surface, it boiled, waiting to spill out and overwhelm her tenuous consciousness.

It wanted to destroy Blake as much as it wanted to possess him. Her fingers ached to dig into his taut muscles, to score his flesh and draw warm blood to the surface of his skin. She fought to keep from biting his lip when he kissed her, to keep from pushing him onto his back so she could straddle him and wrap her hands around his throat.

She couldn't let it win. She wouldn't let it use him up and discard what remained when it was through, not when she needed him as much as she did. Not when she loved him.

Her climax came fast and hard on that realization—an explosion of hot light behind her eyelids, a wash of molten sensation in her core. She moaned and clutched at him, then held her breath while her body shuddered to completion, terrified of what she might become if she relinquished this last shred of control.

Above her, Blake tensed. He had to have felt her come. He smiled against her lips and ran hungry hands down her sides to grasp her hips. "It's good, angel. I'm there with you."

And he was. The energy of his orgasm fed the Cabochon

until its power engulfed every nerve ending in Mel's body. She clung to Blake and cried out, stunned by the heat of it and the intensity of sensations she'd never even imagined before.

She'd lose herself if she let it have her, but she'd have given everything for this—for the moment Blake DeWitt claimed her as his own.

"There, Melodie. There. I've got you." Blake eased her through it. His strong arms around her kept her grounded, kept her in control. He anchored her to reality and held the demon at bay until, finally, her inner tremors ceased, the heat of the Cabochon subsided and she relaxed against him.

"Blake..."

He smoothed her hair and kissed her temple. "Shhh. Just let it be. We're both still here."

She met his gaze, and the clarity in his tawny eyes made her heart skip a beat. "Blake, when this is all over...when—"

He hushed her anxious question with a firm kiss. "Ah, Melodie. I don't think you and I are ever going to be over."

Despite having slept most of the day, Blake would have gladly remained in bed all night as long as he could have kept Melodie safe and warm in his arms. Her deep, rhythmic breathing told him she'd finally fallen asleep with her head on his chest, her hand splayed on his stomach and her legs entwined with his. The moment would have been utterly perfect, except for the steady beat of the Cabochon hiding within her perfect body like a parasite. It would only grow stronger as the night wore on.

He woke her reluctantly with a kiss on each heavy eyelid. She smiled even before she stirred.

"We've slept too long again, and I hear a car outside," he said, letting his gaze roam her curves as she pushed himself to a sitting position beside him. She actually blushed at his perusal and pulled a pillow across her body to cover herself.

He grinned. "Nothing I haven't seen. Or tasted."

"Oh—" She covered her eyes with one hand. "I'm not used to this, waking up with a man...you know."

"Naked?"

"Mmmm."

"If I had my way, you'd get used to it very fast." Outside, the thud of a car door interrupted the quiet evening. Blake rose. "I wonder if that's Calypso."

Melodie flung herself over the side of the bed and scrambled to retrieve her clothes. She was only half dressed when the doorbell rang. "I'll go so you can get dressed," she said, shrugging into her shirt.

Blake stifled a tart remark and opted instead to stare at Melodie's jean-clad rear end as she hurried out of the room.

He'd spent the last hour feeling closer to normal than he had in ten years. He'd finally seen the sunlight, even if it was through a window. Maybe that was enough to hope for. Animate gargoyle by day, supremely satisfied human by night. He could learn to live with that.

Before opening Blake's front door, Mel chanced a peek at the small mirror hanging at the bottom of the stairs. Her reflection stopped her cold. Who was the beautiful woman staring back at her? When had her normally drab, dark brown hair morphed into an unruly chestnut mane? When had her thin lips become so full and red, and when had her eyes started to look smoky rather than shadowed?

The muscles in her belly clenched when she thought of Blake. If this was what he saw when he looked at her, no wonder he'd wanted her.

Would he feel the same way when she went back to being just plain old Melodie?

The doorbell rang again, scattering her self-absorbed musings. She tore her gaze away from the wicked beauty in the mirror and opened the door, expecting to find Calypso.

Instead Palmer stood on the narrow porch. He looked as anxious as she felt. A slim, black-haired woman hovered on the step behind him—definitely not Calypso, though she bore some resemblance to the witch.

Mel sighed and ushered them both inside. "Where have you been? I'm so sorry about the warehouse. Was your uncle angry? He didn't fire you, did he?"

The barrage of questions seemed to startle Palmer. He squinted at Mel, and his companion raised two perfectly sculpted brows but said nothing.

"Fired...uh, well. I don't know, actually. I haven't been to work today. It's probably a safe bet that I'm not only out of a job but out of the will as well." He punctuated his statement with a humorless laugh. "You look pretty...pretty good. Better than I expected."

Mel blushed. She resisted the urge to press her suddenly cold hands to her flaming cheeks. The temperature difference would have probably made her face crack anyway. She led the two into the living room and motioned for them to sit on the sagging couch. Palmer pressed on.

"I spent the entire day researching, and I found someone who knows a bit about the Cabochon. This is my friend from the DHN. Her name is..."

"Helena." Blake's voice sounded like rusty nails. He stood in the living room doorway, his shirt open to reveal places Mel had lately been pressed against. His skin was ashen and his expression hard as granite. "Demon Hunters' Network, huh? Are you serious? They must have done away with the background checks if they let your kind in."

Mel's breath seemed to vanish from her lungs, leaving her

gaping like a dying fish. This was *that* Helena? The half-demon woman Blake had seduced...

The woman rose, and her deep indigo eyes flashed. Mel recognized the look she gave Blake. It was the look of a woman who hadn't quite forgotten having her heart broken. "Palmer, maybe this was a bad idea." Her voice, smoky and sexy, reminded Mel of Calypso's.

Palmer's confused gaze bounced between Helena and Blake. "What did I miss? You two know each other?"

Blake laughed. "Didn't she tell you? I'm surprised she'd show up at all if she knew you wanted to help *me*."

"Not you." Helena took a step forward, and something primal surged inside Mel. She didn't want this woman near Blake. She fought the urge to put herself between them. "Palmer asked me to help Melodie. I found him researching the Cabochon, and I told him about a spell that could be used to transfer the gem from one host to another."

"But you didn't tell him you know about that spell because it's been handed down through generations of your family. Your *demon* family." Blake held Helena's gaze. The look in his eyes was the same one he'd had that first night when he thought only Palmer stood between him and the Cabochon.

"What does it matter how I got the spell? I have it, and I can perform it and remove the gem from Palmer's friend."

"Can you break the curse?" Mel asked. At the moment, that was more important to her than anything.

"You're a demon?" Palmer's question went unanswered. The doorbell rang again, and Blake whirled out of the room to answer it.

Helena turned a sympathetic gaze on Mel. "I'm sorry. I don't have enough power for that. The spell I have was developed as a failsafe in case the Cabochon ever fell into the hands of the lesser demon breeds."

Mel stared at the woman. She didn't look at all demony. In fact, she was lovely. Her dark hair and sparkling blue eyes contrasted with her light skin and delicate bone structure, giving her the look of a china doll. "You mean like Fremlings or something?"

Helena laughed. "Fremlings could never handle the power of the Cabochon. It's been the legacy of the higher-level clans almost since its creation. Controlling the Cabochon requires intelligence, cunning, and a little bit of soul. My people, the Domaré, possess all of that."

Palmer's mouth hung open. "How *did* you get into the DHN, anyway? Does anyone else know?"

Helena tuned to him and placed a hand on his cheek in a motherly gesture. "Don't worry, Palmer. You're not the only one I've fooled. My job is to monitor DHN activities and any demon research that goes on, just to make sure no one finds out anything they're not supposed to know."

"All right. Here's a question, then." Mel gave Helena a discerning once-over. Had she slept with Blake? The thought almost made her forget her more pertinent inquiry, but she forced her muddled brain to focus. "If the 'higher' level demons are supposed to control the Cabochon, what was a Gogmar doing with it? The one that attacked me certainly didn't seem like it had much intelligence, cunning *or* soul."

Helena opened her mouth, but her reply trailed off. Blake had returned with Calypso in tow. The resemblance between the half-demon and the witch was so striking that Mel couldn't hide her shock.

"Maybe you could field this question, cousin," Helena said, her lips curving in a smirk.

"Calypso!" Mel crossed the room to stand in front of her friend. "You're not, are you?"

Cal's indigo eyes, a shade deeper than Helena's, shifted

back and forth, but she wouldn't meet Mel's gaze. "Yes, I'm Domaré," she said. The admission came with a hint of shame.

"To answer your question, the Gogmar had been enthralled as a temporary servant of the Domaré to bring the gem to Calypso, because Gogmars can't absorb the power of the Cabochon. Their hides are too thick...or something." Helena's explanation burned in Mel's ears, and the gist of her words percolated slowly through the fog in her tired brain.

Calypso was a demon as well as a witch. Mel's best friend in Amberville wasn't even human. Not only that, she was destined to be a demon queen as well.

Destined to take Mel's power.

She stepped away from Calypso, and the sound that escaped her, meant to be one of confusion and exasperation, came out sounding more like a warning growl. "The Cabochon is supposed to be *yours?*"

Finally Cal looked up, though her gaze met Melodie's for only an instant, then shifted over her shoulder to zero in on her cousin. "I didn't know the gem was in transit. No one told me...or I wouldn't have taken that night off work."

"The transfer wasn't planned in advance. The death of the previous Domaré queen was unexpected. It shouldn't have happened for another quarter century." Helena's response drew a muttered curse from Blake, and a pang of sympathy twisted in Melodie's aching stomach. Could he have lasted another twenty-five years in this hellish half-life of his?

"I have a phone, you know." Cal actually pouted and crossed her arms over her chest.

"Well, Gogmars don't. And the old queen, I hear she was more demon than human. She didn't even live in this world anymore. The demons who attended her wouldn't have known how to contact you other than to send their thrall to trail you by scent."

"And the Gogmar screwed up royally, didn't it?"

Helena laughed. "Don't blame the messenger. It was sent to find you and given a rough location only. Then Palmer runs the poor thing through with a sword. What could it do but give the gem to the nearest living creature in order to carry out its mission?"

Palmer jumped up from the couch. "Now it's *my* fault?"

"Sounds good to me." Blake mimicked Calypso's pose and leaned against the doorjamb. His attention was focused on Helena, and Mel didn't like that one bit.

Palmer bristled at his cavalier response. "If I recall, DeWitt, I'm the one who saved your hide last night at the warehouse—"

"And I'm *eternally* grateful." From there the conversation degenerated into a four-way argument with Calypso, Palmer, Blake and Helena all shouting at once.

Mel's gut boiled, her skin heated, and finally the part of her that was still human erupted. "Enough! Everybody shut up."

Everyone obeyed, and they all stared at her like she'd grown a second head. Which, considering how awful she felt at the moment, might have been a possibility.

"Now that I have your attention. Calypso...I'm not going to ask why you didn't bother to tell me you were a demon, or rather *the* demon who's supposed to inherit the Cabochon. I'm just going to ask you, if Helena's family has a spell to get it out of me, and you two are actually cousins, why don't you have the same spell?"

"It's not that simple. If I remove the Cabochon and then absorb it, DeWitt remains cursed. I've been trying to find a way to break the curse without damaging the gem's power, because the demon breeds, especially the Domaré, have come to rely on it."

"Nice. Let me say this—if you don't hurry up and get this thing out of me, you might not get the chance, because I'm starting to like the power, and I'm starting to think like a demon. Right now it's taking all the control I've got not to run off again. The Fremlings are out there. I can feel them, and I don't think they'll let me get away the next time they have me."

"Didn't she tell you?" Helena's question was directed at Mel, but it produced a disparaging sound from Calypso.

"Helena, she doesn't need to hear this right now."

"What?" Mel positioned herself between the two women. "I know I'm going to turn into a demon, and I know I'll get so strong that I can't be killed. I can feel that."

Helena's eyes widened. "Is *that* what you told her?"

"No. I didn't want to scare her any more than she already was."

"Scare me? You didn't want to scare me? I spent last night in a rotting boxcar with demons holding me down while the creature in charge prepared to rip my guts out looking for the Cabochon. I've been attacked by living garbage, chased by things that give nightmares nightmares, and you didn't want to scare me? Please, Cal. Spill it."

Calypso sighed and sank to the couch. "You won't become a demon, Mel. Not a full-blooded, nearly immortal demon."

"And that's the *bad* news?"

"No. The bad news is, if we don't get the Cabochon out of you, you'll just die."

Chapter Twenty-Four

Blake stepped into the fray in the wake of Calypso's ominous words. He put his hand on Mel's shoulder. In addition to the electric current surging from the Cabochon, her body trembled.

"What?" Her voice was small despite the power contained within her. The demon had gone dormant while the human suffered.

"You can't sustain the power of the Cabochon. It's hard enough even for demons. That's one of the reasons I took up witchcraft, so I could get used to handling power and channeling it. I didn't want to turn into what the old demon queen had become." Calypso's shoulder's sagged. "You've got another day at most before the power surges kill you."

Melodie only nodded, bobbing her head slowly while she chewed her bottom lip. Her gaze seemed focused on something a million miles away.

Anger bubbled in Blake's gut. Why on earth would Calypso have withheld a spell that could save Melodie's life? He wanted to shake the witch, to squeeze a logical answer out of her alabaster pale throat. "We can't waste any more time then. Helena, are you prepared to do the spell now?"

She glared at him but nodded. He'd take time later to feel remorse for the way he'd used her. She'd told him, upon discovering his true motives for attempting to seduce her, that demons had emotions too, poignant, all-consuming ones, just like humans. He hadn't believed her then, but her eyes still held the depth of the feelings he'd played fast and loose with in an attempt to get what he wanted. She'd cared deeply for him, more deeply than he'd been capable of caring for her or for anyone at the time.

"I have everything I need."

"If we do it here, with you and me present, the Cabochon could go into one of us," Calypso said.

Helena transferred her burning stare to her cousin. "Are you afraid it might be me? Don't worry, Cal. I don't want the power. I never did. It was always meant for you, and I wouldn't stand in the way of the natural succession of things."

"What I meant was, if we can't contain the gem, if one of us absorbs it, Blake may never get free."

Blake shifted his position to face Calypso. Beneath her Goth makeup, she probably looked a lot more like Helena than he'd first realized. No wonder he'd felt an odd sense of familiarity when he'd first looked into the witch's eyes. He crossed the room and put his hands on her shoulders now, letting the weight of them settle on her. "Why does it matter to you? I've never been more than a witch hunter in your estimation. If none of this had happened with Melodie, you would have never given me any more consideration than the old Domaré queen had."

"You're right. I wouldn't have, because I never realized that after Percival died, the curse stopped being about punishment and started being about revenge. If we don't break the curse, it won't just be demon blood on my hands."

Blake wasn't quite sure he believed in Calypso's altruism, but he couldn't dispute it. The bottom line was Mel's life depended on removing the Cabochon from her immediately. He never thought anything would be more important to him than his own freedom, but right now, his only concern was her survival.

He dropped his hands and stepped back. "Do the spell now. We'll worry about the Cabochon later, when Melodie's all right."

More than an hour later, Mel sat cross-legged in the center of a circle of salt Helena had drawn on the floor in Blake's kitchen. Fat white pillar candles burned at five anchor points around her, increasing the already elevated temperature in the room.

Mel felt a little foolish and a bit like a museum exhibit with everyone gathered around, staring down at her. Palmer and Calypso looked anxious, and Helena was all business, bustling around at the stove where a strange-smelling potion boiled in a small pot.

Only Blake's whiskey-colored gaze held sympathy. Everyone else seemed intent only on results, and it was those results that scared Mel the most. Once the Cabochon was removed from her, what would happen to Blake? Did they dare try to destroy the gem themselves?

Palmer had retrieved a ball-peen hammer from Blake's basement just in case, but Mel had noticed Calypso eyeing the tool suspiciously. Would the rightful demon queen give up the source of her power so easily? Mel hated doubting her friend, but if she really allowed herself to think about it, she feared there might be nothing inside Calypso that honestly resembled the woman Mel thought she knew.

"This is ready." Helena's announcement had everyone shuffling around the circle, taking up their pre-assigned positions. Blake reached out to squeeze Mel's shoulder, but Helena intercepted him.

"Don't break the circle. Once the gem is out, we have to be

very careful not to touch it. Now that we know a human can absorb it, none of us should go near it."

"What happens if we just shatter it?" Palmer asked, hefting the hammer. Calypso winced at his question but didn't respond.

"I don't think that's a good idea. The release of power could be deadly. We should leave the gem here inside the circle until the Witches' Council can come for it. They'll have to decide the safest way to proceed."

While Helena spoke, Mel stared at Calypso. She wanted desperately to believe that Cal hadn't known all along how to help her. Now she'd begun to wonder if the mysterious and strangely absent Witches' Council even existed. "Does that mean I have to stay inside the circle too?" Mel asked.

"We can cut you out later," Helena said.

"*Cut* me out?"

"With the athame. We'll create a doorway so you can walk out of the circle."

Mel's sudden panic subsided, and she took a deep breath. "Okay. That doesn't sound so bad. I'm ready whenever you are."

"Good." Helena crouched in front of Mel, careful to remain outside the salt barrier. She addressed the room, but her eyes bore into Mel's. "Listen to me, everyone. Whatever happens, we can't break the protection circle. We can't touch the Cabochon—any of us, for any reason. Do you understand?"

Mel nodded. It seemed reasonable enough. Mel had no intention of ever going near any blue gems again. In fact she would probably chuck all her jewelry in the trash as soon as she got home, just to be on the safe side. She glanced around the circle. "Got it, guys?"

"Yes," Calypso and Palmer answered together, but Blake hesitated.

"Is this safe for Melodie?"

Helena rose, still not taking her eyes off Mel. "It's magick. Of course it's not entirely safe, but it's the only way. Also, bear in mind, it *won't* be painless."

Mel swallowed hard. Up until that moment, she'd been pretty confident. Now a faint shiver skittered down her spine. Her control was slipping, and her blood ran hot and cold beneath her skin. If they didn't hurry, she'd break out of the circle and just run away into the night. The allure of the shadows grew stronger each moment they wasted talking. "Can we just get started, please?"

Helena turned off the burner under the pot and waved away a cloud of white steam that rose under the range hood. She'd set a teacup on the counter next to the stove, and now she poured the contents of the pot into the cup. "Give me the athame." She gestured to Calypso, who retrieved a black-handled knife from the kitchen table.

Helena nodded, and Calypso muttered an incantation while walking around the circle three times, counterclockwise. When she returned to her starting position in front of Melodie, she raised the knife and sliced the air above the line of salt.

Mel could have sworn a faint shimmer trailed behind the dull blade as the witch opened a portal in the magickal barrier. Through the invisible opening, Helena handed Mel the steaming cup. "Drink it all." She pulled her hand back out of the circle, and Calypso reversed her movement with the knife, closing the breach.

Mel stared into the warm liquid and recalled Cal's putrid "calming potion". This concoction looked like coffee and smelled a little like licorice and...dirt, but it was an improvement over the other one, nevertheless. "I usually take cream and sugar in my potions." She chanced levity, but no one laughed. Blake's face might as well have been granite. Not a single muscle moved, even the one in his jaw that sometimes twitched when he was annoyed or frustrated. "I guess this will have to do."

She sipped...prepared for another horrible flavor to slide down her throat, but surprisingly, the demon brew wasn't half bad.

While Melodie concentrated on reaching the bottom of the cup, Helena instructed everyone to hold hands. Out of the corner of her eye, Mel watched Blake slip his fingers into Helena's palm. The demon in her stirred. He belonged to *her*, not Helena. She couldn't allow...couldn't abide...

The chanting began just as her thoughts disintegrated into chaos. Anger and jealousy collided with an overwhelming need to flee the scene, but a heaviness settled in her limbs that left her nearly immobile.

Latin words delivered in a tribal cadence lulled her after a moment, and her eyelids drooped. Maybe if she took a little nap, she could sleep through the pain Helena had warned about. With her eyes closed, she slurped the last drops of the potion and let the cup tumble from her fingers, which tingled a bit, just as her lips and her tongue did. "Mmm...this stuff has a kick to it."

A calm settled over her then, coupled with the faint buzz of the Cabochon. She'd grown used to the odd sensation beneath her skin but not the itchiness. Her throat felt scratchy now that she was without something to drink. Maybe she could ask Helena for another quick sip...?

Before that thought was fully formed, knives twisted in Mel's gut. The pain hit her like a sledgehammer, and she doubled over with a vicious cry. For the first time, Mel knew exactly where the Cabochon was. The amorphous gem seemed to have turned solid in her belly. She wrapped her arms around her middle, and the added pressure on the hard lump beneath her skin only made the agony worse.

Through the white-hot pain, Mel vaguely registered Blake

Jennifer Colgan

reaching for her and Helena and Palmer holding him back. She screamed at the sensation of something sharp trying to work its way through her flesh. No one had mentioned that the Cabochon would actually tear its way free of her body. If she'd known that...

"Melodie, concentrate. Listen to my voice," Calypso crooned to her. Soothing and deep, her voice gave Mel some focus through the haze. "This won't take long. I promise."

"Uh..." She tried to respond, but the words wouldn't form. Her tongue seemed to fill her mouth, leaving no room for sounds. Beneath her shirt, her stomach bulged as the Cabochon seemed to shift position. Would it pop out of her like some alien parasite, leaving her with a gaping wound while it scuttled away in a trail of blood? "Ughod."

"Melodie, hold on. You can get through this." Blake's voice came from somewhere very far away.

"Ikhant...ikhant." Tears blinded her, and her mouth began to water, heralding a bout of nausea. She clamped her tingling hands over her distended stomach and swallowed hard, hoping to clear the knot that seemed to block her esophagus. Above her, Blake struggled with Palmer.

"Get him out of here," Helena ordered. "Don't let him break the circle."

Furniture scraped on the linoleum, and a chair toppled with a crash. Calypso hurried to right it and move it away from the still unbroken barrier of salt.

Mel keened, and beneath her trembling fingers, the Cabochon rolled under her stretched skin.

"How much longer?" Calypso asked. "She can't take much more."

"Soon." Helena crouched before the circle again, and Mel glared at her through eyelids she could barely keep open. "As soon as she stops breathing."

228

"What?"

Mel tried to concentrate on Calypso and Helena screaming at each other. The demon cousins seemed so far away now, but she heard Helena's final words with perfect clarity. "You know as well as I do, there's no way to get the Cabochon out of her while she's alive."

Blake heard Helena's words too, and every raw nerve ending in his body caught fire. He threw himself toward the kitchen doorway, but Palmer placed his hands on Blake's chest and heaved him backward.

"We'll bring her back," he said, bracing for a linebacker's tackle. "Helena has a resurrection spell."

"A *demon* resurrection spell?" Blake roared. This was not happening. He couldn't lose Melodie now. "How stupid are you, Van Houten?"

"Don't worry. Helena told me how it works. She can bring Mel back to life."

"Yes, as a thrall to the demon who resurrects her. She'll be Helena's slave."

"No—"

"Yes!" Blake put all his strength into moving Palmer out of his way. He grappled with Golden Boy in the living room while Melodie's screams of agony echoed from the kitchen. "You of all people should know, never trust a demon."

"I didn't know she was a demon. She—"

"Exactly." Blake swept his opponent aside and feinted. They jockeyed position for a moment and came up chest to chest.

"I can't let you in there, DeWitt. You'll ruin everything."

Blake backed down. He hung his head and sighed. "You're right, but how can I just stand here and listen to that?"

Palmer flicked a glance over his shoulder, and that's when

Blake hit him. The crack of his knuckles against Palmer's square jaw reverberated up his arm. The All-American went down like a sack of cement, moaning while Blake shook the numbness out of his aching fingers. "Sorry. I didn't have any pixie dust handy."

Without remorse, he stepped over Palmer and vaulted into the kitchen.

Helena and Calypso didn't bother to intercept him. They let him rush to Mel's side and break the circle as he scooped her up in his arms. "Is it done?" he demanded, cradling her limp body. Her skin was splotchy, her eyes appeared swollen and bulgy and her breath came as a harsh rattle from somewhere deep in her chest.

"No. Something's wrong. She's supposed to pass out, to stop breathing, but this isn't normal," Helena said. Her voice shook.

"No human has ever possessed the Cabochon. Maybe it works differently," Cal said. She leaned over Blake's shoulder and stared at Melodie.

Blake ignored the witch's scrutiny. "Melodie? Lass, can you hear me?" Blake placed her flat on the floor and knelt over her. He patted her face and lifted one of her limp hands. Her fingers seemed unusually thick, almost bloated. She gurgled something at him and gaped like a fish, struggling to draw in air through her mouth.

Her swollen tongue lolled. "She's having a reaction!" Blake hauled her back to a sitting position. "She's going into shock. She must be allergic to something in the potion."

"Like what?" Helena and Calypso gathered close as if staring at Mel while she suffocated to death might somehow give them answers. Palmer stumbled in from the living room, clutching the side of his head. When the demon hunter saw Melodie, he raced across the room and knelt on the other side of her shivering body.

"She has food allergies. What did you put in the potion?" Blake said.

Helena jumped up to survey the spread of items she'd set out on the counter. "All the ingredients are here...which one? Which one?"

Blake ignored her panic. "In her purse, she has one of those rescue pens. Palmer? Can you get it? I think it's in the bedroom."

"I'll be right back." Palmer lurched out of the kitchen, and Blake tilted Melodie's head back, hoping to clear an airway in her constricted throat.

Calypso tore through the items Helena had arranged on the counter. "There's nothing here. Mel's allergic to nuts and...oranges I think. There's none of that here."

Helena gasped. "The bottle on the end. It's hazelnut oil. But there's only a drop of it in the potion for flavor."

"A drop is enough..." Blake patted Melodie's swollen cheek. "Come on, lass. Stay with us. Fight it! Calypso, call 911, now."

Before Calypso reached the phone, Melodie began to convulse. Tremors racked her body so violently that Blake almost lost his grip on her. Her swollen eyes flew open, and she gaped. For a moment, her breathing sounded like sandpaper on glass—then it stopped.

The sudden silence froze everyone in the room, and Blake's heart seemed to collapse in his chest. After ten years in the dark, he could not allow the only light in his life to die in his arms.

He shook her, more out of fear and desperation than anything. Then he placed her flat on the floor again with her head just outside the salt circle and her body within it and cupped his hand around the back of her neck.

He was no expert at CPR, but he could at least keep her

breathing until an ambulance arrived. He was about to begin when Palmer flew into the room. He held the fat, pen-like object Blake had found in Mel's purse.

"Take her jeans off," Calypso instructed as she dialed the phone. She reached for the pen and shoved the receiver into Helena's hands. "Hold this and give me the pen. Mel showed me how to use it once."

Palmer and Blake slid Melodie's jeans down her legs, exposing her thighs. Calypso yanked the safety cap off the epinephrine dispenser and jabbed the dull end of it against Melodie's flesh. Blake heard a faint click as the pen activated, releasing the hidden needle and pumping the rescue drug into her ravaged system.

He waited only the space of one breath before resuming CPR, and after one puff of air through her blue-tinged lips, all hell broke loose.

A brilliant, cold light flared from Melodie's midsection, and her body went completely rigid in Blake's arms. The flash blinded him, and the noise of it left his ears ringing. The windows rattled, and something thumped hard against the front door.

"Fremlings—" Calypso muttered. "They're swarming."

"Don't touch it!" Helena's reverent words drew everyone's attention. At first Blake had no idea what she was talking about; then he saw it. The Cabochon tumbled onto the floor next to Melodie. The sapphire blue gem glowed with a pulsating inner light. His salvation finally lay within reach, yet all he could think about was the woman he held gasping in his arms.

Gasping.

Melodie's body trembled now, but at least she was breathing, great desperate gulps of air. He cupped her face and cradled her against him. "It's okay now, lass. You're gonna be fine."

"Back away!" Helena pulled Palmer away from the circle. He scrambled for the discarded hammer, but the two Domaré women jumped him and wrestled it from his grasp.

"You can't destroy it!" Calypso bodily held Palmer back from retrieving the hammer. "Not now. Let it be."

"Get Melodie out of the circle, and don't touch the gem," Helena instructed Blake. "If you accidentally touch it—"

"I won't touch it." Blake scooped Melodie up in his arms. Though still limp, she looked better. Her breathing came in short pants now, and her eyes were mere slits, but her gaze was focused on him, and she seemed coherent. "It's okay, Melodie. Help's on the way. You're going to be okay."

She croaked his name, and he shushed her. "Don't worry about me, angel. I'll be just fine."

They vacated the kitchen, leaving the Cabochon pulsing and alone in the salt circle.

"What are we going to do about the Fremlings?" Calypso asked. She peered out the living room window.

"The sirens will take care of them." Palmer swept the curtains aside. The red and blue flash of emergency vehicles illuminated his features as Blake placed Melodie on the couch. "The ambulance scared them away, but they won't stay gone for long with the Cabochon lying around like that. We need to do something with it."

The doorbell rang then, and Palmer dashed out of the living room to let the EMTs inside. A moment later, two ambulance attendants and a police officer surged into the room. They crowded around the couch, making it clear by their actions that everyone else should stay back and give them room to work.

Blake caught the odd glance that passed between Helena and Calypso right before the rescue personnel started firing questions at him. He answered them dutifully and squeezed Mel's still-puffy fingers as they settled her on their portable stretcher and wheeled her toward the front door.

She smiled through the plastic oxygen mask they'd placed over her face, and Blake fell into step behind the entourage.

Calypso stopped him before he crossed the threshold. "Where do you think you're going?"

"To the hospital. Melodie shouldn't be alone."

"It's almost dawn."

Those words halted his forward momentum, but his gaze followed the stretcher down the front stairs. His neighbors had gathered at the curb, watching the EMTs load Melodie into the ambulance and no doubt wondering what he'd done to the poor girl.

"I don't know what's going to happen at sunrise, but I know you won't remain human."

Blake cursed and stalked back into the living room, where his sullen gaze met Palmer's.

"I'll go with her," the demon hunter said. Blake might have argued, but all things considered, Van Houten was the only logical choice. Blake waved him off. "Tell her I'll be there as soon as I can."

"I will."

"Thank you. And I am sorry about the sucker punch. You saved her life. I owe you for that one."

"Yeah, you owe me, but not for saving Mel. We'll talk about it later, when we're sure she's okay," Palmer said before hurrying out the front door.

Exhausted, Blake sank to the bowed couch cushions and lowered his head into his hands.

Now Melodie was out of the equation. He should have been relieved—and he was—but his problem remained. What if the Witches' Council still refused to break the curse?

A delicate hand rested on his knee, and he glanced up into

Helena's ocean blue eyes. "You care about her, don't you?"

"It doesn't matter. Until the curse is broken, what have I got to offer her or anyone?"

"They'll find a way. The witches know the curse has gone on long enough."

"And what about the Domaré? Will they agree to give up the source of their power?"

"The Domaré won't have a choice if the witches make a decision. They're more powerful than we are, but we're not weak. We'll find ways of holding our own, even without the Cabochon to help us."

"I'll believe in the witches' power when someone uses it to break the curse. Until then, it's all just empty promises." Blake looked away. Staring into Helena's eyes reminded him of his darkest hours, the times when he was desperate enough to hurt another living soul to save himself. That all-consuming quest for freedom no longer controlled his actions, but the shame of it lingered.

The soft sound of the door closing interrupted his melancholy thoughts. Both he and Helena glanced toward the kitchen. The insistent blue glow of the Cabochon had ceased, and the doorway was dark.

Their eyes met for a moment; then they both bolted across the room. In the kitchen, the circle of salt still lay unbroken, but the white candles, now extinguished, lay on their sides, anchored to the floor by puddles of hardened wax.

Calypso was gone. And so was the Cabochon.

Chapter Twenty-Five

At half-past ten the next morning, Melodie made her way out of the labyrinthine emergency department of Amberville General Hospital. She carried a cup of ice chips, a plastic bag with three sample doses of Prednisone and a prescription for a new epinephrine rescue pen.

She felt pretty good, considering she'd probably been dead for a second or two the night before.

The rumbling in her stomach was honest-to-goodness hunger, and the sleepy feeling that made her glance longingly at the couches in the ER waiting room had to do with the fact that she'd been up all night while an endless stream of nurses and doctors had taken her blood pressure and shined bright penlights into her eyes and down her throat every few minutes.

She needed sleep. She really needed a burger, and most of all she needed Blake.

When Palmer met her in the lobby, she mustered a smile to hide her mild disappointment. He hugged her, and she had to admit, the contact felt good.

He led her to the lobby exit and opened the door, releasing her into the brilliant sunlight. "How are you?"

She blinked and shielded her teary eyes. "A lot better. At least I don't feel like a balloon with a slow leak anymore."

"I'm sorry I couldn't be with you. They wouldn't let me in

the ER since I'm not family."

"That's okay. Everyone took good care of me." *Where's Blake?* Her mind tacked on the last question silently. If Calypso had gotten the witches to break the curse during the night, he'd be here now, wouldn't he?

"Do you want to stop at the pharmacy before I take you home?" Palmer asked as they headed toward his Jeep. Mel eyed him. He seemed almost too cheerful. Something wasn't right.

"Or maybe we should get you some food? What would you like? Breakfast, lunch? Both? We could stop at Brunch Palace—"

"What's wrong?"

"Nothing."

"Liar. Something's not right. I can tell by your voice."

He squeaked out a word or two, then cleared his throat and began again in a purposely lower pitch. "My voice is fine. I'm starving. I could go for pancakes. How about you?"

"It's Blake, isn't it? What happened?"

"He's fine."

"Fine-fine like great-fine or fine like not-dead-but-close fine?"

Palmer squinted at her. "Why would he be dead?"

She growled in exasperation and refused to hop into the passenger seat when he held the door of the Jeep open for her. "You know what I mean. There's fine as in perfectly normal and then there's the fine you tell people you are after you've just been in a three-car pileup but you don't have any broken bones."

He assessed her with a critical stare. "What kinds of drugs did they give you?"

"Palmer!"

He held up his hands in surrender. "All right. I guess you

could call it three-car-pileup fine."

"The Council wouldn't break the curse?" Defeat settled in her chest, and tears threatened, but she held Palmer's gaze.

"They can't at the moment. Helena called me a little while ago... Calypso...disappeared with the Cabochon. She probably absorbed it. She had to have if she touched it. They don't know where she went, but Helena has been out looking for her."

Mel slumped. Her bones seemed rubbery, and vaguely she registered Palmer helping her slide into the bucket seat. "How could she do that to Blake? How could she do that to *me*?"

"I don't know, Mel. I'm sorry." Palmer settled into the driver's seat and placed a hand on her knee. "Once I get you home, I'm going to look for her too. Between Helena and me, we'll track her down."

"I don't want to go home. I want to see Blake. Take me to his place."

"He didn't want me to do that. He doesn't want you to see him while he's—"

"Palmer, if you don't take me back to Blake's house, I'll pixie dust you until you don't remember your own name." She pinned him with a glare that she hoped left no room for argument. The Melodie-demon might be gone, but she could still conjure a solid death stare if she had to.

He sighed and drove her to Blake's. When they pulled up in front of the house, she gave him a quick kiss on his bruised cheek, and he winced. "Call me if you find her," she said as she climbed out onto the sidewalk. "Try the rail yard. That's where I'd go if I was a demon."

"Uh...sure. Will you be okay? I mean, things looked pretty bad last night. Are you sure you should be alone?"

She smiled and waved her baggie of drugs at him. "I'll be fine, and I won't be alone. I'll be with Blake."

Palmer muttered something before he pulled away, but Mel

didn't quite catch his comment. She waited until he turned the corner, then hurried up the stairs.

Panic seized her when she realized she didn't have a key, but disappointment at the thought of having to leave Blake alone all day morphed into another emotion entirely when the front door swung open and Helena stepped out onto the porch.

"Melodie! I'm so glad you're all right. I've never seen an allergic reaction before. I had no idea they could be so bad."

Mel stared at the Domaré woman, rendered speechless by a tumult of thoughts she probably had no right to think. Had Palmer lied about her being out looking for Calypso? How long had she remained with Blake after the ambulance took Mel away?

"Where is he?" She tried to keep her tone neutral and failed. The question sounded like an accusation, and Helena was clearly perceptive enough to take it that way.

She glanced over her shoulder into the house. "Upstairs. In his bedroom. He's...he transformed back to stone at sunrise."

In his bedroom. And why would he be in his bedroom? The words never reached Mel's lips, which compressed tight over her clenched teeth.

"Melodie, I know that look."

"Oh?" Her brows shot up, tightening the still slightly swollen skin of her forehead. She probably looked awful with sweaty hospital-bed head, blotchy cheeks and cotton balls taped over the IV marks on the backs of her hands. Meanwhile Helena looked fresh as some exotic tropical flower, as though she'd had a satisfying night's sleep...or something.

"You don't have to be jealous of me."

"Oh?"

"I never had anything real with Blake. I was just a means to an end for him. He'd traced the Cabochon to the Domaré clans, and I was assigned by my family to run some interference. Once he discovered what I was, he turned on the charm and, stupid me, I fell for it and for him. How could I not?" She gave a fluttery laugh. "Those eyes? My God. And that hint of an accent can make a woman's clothes fall right off."

Mel swallowed hard but said nothing. She was too busy listening to the message hidden in Helena's words.

"He made me feel human. You know, a lot of us want that. Being a demon, or even half demon in this world isn't easy. All the hiding, all the secrets, it gets to you after a while. I hope you can forgive Calypso for not telling you. Most people don't believe us, and those who do...well, they usually run screaming in the other direction. Blake didn't."

Mel tried to muster a response, but Helena pressed on.

"He reached out to me, and we shared...our fears. He told me how lonely he was and how terrible his existence had become, and I told him how isolated I felt in a world that would never accept me for who I was. Domaré men are a bit domineering. Marriages are more like contracts, and love isn't usually an issue. Like Calypso, I dreamed of something a little more than what my family dictated, so I began to think life with a gargoyle might be an improvement over what I had to look forward to."

"Calypso was married. Twice. To Angelo."

"He's Domaré. That's why they were divorced twice. She doesn't really love him as much as she's bonded to him. They fight all the time, but she can't really break free of his hold over her. I didn't want a life like that, so Blake seemed...perfect. When I found out all he really wanted was for me to lead him to the demon underworld so he could track down the Domaré queen, it hurt." The odd lilt in Helena's voice might have been to hide the depth of her emotion, or it might have been a challenge.

"Are you warning me to be careful?"

"What? No! Blake really cares about you. He was devastated last night when he thought he would lose you. He only *glanced* at the Cabochon while you were...dead. Besides, you were together before you absorbed it, right?"

Surely Helena knew the answer to that. Mel shook her head.

"Oh. You met after?"

"I don't like the direction this conversation is taking."

Helena reached out and placed a warm hand on Mel's arm. She tried not to flinch. "I'm not in the market to get Blake back. I came here to help you because Palmer is my friend. The odds are, Blake is really serious about you regardless of the Cabochon, so you probably have nothing to worry about, but just in case his interest in you was dependent on what he thought you could do to help him...well, at least you won't be surprised if he treats you differently now."

Mel smiled to hide her seething. When one looked close enough, it wasn't hard to see the demon side of Helena. "Thanks for that," she said and turned to skip down the front steps.

"Aren't you going inside to be with Blake when he 'wakes up'?" Helena called as Mel's feet hit the sidewalk.

"I'll be back," she said. "Don't lock the door."

"Where are you going?"

"To do what you should be doing. I'm going to find your cousin and get her to break the curse. Now."

Mel didn't listen for a response from Helena, and she didn't care if the demon woman stayed at Blake's place or not. She strode down the street, her anger carrying her on her quest.

Once again, by the light of the full moon, Percival stood at the foot of Margaret Thorne's grave. This time, rather than a hand-tied noose, though, he held in his hand a single white rose.

Since he'd purchased the Thorne property from her grieving husband, no flowers had ever adorned the once-fine lady's grave. Emmett Thorne and his three sons, in their haste to be rid of the estate and settle their mounting debts, had not requested the relocation of Margaret's remains.

For a time, after taking up residence, Percival had ignored the tiny plot, fenced in wrought iron and set on a small hillock where Margaret, in her eternal rest, could survey the house over which she'd once presided and the back gardens that had been her joy to tend each spring.

Weeds grew thick over the grave for a time, obscuring the headstone which read simply: Beloved Mother—Devoted Wife, along with the date on which Percival had snapped her neck. His first visit here had been to gloat, to promise her tarnished soul that he would stop at nothing to rid the world of her insidious brand of evil.

Today he hovered at the gate, a cold hand curled around one of the filigreed posts, not to taunt her spirit but to offer an apology.

"I've tried everything, Mum." He'd come to call her that...not to mock, but because over time he'd developed a kinship with this woman who shared his home, who slept on his land. Had he married Rebecca, he might have called her that name lovingly... He squashed that thought, having taught himself over time not to dwell on what might have been but to live only for the moment, since he never knew which might be his last.

"I've paid great sums for charlatans to cure me. I've walked such dark places, I fear even your lord and master would cringe at the things I've seen. I've begged and pleaded and threatened the lives of creatures I could never have imagined existed. And none of it has worked." Percival shook the sturdy bars. A cold autumn wind stirred the grasses that had withered on the grave, and the scent of the rose he carried wafted from its silken petals, a cruel reminder of the world's false beauty.

"I've only this left." He opened the gate and stepped into the small space in which Margaret Thorne had dwelled for all these years. Reverently, he placed the rose upon her grave and stepped away, his back stiff, old bones creaking. "I am sorry, Mum. I should have let you live."

Percival remained at the graveside until moonset, when the darkness grew so thick he could barely see to close the gate. Determined to continue this last, desperate bid for absolution, he trudged toward the main house with the Lord's Prayer on his lips. This time he recited the familiar words not as a litany meant to cleanse his own soul, but as a gift to Margaret Thorne.

With this burden gone from his psyche at last, he could concentrate on his most important mission. He would find the witch who cursed him and tell her what he'd done.

Silence greeted Mel's first tentative knock on Calypso's door, so she graduated to pounding with her fist and yelling. "I know you're in there, *Eugenia Maria Philomena Slovetski.* And if you don't answer this door by the time I count to—"

The door flung open, and Cal reached out and dragged Mel into her dark apartment. "My real name? You had to stoop to using my real name?"

Mel put her hands on her hips. "The things we confess after ten tequila shots come back to haunt us sometimes, don't they? And besides, you deserve it. How could you...*how could you* take the Cabochon and leave Blake like that?" Tears threatened Mel's resolve. The long walk from Blake's house had left her legs trembling and her throat tight. She probably needed a dose of the medicine they'd given her at the hospital, but it would have to wait until she'd said her piece. All the way over, she'd rehearsed what she wanted to say to Calypso when she found her, and now the eloquent words left her in favor of this pleading.

"How did you know I was here?" Cal asked, avoiding the question along with Mel's stare.

"I saw your car around the block. I know you park it there when you don't want the landlord to know you're home."

Cal sighed. "I'm sorry."

"Sorry isn't enough. We could have helped him, Calypso. We could have ended it."

"No, we couldn't." Indigo eyes flashed, and Cal whirled away. She paced the length of the cluttered living room, hands massaging her lower back above the waistband of her tight black jeans. "Helena was right. The release of all that power would have killed us."

"Then why not give the Cabochon to the Witches' Council?"

"That's exactly what we shouldn't have done. Don't you see, Mel? Once the gem was out of you, the urgency was over. They were trying to figure out a way to transfer the gem safely in order to save your life. Now that you're not in danger anymore, they're more likely to keep the gem and study it rather than destroy it. No one casts spells like that anymore. The Cabochon is a rare antiquity, and there would have been those opposed to damaging it for any reason."

"I'm not sure I believe that." Mel wanted to. She really did want to think that everything Calypso had done had been with Blake's interests at heart, but she also had to keep reminding herself she was dealing with a demon.

"I don't know how I can convince you, but the fact is, if I hadn't absorbed the gem, someone else would have, either by accident or on purpose. Now that it's in me, you're safe. Palmer is safe, and—"

"Don't say Blake is safe." The venom in Mel's voice

surprised her. Her heart had never ached so badly as when she'd spent the day watching Blake stare out the window on the world he'd been denied access to for ten years. Not even when she'd realized her marriage to Larry was over had she felt such an acute yearning for something she couldn't have.

"I wasn't. I was going to say the balance of power in the demon world is safe."

Mel turned her back on Calypso, partly to hide her growing rage. "And why is that? Because you're the queen now? Because you've got all the power?"

"Yes." Cal's response wafted across the room.

"Well, that's just—"

"Wait, Mel. Hear me out. Please?"

"I don't want to hear why you can't help Blake."

"Then will you listen to how I *can* help him?" Calypso touched her shoulder, and this time Mel allowed herself to flinch away from the contact.

Guilt washed through her at the reaction, but she couldn't bring herself to apologize. "Go ahead."

"I probably have enough power to break the curse myself, but if I don't, if it doesn't work, the Cabochon will have to be transferred to another demon, preferably to Helena because she's Domaré also."

"Why would it need to be—oh."

Calypso's unspoken words sank in. She would have to risk her own life to save Blake, and if her spell failed, if she died, nothing would be able to save him.

"The Cabochon is too strong for us to break it, isn't it?"

"Yes. The gem can't be shattered. If it was, the release of power would be like setting off a bomb."

"So if this doesn't work, Blake will never get another chance in his lifetime, will he?"

"Probably not."

Mel lowered herself to Calypso's couch. "He told me the curse ends with him. He's the last of his bloodline. What happens to the Cabochon when he...dies?"

Calypso shrugged. "I think it will just keep getting stronger. The power of the curse will live on beyond DeWitt."

"Maybe that's not a good thing."

"It probably isn't. If I break the curse, the power of the Cabochon will be diminished if it's not destroyed outright."

Mel thought of Blake. He might once have been willing to sacrifice anyone or anything to get his life back, but he wasn't like that anymore. Regardless of what Helena believed or wanted Mel to believe about him. "He might not let you do it. He wouldn't want you to take that kind of a chance."

"That's why we have to do it before sunset, so he won't be able to stop me."

Mel should have stopped her. She should have said no, but she couldn't make that choice for Blake. He deserved his freedom—not at Calypso's expense, even if she was a demon, but there was no alternative except to let him continue to live his life in darkness. She'd seen what little Cal could do for him without breaking the curse. He'd gotten to see the sunlight, but he'd been too weary to enjoy it, his form too monstrous to allow him to walk safely outside. That wasn't a good-enough life for him. He deserved so much more. "What do you need to get started?" she asked, rising on shaky legs.

"Nothing, except some moral support. Can you round up Palmer and Helena and have them meet us at Blake's house just before sunset?"

"Why not right now?"

Calypso gave her a sad smile. "I need to talk to Angelo first."

Mel stiffened. Surely Angelo would stop her. "Helena told

me he's Domaré too." She didn't need to voice her concerns. Cal seemed to sense them.

"I won't tell him about this. I can't. I just want him to know a few things, just in case something goes wrong."

"Do you love him? Really?"

"I used to think I did, but that was just the Domaré mating bond. Sometimes I can't resist him, but it's not really love."

"Oh, Cal."

Calypso patted Mel's shoulder and guided her to the door. "I'll be okay. I promise. Now go."

Melodie left Calypso's apartment, ignoring the nagging fear that on the one hand she might never see her friend again and on the other she might have just been taken for a fool.

She shook off her doubts. What choice did she have but to trust Calypso? And, if it didn't work out, she'd find another way to break the curse. If she had to track down every witch and every demon in the world, she'd find a way to give Blake back his life.

Chapter Twenty-Six

Half an hour before sunset, Calypso appeared on Blake's doorstep. Mel felt like she'd finally let out the breath she'd been holding all day, and her head swam a little from the sudden rush of oxygen. Palmer hadn't believed Cal would return, and Helena had remained noncommittal, though Melodie hadn't actually sought her opinion on the subject.

The two of them waited now in Blake's bedroom. They both gave the witch curious looks but said nothing as she began emptying the contents of her voluminous purse onto the bed.

"I thought you didn't need anything for the spell," Mel said. She eyed the usual witchy paraphernalia as Cal arranged familiar objects on the bedspread. A canister of sea salt, two white taper candles, a quartz crystal and a small bottle of vodka completed her array.

"What's this for?" Mel picked up the bottle. No more than a shot's worth, it looked like the ones sold on airline flights.

"Courage." Calypso laughed, and Mel felt a pang of sympathy for her. "Why isn't the Witches' Council helping you do this? Shouldn't someone be here...?"

"It's too dangerous. They don't want me to do it at all."

"I guess the Domaré don't want you to either."

Cal nodded and glanced at Helena. "I'm pretty much on my own." She put up a hand to stop Mel's protest. "It's fine. It's got to be done. Two hundred and seventy-four years is plenty of penance for Percival's soul. Another minute is too long for Blake to endure this."

Mel hugged Calypso, and she swore she felt the Cabochon's power surge over the witch's skin. She wondered what Cal might become over time with all that bottled up inside her. Maybe draining off the Cabochon's power would be a good thing in the long run. "What do you need us to do?"

Calypso instructed them to set up a circle of salt with a white candle at either end, a makeshift altar. Before kneeling between the flickering flames, she opened the vodka bottle and downed the clear liquid in one convulsive swallow.

She handed the bottle and its tiny aluminum cap to Palmer and closed her eyes. Her incantation was long and complicated, half prayer, half song. Mel wished someone could translate, but it appeared even Helena didn't understand the words.

Finally Calypso bowed her head. The candlelight glinted off her shiny hair, and for a long, long time, nothing moved.

Then she exploded. Light and sound akin to that which had accompanied the expulsion of the Cabochon from Mel's body arced around the room. From the witch's eyes and mouth a brilliant blue glow burst forth, obscuring her features.

Helena and Mel jumped, and Palmer skittered back a step, reaching for Cal and heading for the bedroom door at the same time.

Through a conflagration of cold blue flame, Calypso moaned. The sound was desolate and inhuman, and it set Mel's teeth on edge. When the flames shot out farther from Cal's body, licking the icy pillars of Blake's granite legs, Mel rushed toward him.

"Don't touch him!" Helena lunged after Mel. "Let it happen."

Calypso's body stiffened, and her head fell back. Tongues of sapphire energy danced over Blake's body and finally, as had happened before, a small patch of his sleeve changed color, morphing from gray stone to white cotton. Inch by inch he transformed. Cold rock became warm human skin.

His knees buckled, and Mel caught him and struggled to hold him up. He turned his head slowly to meet her gaze.

"Hi there," she said, grinning so wide she thought her face might break. He stared, uncomprehending for a moment, then he smiled back.

"Hi."

"Cal broke the curse."

"What?" he whirled around in time to see Calypso sink to the floor.

Paler than usual beneath her Goth makeup but still breathing at least, Calypso stared up at the anxious faces hovering over her. Palmer helped her sit up.

"She looks okay," he said. "*Are* you okay? Should we call someone?"

"Nn—o—no. I think I'm all right." She snaked a trembling hand across her stomach. "It hurts a bit."

"It feels like you drained the Cabochon almost completely," Helena said. "I can barely sense it."

Calypso nodded. "Hopefully it will recharge."

"What if it doesn't?" Mel asked. "How will it affect you?"

Cal's weak smile really wasn't all that reassuring. "I don't know. I guess I'll find out. Help me up, will you?"

"No, you should rest a while. DeWitt, help me put her on the bed," Palmer instructed.

Blake didn't respond, and Mel turned to find him staring out the window in much the same position he'd been in when she returned from Calypso's earlier in the day.

"What is it? Fremlings?" she asked.

"No. It's just after sunset," he whispered.

Mel glanced at Palmer, who had hoisted Calypso in his arms. "Sunset was officially when?"

Palmer shrugged and settled Cal on the bed. "Eight-oh-two."

"That was two minutes ago—the same time Blake transformed."

Calypso shook her head. "I gave it all I had. I know it worked."

Mel smiled at Blake and slipped her arm around his shoulders. "I know it did too. We just have to wait and see."

Blake climbed the stairs to his front door and let himself into the house after a deep breath of cool night air. The evening was quiet. The only sound was the rumble of Palmer's engine receding into the distance as he followed Helena and Calypso back to Calypso's apartment so the witch could get some more rest. No Fremlings stirred the shadows, and the buzz of the Cabochon that had made his very bones itch for ten years was gone as well.

Whether that was truly because the curse was broken or merely because Calypso had drained its power beyond his capacity to sense it, he couldn't be certain.

He wanted to believe the demon witch had saved him, but he had to be realistic. He'd felt nothing unusual when coming out of his stone exile tonight, and he felt nothing different now except the nagging certainty that Percival, for all his crimes, had ultimately deserved absolution, whether he'd ever received it or not.

He tried to tell himself what Percival got or didn't get was immaterial. Blake himself deserved to live the life he'd been born to. He deserved the sunlight, and at least for tonight, he wanted to believe he'd wake up to the world of daylight tomorrow.

No. He wouldn't wake to anything. He planned to keep his eyes open all night long. The last thing he wanted to do was sleep. With that thought in mind, he stalked through the house and found Melodie in the kitchen attempting to sweep up the salt that remained from the previous night's spell. He eased the dustpan out of her hands and helped her to her feet. "You don't have to do that."

"You shouldn't waste time with it. It'll only take me a minute; then maybe we could go out. Would you like that? Someplace bright with lots of people to help take your mind off—"

He engulfed her in his arms and hushed her with a kiss. "My mind's already on the only thing I want to think about. You."

She tucked her head under his chin and wrapped her arms around his middle. It felt good. After a contemplative moment, he said, "Isn't Arnold expecting you back at work?"

She sighed. "Not tonight. I called him earlier today. We're going to talk about me switching to the morning shift."

Blake leaned back to meet her sleepy gaze. "Why? Finally ready to rejoin society?"

She laughed and fell into step with him. They moved out of the kitchen toward the stairs, arm in arm. "It's not really that. I just thought if I worked days, I could spend my nights with you."

"If the spell didn't work, you mean."

"No. I *know* it worked." She put her hands on either side of his face and made him look at her. "I know it did. But either way, I want to spend my nights with you, if I can."

He kissed her again, quickly, and that led to three more longer kisses. Finally he broke away. "The nights might be all I ever have to give you. Nothing more. Ever. No walk down the aisle. No honeymoon. No babies."

Her chocolate eyes filled, but she held back the tears through sheer force of will. "That's okay."

"No. It's not. You deserve more than just hanging around in the dark with a brooding gargoyle."

She swept the tears away before they fell and gave him a tremulous smile. "You are not a gargoyle. And I happen to like brooding."

"I don't know if I can put you through that kind of a life, lass. The curse didn't just take the lives of ten generations of men, but their women as well. A lot of heartache comes with this life."

"That's because none of those women knew what was happening to the men they loved. They always kept it a secret, but I already know the secret, and I can live with it."

The men they loved. Blake's heart reacted to her words with a quick thud, as if trying to escape his chest. He wrapped his arms around her and squeezed as hard as he dared. "Ah, lass. I'm just not sure *I* can."

By the time they reached the bedroom, Mel's heart was pounding so hard she was certain Blake could hear it.

She shivered when he ran his fingertips up under her shirt and around the waistband of her jeans, tantalizing her nerve endings. She went up on tiptoes and kissed him while he explored, letting him maneuver her toward the bed.

They fell together in a tangle and rode the soft undulations of the mattress while they worked at pulling off each other's clothes.

"I'm sorry it can't be more than this," Blake whispered in her ear as he covered her with his body. "I'd give you a future if I had one."

She hushed him with trembling fingers across his lips and paused to sigh as he sheathed his erection in a condom and guided himself into her. "This is enough. If this is all there ever is, it's enough."

She wouldn't let him argue and distracted him from any further protests with eager movements of her hips. He smiled against her neck, nipped at the taut skin there and laughed.

"You do know how to control the conversation, don't you?"

She nodded and gasped at his next deep thrust. "Less talk and more of that."

"Who am I to argue?"

Their whispered conversation ceased, and Mel lost herself in the moment. The friction of skin on skin, and the heady, spicy scent of man chased any worrisome thoughts out of her head. She hoped that, for a little while, she could make him forget that he might not have tomorrow or any other "day" to look forward to.

When the rhythm of his movements increased, she urged him on with a moan and told him with her body she could take all he had to give. A moment later, she shuddered with her climax, and Blake followed. They trembled together, and he caught her lips in a desperate kiss that left them both panting.

"Is it wrong to say I'm in love with you?" Blake asked finally. He stroked a thumb over her lower lip and followed its path with his tongue.

Content and cozy beneath him, Mel brushed a dark strand of hair from his eyes and smiled. If this was all there ever was, it would be enough. "Why would it be wrong? I love you too, and that's all we need, isn't it?"

He kissed her again and smirked. "That...and maybe a sturdier mattress."

They both laughed and loved again and finally, they slept.

Anticipation of this moment made every beat of his weakening heart more painful than the last, but still Percival trudged toward his goal. Cold mud gripped his boots, and the torch he held aloft with his aching left arm dripped pitch on the sleeve of his tailored greatcoat. Heedless of the last of his expensive clothes, he pressed on through the fallow field surrounding the lone cottage. Moss and ivy-covered walls the of rough-hewn stone, and the roof thatch was bare in spots, attesting to both its age and the financial straits of its resident.

A gibbous moon lit the damp spring night, casting long shadows from the few pieces of chipped granite in the small yard bordered by a rotting fence. This had once been the home of a sculptor and lapidary. Castoffs of his work littered both the unkempt garden and the small patch of overgrown land to the south of the cottage. The man who'd lived here decades past carved headstones and statues, and his skill had finally afforded him a nicer home in London.

Now his abandoned cottage belonged to a witch.

Not any witch, of course.

She was the *one.* Birgid Cooper was her name, so said the woodsman as well as the villagers who spoke of her kindly enough but rarely paid her a visit.

She lived alone, having lost a husband and young son to consumption three winters past, he'd been told.

When Percival first heard that rumor, he'd consoled himself with the unkind thought that perhaps the Lord had seen fit to punish her, but he'd quickly repented.

The punishment was his alone, and he'd borne it for nineteen years. He could bear no more.

A wilted wreath of lavender hung on the whitewashed planks by the door. It rattled when he knocked, and shriveled leaves fell to the flagstone beneath his feet. She came to the door immediately, an oil lamp in one hand and a shock of dried thistle in the other.

"Day will break soon, my lord," she said by way of greeting, as if she'd been expecting him. "You've only a few minutes to kill me, if that's your intent."

Her blonde hair had darkened to dull gold and hung in heavy braids, shot through with black ribbons of mourning. Those jewel blue eyes he remembered so well had faded to slate and bore wrinkles at their corners that might have been laugh lines from earlier times when she had occasion to smile.

Here was a woman hardened by circumstance, her once-brilliant colors leached away by years of strife. Like him, she might have welcomed death, but that wasn't what he had come to offer.

He knelt before her, and the mud from his boots soaked instantly through the worn knees of his trousers. Pain shot from his shoulder through his chest when he doused his torch in the rain bucket beside the door.

"Killing you won't free me. I know that. I've come to beg forgiveness." Those long-rehearsed words burned like bile at the back of his throat. How many times had he vowed vengeance? How long had he prayed for one moment within arm's reach of the creature who'd stolen his life? Now, for the first time, he saw her not as the personification of evil, but as a human being, a woman as weary of her worldly burdens as he was of his.

She stepped back, bare feet scraping the thrush-lined floor of the cottage. "Have you now?"

"My son will marry on the Sabbath at noon. I have few days left, and I've long ago lost any joy in living, but this one day I covet. He's begged me to see him wed." The weight on his chest grew, and the rattle in his lungs forced a harsh cough from him. The months he'd searched for the witch had been long and cold, and he'd gotten little rest for his weary bones.

When he'd regained his breath, he looked up at her as he had to the altar of the Lord so many times, beseeching.

"Lift this curse, if only for a day."

"There's so much blood on your hands, *my lord*." The title held no reverence. She used it as an insult, but he hadn't the strength to take offense. He'd welcome insults if it meant he could see the sun once more.

He clutched his chest and waited, head bowed again, for her decree. "I beg you. Since that night, no other woman has died at my hands, and no other will. I give you my word."

Her breath caught, and she set the lamp aside, casting her lithe shadow long across the floor beside her. Percival closed his eyes, hoping to squeeze away the pain that racked his chest. His left arm had gone numb from the exertion of wielding the heavy torch, and the very air seemed to weigh on him, pressing him toward the earth.

"They were my sisters, Percival. Each one of them as close as if we'd come from the same womb. Five of the dozens you killed belonged to *me*."

He nodded and folded his hands in supplication. Gnarled fingers rubbed together, parchment skin, bone on bone. He'd worn himself down to nothing over the years, searching for her, praying for salvation through the long nights until dawn stole his breath and turned his body cold and stiff. "I will give you anything you ask. I will do anything within my power."

"You have nothing I want, my lord. And I imagine you have nothing *you* want either."

Percival tugged a small coin purse from his coat and dropped it on the floor at her feet. "If nothing else, surely gold will be of use to you. Take this, and I will give you more anytime you ask."

"I should have to ask you for nothing, my lord. I *will* ask you for nothing except this..."

He raised his head. The effort made his chest hurt. So tight were his lungs, he feared he would not be able to draw another breath, but he would have given her the very blood from his veins if she'd asked for it. "Anything."

"Pay homage to the witches for every life you took. Your gold will certainly buy a monument to them, open and free for all to look upon. Percival Blake should beg forgiveness of the women he murdered, bear his shame in public and face the consequences of his crimes."

A small price indeed. He almost laughed. He could pay the very sculptor who'd once resided here to carve a statue in honor of them all, with his beloved Rebecca at the center. He smiled and bent to lay a kiss upon Birgid Cooper's feet.

He never rose.

Death took him swiftly before she could raise a hand to break the curse. She buried him there, in the overgrown field to rest eternally in the shadow of her cottage.

His gentleman son didn't marry on the Sabbath because the curse stole daylight from him on the very next morning. He went into hiding for decades, and rumors persisted that he'd lost his mind as well as his bride.

Though she searched, Birgid never found Rene. She died barely a year later and was laid to rest in the same field, a stone's throw from the remains of Percival Blake.

Chapter Twenty-Seven

Blake swam toward consciousness, unsure of where he was, or who, for that matter. Percival Blake was dead—he had been for two hundred and sixty-one years, yet Blake woke with the smell of moldering earth in his nostrils and a heaviness in his limbs that made him fear he might suffer the same end as his murderous ancestor.

He dragged his heavy eyelids open, gasping for breath as if he'd been buried alive. Panting, he lay in the dark, staring at the ceiling and trying to piece together what he'd just seen.

In all the years he'd been forced to live Percival's life, he'd never experienced the man's death before. Did that mean the connection had finally been severed? Was Percival's soul free because the curse had been broken, or was he doomed to these visions of a madman's existence even in his sleep?

He sat up slowly, careful not to disturb the woman sleeping next to him. Mel was the first person he'd permitted to share his bed in ten years. The only person he'd considered making room for in his complicated life.

He reached for her but stopped short of touching her bare shoulder to rouse her when his bleary gaze focused on the clock beside the bed. The glowing numbers read 5:34. Sunrise would happen any moment.

He jumped up and stumbled in the dark, searching for his

pants. Dear God, if he'd forgotten—if he hadn't woken up, he might have crushed her or at the very least destroyed the bed.

His heart thudded unevenly in his heaving chest. He had to get dressed quickly. Turning to stone was bad enough; he refused to spend the day as a naked gargoyle.

Bypassing his discarded briefs, he jammed one leg then the other into his jeans. Instinct sent him out of the bedroom and down the stairs, heading for his secret lair where he could hide his shame.

She'd understand, he told himself when his bare feet hit the landing. She had to realize he couldn't risk the transformation while he lay next to her.

Her voice stopped him at the foot of the stairs, and he dared to glance up at her shadowy form, wrapped in a sheet. She looked like a goddess, demure but so sensual she took his breath away. He'd have given the world to be able to climb back up the stairs and take her in his arms.

"Go back to sleep."

"Blake. Don't leave me." She gathered the sheet in her hands and started down the stairs.

He held up a hand to stop her. "Don't. Please, Mel. If I change, I can't bear for you to see it again."

Her expression hardened. Determination narrowed her eyes as she made her way down the last few steps.

"Come with me." She took his hand, held it fast even when he tried to twist out of her grasp. She tugged him toward the kitchen, to the door that led to the backyard.

When she pushed the screen door open, flooding the kitchen with icy morning air, he reared back. "Are you nuts? What am I going to do, stand in the yard all day while the neighbors gawk?"

"The neighbors might gawk if they're up at this hour, but who cares? Come on outside with me now, Blake. Show me you love me."

"Uh, angel, I thought I did that last night...twice in fact." He would have smiled at the memory of it, but she scrambled around behind him and shoved. The woven mat on the back porch tickled his bare feet. The bricks of the back stairs were cold and sharp, but he let her lead him down into the dewy grass.

"I believe in you, Blake. And I believe in Calypso. I won't have it any other way."

"Lass..."

She pointed at the sky above the old, scrubby apple tree that dominated his backyard. A sprinkling of stars paled while they watched, the pinpricks of light winking out one by one.

Next to him, Melodie shivered, and he put his arm around her. If he turned to stone now, she'd be trapped against his granite body all day, wearing nothing but a sheet. She didn't seem the least bit concerned, though.

Her gaze was fixed on the sky which, as they watched, turned from indigo to lavender.

Blake rubbed his eyes and blinked. Birds chirped in the high branches. Shades of gray brightened into the muted colors of early dawn.

Dawn.

He held his breath and stared down at his hands, expecting the change to come over him. If not stone, then at least the rough flesh of his gargoyle form...fangs, a tail? He didn't feel any different.

"Blake, it's sunrise, and you're still you." Her voice trembled. "You're still you."

No. He couldn't believe it. After all this time.

Dragging Melodie by the hand, he raced around the side of the house and out onto the sidewalk. Here, facing east, the sky was even lighter—a nameless color somewhere between pink and yellow and blue but none of those and all of them at once. A car turned onto the street up at the corner, and Blake resisted the instinctive urge to flee from prying eyes. Maybe the sunlight had to touch him. Maybe in a few moments, he would turn, and whoever drove the car would see a gargoyle standing at the curb.

But it didn't happen. The car slowed as it passed his house, and out of the passenger window, a teenage boy flung the morning paper at his feet.

The car sped up and drove on, and beside him, Melodie laughed.

"Sorry, lover, but I don't think you're going to make front-page news. You're just a man today, not a monster."

He met her gaze and broke into a grin so wide it hurt. "She did it. She broke the curse."

"I told you. Have a little faith." Melodie slipped her fingers into his and tugged him toward the front steps. "Now can we go back to bed?"

He didn't miss the suggestive tone in her voice, and he wanted to. Lord knew he wanted to...but there'd be time for that later. There'd be time for everything later.

"Sorry, lass. I'm not going inside today."

"Umm...the neighbors might talk if we hang out on the curb all day watching traffic go by."

"Hmm. You're right." He scooped her up and swung her around, ecstatic and a little bit hard. "Let's go in the back. There's a shady little spot under the tree where no one will be able to see us."

"Blake!" she shrieked when he tossed her over his shoulder and carried her off.

"Let 'em gawk, lass. Let 'em gawk."

Melodie was still picking twigs out of her hair three hours

later, but she didn't care. She'd finally gotten Blake to come inside with the promise of a shared bubble bath, which she'd sent him upstairs to prepare.

She listened for the sound of running water while she dialed Calypso's number. A familiar voice answered after the fifth ring, but it wasn't the witch.

"Helena? Is that you?"

"Hmm...Melodie?"

"Yes, it's me. I'm with Blake, and he's human. It worked. The spell worked. Can I talk to Calypso? How's she doing?"

Helena's long silence had her pacing the kitchen in a panic. "Helena?"

"She's gone, Melodie."

"Gone? What do you mean she's gone? She's not...?"

"She left. I don't know when. I dozed off on the couch, and when I got up to check on her, the bed was empty. It looks like she packed a few things. There are hangars all over the floor, and her toothbrush is gone."

Mel squinted at the sunny front window and gripped the phone tighter. "Why would she leave? She was so weak last night. Will she be all right?"

"I think she had to leave. The Domaré aren't going to be happy about what she did. She was the custodian of an immense amount of power, and she threw it away...most of it, anyway."

"She's going to be in trouble?"

"Definitely."

"Can you do anything to help her? What about Angelo and the Witches' Council?"

"I don't know about the witches. I'm not one, so I have no idea how to contact the Council. And Angelo is more part of the problem than the solution. He won't be happy at all about what she did."

"So she's running away from him?" A sense of desolation gripped Mel, and she sank into one of Blake's kitchen chairs. "She's in danger because she helped us."

"That was a given from the beginning. Don't act surprised."

Mel bristled a little at Helena's tone. The spell had been Calypso's choice, after all. If she hadn't wanted to do it, she could have disappeared the night before and left Blake to fend for himself. "We'll find her," she said after she'd regained her temper. "We'll help her."

"There's not much two humans can do for her. Unless you want to end up dealing with another curse or a horde of vengeful demons, I'd suggest you stay out of it. Remember, Calypso might have made an unpopular decision, but she's still the Domaré queen at the moment, and she's entitled to some respect."

"She still might need some help. Will you help us find her?"

Helena laughed, and the sound grated on Melodie's nerves. "No. She's my cousin, but she's not my friend. I have to side with the will of the clans on this. If it comes down to a choice, I'm with them."

"I guess demon blood isn't thicker than water." Mel wished she'd used Blake's regular phone to call, because then she could slam down the receiver to end the frustrating conversation. Instead, all she could do was jam her finger on the disconnect button and toss her cell phone across the table.

"Damn demons."

Blake appeared in the doorway then, still shirtless and so gorgeous Mel felt light-headed just looking at him.

Her body responded to his appreciative gaze immediately, but her mind put the brakes on any repeat of their performance under the apple tree.

"What is it?"

"Calypso ran away." She relayed everything Helena had told her and let him wrap her in a reassuring hug. "We owe her something, don't we? We can't let the Domaré punish her for helping us."

"We may not have a choice. It's her world, her family. One thing I've learned over the years, it's best not to get involved with demon politics."

"She was my friend. She still is. I have to help her."

Blake leaned his forehead against hers. "Then we will. Come upstairs and get cleaned up with me, and then we'll start looking for her."

"Where do we begin?"

Blake shrugged and guided her out of the kitchen. "With a demon hunter, of course."

"We'll check in with you every six hours," Melodie told Palmer two days later when he pulled up outside of Gleason's with his Jeep loaded to the roll bars with luggage and equipment.

"She will. I won't," Blake added with a rueful smile. It had taken him this long to convince Melodie that the best thing the two of them could do for Calypso was to let a professional make the foray into demon territory to search for her.

Unfortunately, they didn't have a professional. The All-American would have to do, the upside of the arrangement being that Palmer would be out of town and not making any more sketches of Melodie.

Blake reached into the Jeep and offered his hand. Van Houten shook it and met his gaze head-on. "Be careful. I don't fancy coming to your rescue again."

"My rescue? *My* rescue? Who saved your ass from the Fremlings again? Oh yeah, that was me."

"No more arguing, you two." Melodie opened the passenger

door and leaned inside. She planted a smacking kiss on Palmer's cheek, and Blake stood back, studying the sidewalk and pretending it didn't bother him to see the woman he loved putting her lips on another man. "Remember, if you need us, just call. Don't get into trouble."

"Ever since I met you, sweetie, that's the only thing I've been doing." Palmer laughed, but Blake noticed he did look a little pinched around the eyes. This was a tall order. Tracking a Domaré queen, even in a weakened state, was a lot harder than skewering Gogmars.

"You have that paper I gave you, right?"

Palmer patted his breast pocket. "Right here. I promise to open it only in a dire emergency."

"Good. Now you'd better get going. Take care." Mel kissed her fingertips and waved as Palmer revved his engine for effect and pulled away from the curb.

With his arms wrapped around Melodie, Blake watched the demon hunter drive away. "What was that about? Some kind of spell?"

Melodie grinned. "Sort of. I gave him a secret incantation that's guaranteed to get Calypso's attention when she's being stubborn."

"Really? And I thought you didn't know anything about witchcraft."

"Oh...every girl has an ace or two up her sleeve."

"Have you got any spells that are guaranteed to get *my* attention?"

She laughed and whispered one in his ear. He immediately stood at attention, or at least part of him did. Unfortunately he couldn't do anything about it at the moment. He and Mel had work to do. While Palmer searched for Calypso, they planned to track down some of her witchy friends. Someone with access to the Witches' Council might know how to help her avoid the wrath of the demon clans.

"Are you sure you want to take on the Witches' Council?" he asked as he led her toward the front door of the bakery. "I thought you wanted to have as normal a life as possible now that the curse is broken."

"Mmm." She kissed him lightly. "I do, but nothing will be normal until we find Calypso. Once we find her and make sure she's safe from the demon clans, we can have all the normal we want. You've got a lot of sun to catch up on, and I want to share that. I can work at night, and so can you so we can spend our days together."

Blake caught her in his arms, reluctant to let her go just yet, even if it was only for a moment. "Even if we just spend the day in bed?"

"Especially if we just spend the day in bed. Now, I've got to go make some calls to Cal's friends. I'll be back soon." She kissed him again and slipped away to start her search.

Blake watched her go and sighed. He'd have preferred sharing Melodie's days and her nights, but he could definitely learn to live with this arrangement, once he set the Council straight about a few things himself.

After all, getting hard certainly beat turning to stone.

About the Author

To learn more about Jennifer Colgan, please visit http://jennifercolgan.com/.

Send an email to Jennifer at jcolgan@newoa.com, join her Yahoo! Group to join in the fun with other readers at http://groups.yahoo.com/group/electricromance or stop by her Two Voices blog at bernadettegardner2.blogspot.com.

Magick made him human. Only love can keep him that way.

Uncross My Heart
© *2011 Jennifer Colgan*

After a century of living *la vida muerta*, Julian Devlin's closest ally casts a de-vamping spell that leaves him defanged and demoted from his hard-won place in Baltimore's vampire hierarchy. Disoriented by his transformation, he can't even find his way home.

The indignities don't end there. Before he can explain to the quirky consignment shop owner why he's hiding in her basement, she's punched the newly re-acquired breath out of him and smacked him upside the head with her knock-off purse.

Zoe Boyd's scream could have peeled paint from the walls—if she could get her heart out of her throat. Common thugs aren't supposed to have a smile so panty-melting that she finds herself apologizing for scaring *him*.

She's also too busy managing her friends' love lives to take on an ex-vampire with revamping and revenge on his mind. Until she guides him home and ends up neck deep in his world of trouble.

As Zoe risks her life to give him back his death, she warms the soul Julian never thought he'd own again. And when he tracks down a devilish witch who can reverse the spell, immortality without Zoe suddenly seems like cold comfort...

Warning: This novel contains sensual love scenes between a fashion-forward hero and a fashion-unconscious heroine, abuse of Italian loafers, and a few love bites. Don't worry, freshly sharpened fangs don't hurt. Much...

Available now in ebook and print from Samhain Publishing.

Their desire could be their destruction...or their greatest strength.

Cipher
© *2011 Moira Rogers*
Southern Arcana, Book 4

Fourteen months ago, Kat Gabriel learned a brutal truth. Under the wrong circumstances, her empathic ability is no gift. It's a deadly weapon. Now her soul bears the inescapable weight of those deaths—and it aches for the loss of the easy relationship she once shared with Andrew Callaghan. Unleashing her power saved his life, but she couldn't save his humanity.

Since the attack that turned him into a werewolf, Andrew's sole focus has been to make himself stronger. Pushing her away hurt like hell, but Kat doesn't need a friend. She needs a protector strong enough to shield her from the supernatural world that forced her to kill. Strong enough to resist their volatile connection.

As Kat's quest to understand the violent legacy of her past leads her into the darkest underbelly of the psychic world, Andrew is at her side. Yet every step forward rips open old emotional wounds and shakes their control. Where they're headed, distractions of any kind can be fatal—especially when the greatest threat they pose is to each other.

Warning: This book contains a dangerous shapeshifter who could kill you with his bare hands, an empathic hacker who could kill you with her mind, a psychic cult determined to kill everyone, a lot of violence, a little bit of hope, and a happily-ever-after seven years in the making.

Available now in ebook and print from Samhain Publishing.

www.samhainpublishing.com

Green for the planet.
Great for your wallet.

It's all about the story...

Romance

HORROR

www.samhainpublishing.com